Acknowledgements

A special thanks to Jackie Wyatt (president of Vore Buffalo Jump Foundation) and Ted Vore (historical expert) for the personal tour of the Buffalo Jump site. Trent Tope, the owner of the Aladdin General Store, offered great insights into Aladdin and regional culture. Mike Frolander, the Crook County Coroner, offered insight into the identification of human remains, and allowed me to use him as a character. Their comments added seasoning and texture to my depiction of the sites, their history, and the location. As always there are a legion of people who contribute to my books. Julie continues to endure my distracted writing while she keeps the house and family together. Deanna Wilson edits and proofs the roughest pieces of the first draft, correcting cop, horse, and legal mistakes while suggesting overall changes that make the book better. Natalie Lund, the sentence structure and preposition rule enforcer, marks up a later draft and improves the readability of the book. Fran Brozo, Clem MacIlravie, Brian Johnson, and Marybeth Johnson, catch plot issues and correct details specific to their background and experience. Anne Flagge and Deanna Wilson make a final post-editing sweep to catch the final typos, punctuation errors, misspellings, and truncated words. Without the dedicated assistance of all these people, the books would be much less than they are. Finally, thanks to Jude Pittman and my BWL editor for your contributions and continued support.

Western Justice
Doug Fletcher Book 14
Dean L. Hovey

Print ISBNs
Amazon Print 9780228628866
Ingram Spark 9780228628873
BWL Print 9780228628880

Copyright 2024 by Dean L. Hovey
Cover art by Michelle Lee

Dedication

To Clem, Lorna, and Rosa

*"There are three
kinds of men. The ones that
learn by readin'. The few
who learn by observation.
The rest of them have to
pee on the electric fence for
themselves."*

— Will Rogers

Table of Contents

Prologue

The leafy camouflage of Jake Foster's outfit was out of place among the pines and junipers surrounding him in the Black Hills National Forest. Enjoying the sun and southerly breeze brought by January Chinook winds, Jake felt invisible hiding behind a clump of junipers. Seated as he had been for the previous two days, he picked up his binoculars and focused on the rear of the few buildings making up Aladdin, Wyoming, population 15. Lulled into daydreaming by boredom, he was startled by a man's voice.

"Whatcha doing?"

Lowering the binoculars, Jake turned to face a man and horse who'd walked up behind him.

"Hunting."

The interloper wore stained Carhartt coveralls and a red and white plaid wool cap with earflaps that hung down like a basset hound's ears. He glanced around the area where Jake was sitting. "You don't have a gun and all the hunting seasons are over."

Lifting a camera, Foster sighed. "I'm camera hunting."

"What kind of game do you expect to walk out of the door you're watching through those binoculars?"

"There are lots of birds this time of year."

The newcomer cocked his head and looked past Foster toward the Aladdin General Store, down the hillside from their perch. "It seems like you're looking at the window of the RV parked behind the store. Are you some kind of pervert window peeper?" After a pause, he added, "You're trespassing."

Jake sighed, "I'm on national forest land. It's public property. I'm not trespassing."

"What are you up to?"

Grumbling, Foster tucked his binoculars inside his coat and picked up his camera. Standing, he said, "Fine. I'll be moving on."

"You haven't explained what you were up to."

"I don't owe you an explanation. I'm leaving."

Jake had taken only two steps when something flashed past his eyes, and he felt a rough rope bite into his neck. Before he could pull the rope free, he was jerked from his feet and dragged through the timber. Struggling to crawl fast enough to relieve the pressure, he clawed at his neck. An ATV engine roared, then the forest raced past him as he bounced across the ground hitting rocks, branches, and stumps.

Chapter 1

April 2024

Peggy Landin's crew arrived at Vore Buffalo Jump to begin the spring cleanup. With her group of volunteers, they had previously locked the buildings and closed the entrance gates after Labor Day. They were now reversing the process before the first spring school tours arrived before Memorial Day. Although the Vore Buffalo Jump Foundation operated the facility, it was designated a National Historic Site. The US Park Service affiliation with the non-profit foundation was largely symbolic because the foundation's volunteers funded, cared for, and staffed the park.

The archaeologically significant site was "discovered" during the survey prior to construction of I-90 when holes were bored to determine the suitability of underlying rock for support of the future highway. The bore samples revealed a layer of buffalo bones over 100 feet deep. Subsequent evaluation by the University of Wyoming determined that the site had been used by local tribes from 1400-1800s as a location to trap buffalo where they could be killed easily with arrows and spears.

Peggy turned on the interior lights, exposing the dusty displays to be cleaned prior to the arrival of spring tourists. Before she could even contemplate the work to be done, Charlie Smith rushed in. "We've got a problem, Peggy. Follow me."

Following Charlie to an area behind the building, Peggy found three of her volunteers staring at a non-descript lump tangled in the chokecherry bushes lining the steep slope behind the building. Charlie stopped on the fringe of the group and gestured toward the lump.

"What is it?" Peggy asked as she stopped behind Charlie.

"I think someone left us a body."

Peggy focused on the heap, recently exposed by the melting snow. Frost covered the surface, but the distinctive shape of a foot extended from the otherwise nondescript pile. Taking time to examine the remainder of the pile partially hidden by shadows and brush, she discerned a camouflage coat and pants. Moving to the side, she saw an ear and hair through the chokecherry branches. With a sharp intake of breath, she reached into her back pocket for her cell phone. She punched 911 into the keypad and waited two rings before the dispatcher answered, "Crook County emergency services. How can I assist you?"

Not having considered what she was going to say when the phone was answered, Peggy stated, "I'm looking at a dead body. Could you send someone over to fetch it?"

"Is the body human?"

Peggy cocked her head to examine details that became clearer as her eyes adjusted to the shadows behind the building. "It appears so."

"You can't tell?" the dispatcher asked.

"It's complicated. It's kind of tangled in some brush partway up a hill."

"Do you need an ambulance?"

"No, this soul is well past the ambulance stage."

"Where are you, ma'am?"

"I'm standing behind Vore Buffalo Jump's Museum building."

"Where exactly is that?"

"It's along the interstate, between the Beulah and Aladdin exits."

"I'll dispatch a deputy to your location. The nearest officer is in Hulett, so it might take him the better part of a half hour to get there, if he's through with lunch."

"There's no rush. Whoever this is, isn't going anywhere."

Chapter 2

I looked at my watch as I set a flat of plants next to my wife, Jill, who had decided it was the day to plant flowers in front of our new Port Aransas home. As I brushed dirt from my hands, the cell phone rang displaying CCSD with a 307-area code. If not for my suspicion that the acronym might represent a sheriff's department, I would've dismissed the call as spam and gone back to dealing with the next flat of yellow and blue flowers.

"Doug Fletcher."

"I don't know if you remember me, but this is Hank Stoddard. I'm the Crook County sheriff in Wyoming."

"I remember you, Sheriff. Have there been any shootouts lately?"

After a chuckle, Stoddard replied, "Well, we haven't had to shoot anyone, but a body was found on a National Park Service site. I was wondering if you happened to be in the neighborhood and would be willing to take a look at it."

"I'm in Texas right now. But you've intrigued me. Did you have another person fall at Devils Tower?"

"This time a volunteer found a body at Vore Buffalo Jump during their spring cleanup."

I vaguely recalled a sign for the historic site but couldn't remember its location. "Where is the Buffalo Jump?"

"It's just west of Beulah, within sight of I-90."

"That's just across the border from South Dakota, right?"

"That would be the spot. I was hoping you were visiting your South Dakota in-laws and might be willing to take a peek at the mess that was once a person."

"As tempting as that sounds, I'm helping Jill plant flowers in Texas, and we're nowhere near you."

Stoddard sighed. "I'm down a deputy and stretched a little thin right now. Since the body was found on a national historic site, I was hoping the Park Service might be willing to give us a hand." The sheriff paused. "The locals would be happy to see you again. We haven't heard much about you and Jill since the Devils Tower investigation. How are your in-laws? Are they still living on the Spearfish ranch and trying to get you on a horse?"

"Yeah, they're still on the ranch. The horse riding is still up for discussion." Pausing, I reflected on our most recent phone call with Jill's mother who was frustrated over what she saw as her slow recovery from a recent fall. "Let me make a couple of calls, Sheriff. We may need to make an unexpected trip to Spearfish."

"I'd be mighty appreciative if you could make that happen. This death is strange. The coroner and I have stewed over this a lot. It appears the victim was dragged across the prairie like a horse thief, then dumped at the Buffalo Jump site at some point over the winter."

"Dragged like a horse thief?"

"Dragging a horse thief across the prairie was called western justice. Our victim is missing his boots and hat. His clothes are ripped to shreds. The coroner says the victim, who he's unable to identify, apparently died of asphyxiation from the rope tied around his neck." The sheriff chuckled. "Considering the scrapes and bruises on his body, I think he'd rather have been shot. His death wasn't quick or pleasant."

"I'm intrigued. Let me make some calls, Sheriff. I'll get back to you in a bit."

"Vore Buffalo Jump is just a few miles from a small motel in Aladdin. It's not the Ritz, but they have clean rooms, a café, and it's near the murder scene."

"I'll keep that in mind. Thanks."

Listening to half the conversation had piqued Jill's interest. Pulling off her gardening gloves, she sat on the steps with her back against the house. "Which sheriff called?"

"The Crook County sheriff may have an investigation for us."

"Why would Hank Stoddard call you instead of contacting the FBI?"

After recapping my discussion with the sheriff's office, Jill said, "Mom's been hinting she'd like us to visit. I think she's getting tired of relying on your mother's cooking since hurting her wrist."

"I've been talking to the superintendent at Glacier National Park about a pair of missing hikers. His law enforcement rangers are handling the investigation. I thought we should assist them." I waited for a response.

Jill got a sly look, which signaled an imminent change in my plans. "Let's talk to Jack about this Wyoming death. The sheriff has requested assistance, and there are no Park Service employees on the site. The Vore Buffalo Jump Foundation operates the park with volunteers, so they have no one other than the local sheriff for law enforcement support, and Stoddard told you he's short a deputy."

"The sheriff said it looked like the victim had been dragged across the prairie like a horse thief. That's intriguing you, isn't it?"

Jill raised her eyebrows. "It kind of sounds like something out of *Gunsmoke* or *Bonanza*. Call Jack."

"The boss might say no."

Jill slid across the step until we were seated hip to hip. "I'd really like to see my folks and ride the horses."

"Vore Buffalo Jump isn't even operated by the Park Service."

Leaning against my shoulder, Jill looked up at me. "My folks replaced the squeaky mattress. A trip to the Black Hills might make me very romantic."

"Jack said you'd missed your calling when you didn't go to work in the diplomatic corps. I'll call our boss while you plant the rest of the flowers."

My conversation with Jack was brief. "If a local sheriff is requesting your assistance at a Park Service property, you should get your butts on a plane and do whatever you can to help him. You know how hard it is to build bridges with local law enforcement agencies. Get yourselves to Wyoming and give them your usual charm..." Jack chuckled. "It's Jill who charms them, isn't it? You're the one who tries to stay in the background."

I watched Jill gather the last of the plastic flower containers and put them into a recycling bin as I ended the call. Pulling off her gloves, she said, "I'll call the travel agency and book a two-week trip."

I held the phone out to Jill. "Call our mothers while I shower."

Instead of reaching for the phone, Jill put her hands on her narrow hips. "Call your own mother. I'm taking the first shower."

As she walked into the house, I called after her. "She'd rather talk to you."

"She's your mother. It's your turn to call her."

My mother, now living with Jill's Uncle Chet in South Dakota, answered on the second ring. "Is this really my son calling?"

"Yes, Mom. It's really me."

"What's wrong?"

I paused. "Nothing's wrong. Why would you ask that?"

"You never call unless Jill's been hurt or there's some crisis and you want to soften the blow before we hear about it on the news."

"Everything is fine. We've got an investigation in eastern Wyoming. We'll be in the area for a couple of weeks, so I'm sure we'll see you."

"You'll *SEE* us? You'd better plan on staying with us unless your investigation takes you farther away than Cheyenne."

"I'm not sure of the geography, Mom. It'd be best if we stayed close to the scene of the crime for at least the first couple of nights."

"Fine. I'll give you two nights of investigation. After that, I expect you to be at our ranch or Rickowskis' for supper and breakfast."

"Let's see how things go. Okay?"

"Have you had your hearing checked, Douglas? I said two days, then get your butts over here."

"Mom, this is a federal investigation. It really takes priority over supper with the family."

"Put Jill on the phone."

"She's in the shower."

"Fine. I'll call Molly Rickowski as soon as we hang up. Have Jill call her mom, and we'll set things straight. Jill's always been more reasonable than you."

"Goodbye, Mom," I said as I ended the call.

Jill was drying her hair when I walked into the bedroom. "Is your mom excited that we're flying back?"

I paused too long before replying, "Yes, she's excited."

Jill froze. "What did you say?"

"I told her we were going to stay in a motel close to the crime scene. That was unacceptable."

"Geez, Doug. Just because there's a cow pie in front of you, doesn't mean you have to step in it." Jill held out her hand for the phone. "Couldn't you have just left the discussion of where we're staying sit until we got there? We could've called and told her we were tied up and unable to get back before supper. It would've softened the blow and she would have been sad instead of irritated."

I handed Jill my phone as I stripped off my shirt. "Spread oil on the maternal waters while I shower."

Setting my phone aside, she reached for her own phone from the nightstand. "Let's pick up our computers and 'go bags' from the park after you clean up."

                    * * *

We found Mandy Mattson setting the kitchen table when we arrived home after collecting our computers and gear from our Padre Island National Seashore offices. The aroma of boiling shrimp filled the house. I set my pistol and holster on the closet shelf as Jill slipped past me. "Thank you for making dinner," she said to Mandy.

Brushing off the thanks, Mandy hugged Jill. "All I did was show up with food, beer and margaritas, and turn on the stove. Y'all have to pack for the trip. That's the hard part."

Matt, her husband, handed me a beer. "Now that you're disarmed, I assume it's safe to give you alcohol."

I touched the neck of my beer bottle to Matt's. "Thanks."

"Mandy gave me an edited version of what Jill told her. What's the real story behind your sudden trip?"

Nodding toward the patio, I led Matt, my former Park Service boss, outside while Jill and Mandy finished supper preparations. "There's an obscure Park Service location in Wyoming along I-90, a few miles from the South Dakota state line. Vore Buffalo Jump National Historic Site is staffed by volunteers and only open during the summer. When the volunteers arrived to prepare the site for their Memorial Day opening, they found a body behind one of the buildings."

"That seems like something the local cops would handle."

"The Crook County Sheriff's Department is small and currently understaffed. We worked with the sheriff during our Devils Tower investigation and apparently impressed him enough that he requested our assistance directly."

"The investigation must be more complicated than a spouse killing or a hit-and-run."

"The coroner is unable to identify the body, which makes the entire investigation more difficult."

"Huh. So, no car sitting nearby or driver's license, and the killer didn't have the decency to drop his cell phone or a credit card with the body."

"None of the above. The killing has the hallmarks of an old-time horse thief getting a dose of western justice. The official cause of death is asphyxiation caused by a noose around the victim's neck."

"He was hung?"

"It appears he was dragged across the prairie by a noose tied around his neck."

"That sounds like something out of *Longmire* or *Yellowstone*."

Opening of the patio door interrupted our conversation. Mandy smiled, "If you boys are through solving the world's problems, supper is on the table."

With paper napkins on our laps, we dove into Mandy's traditional going away dinner of boiled shrimp, potatoes, corn on the cob, and smoked sausage. Wiping her fingers before sipping her margarita, Jill said, "Mandy is picking us up at six o'clock tomorrow morning."

Before I could protest and say that the government would reimburse us for an Uber, Mandy put up her hand. "I like to say my goodbyes properly, at the airport."

Glancing at Matt for support, I got a headshake. "I appreciate your taxi service, but I hate to put you out."

Mandy's smile hid whatever irritation she felt over the argument we had about departure arrangements before every trip. "Douglas, helping friends is a blessing, not a burden."

"Only my mother calls me Douglas, and only when she's angry with me."

Smiling, Mandy nodded, "Jill said you were marginally trainable. I've been unconvinced, but you seem to be catching on."

Caught with a mouthful of corn on the cob, I was unable to respond, which caused the others to break into laughter.

Being on a roll, Mandy added, "Are you bringing the bottle of expensive booze you're going to lose to Jill's father while playing cribbage, or do you plan to purchase that after you arrive?"

Wiping my mouth, I replied, "I plan to investigate, not play cribbage."

"Try not to get into any wrestling matches with bull riders," Matt said, referring to an incident during our visit to the Black Hills Roundup.

"It wasn't a wrestling match; I was sucker punched." Realizing there was no way to win the argument, I decided to move on. "The sheriff suggested we stay near the investigation rather than commuting from the Rickowski ranch. There's a mom-and-pop motel a few miles from the site where the body was found."

"I checked out the area on Google Earth," Mandy replied. "Aladdin, Wyoming has a population of fifteen. I'm sure that calling the motel a mom-and-pop operation is an overstatement of the accommodations."

Jill drew a breath. "I'm not sure we'll be able to convince our parents that a nearby motel is a superior option to sleeping in my childhood bedroom."

Our banter continued through supper. Mandy refused to let us clean up, and even took the garbage home so there's no "stinky shrimp shells" in the trash while we were gone. Jill was packing her suitcase when I exited the bathroom. "How do you feel about going back to the Black Hills?" she asked as she folded Park Service green uniform pants.

"I'm fine with it as long as we're buying round-trip tickets."

Carefully placing a folded gray uniform shirt on top of the pants she said, "Someday we'll have to move there."

I pulled her into a hug. "We've just moved into a new house. Let's enjoy a few years here and defer the Black Hills relocation talk until some time in the future."

Jill leaned her head against my shoulder. "Our parents aren't getting any younger."

"They're doing fine. My mom is happy living with your Uncle Chet. Your parents are nearby. They're living their lives without our involvement."

"They are, but I feel like I should be there for them."

"Honey, we have jobs, a house in Texas, and lives of our own."

Jill eased out of my hug and zipped her suitcase. "Winters in the Black Hills aren't as terrible as you think."

"Tell that to the guy they found frozen like an icicle in Vore Buffalo Jump."

Chapter 3

Unsure of what roads, or lack of roads we might encounter during our investigation, I rented a 4-wheel drive pickup at the Rapid City airport while Jill called her mother. After an unhappy discussion, Molly Rickowski conceded we were there to work, and it might be logical for us to go directly to the Wyoming murder scene to start our investigation instead of stopping in Spearfish, which was *right on the way to Wyoming.*

The conversation stressed Jill. "Are mother's born with a gene to cause guilt in their adult children, or do you think that's an acquired skill?"

"I think there are adult education guilt classes taught at churches and schools."

"Is that why you never called your mother when we first met?"

"Mom had given up on trying to coerce me through guilt. Without being able to play the guilt card, I guess she felt there was no need for us to talk."

"At the time, it seemed like you were being an insensitive jerk. Now, I get it. Mom's guilt trips really eat at me."

"How long is the drive from Rapid City to Vore Buffalo Jump?"

Jill punched information into her phone and waited. "It's a little over an hour drive from the airport."

"So, we won't be that far from the Rickowski ranch?"

"Less than half an hour away. I think that's part of Mom's frustration with our decision to stay in Aladdin."

I glanced at Jill. "Would it help if we stayed in Sundance or Hulett?"

"No, smartass. Finding a motel farther from my parents and the murder scene would *not* be helpful."

I reached over and put my hand on Jill's. "Look at it this way, it'll be easier to have a glass of wine and a beer with supper and retire to our motel room for a night of romance than it would be if we ate at the ranch with them and sat up talking about health issues all night."

Jill snorted. "Are you saying that discussing senior citizen bowel issues is a romance killer?"

"If only we could limit the discussion to irregularity." I paused, thinking ahead to the investigation. "Why don't you call the sheriff and ask if he can meet us at the Buffalo Jump in an hour."

Jill called the sheriff's department. After a brief conversation, she was smiling as she ended the call. "Randy Pannell is meeting us at the Buffalo Jump."

"He's the deputy you pulled off the highway, right?"

"That's him. The sheriff said Randy's shoulder is healed and he's excited about working with us again."

Glancing at Jill I said, "If we're exciting, Randy's life must be very boring."

"I think you told me a cop's life was hours of boredom and moments of terror."

"I don't think I said, 'moments of terror'. More likely, I said 'moments of excitement.'"

"I'm sure you said terror. I think that quote came up right after we moved to Texas. It was when you chased the guy loading toxic waste into a boat. You sent me to call the local cops while you got in a shootout with the guy trying to escape down the canal. Yep, I'm sure you used terror to describe your feelings about hiding behind a wooden piling while he emptied his gun at you."

The interstate through Rapid City was lined with chain motels and strip malls. After we passed the city's commercial areas, the landscape gained altitude and we climbed toward the pine-covered Black Hills. Relatively new houses dotted the hills, each with a steep driveway leading to a home with a commanding view of the valley. After a few miles, I-90 turned northwest, toward Sturgis. The development ended, and the interstate cut through acres of prairie nestled between forested hills.

Jill gestured toward an area ahead of us. "The hillside on the right burned. It's strange how the trees in one canyon burned while hillsides a few hundred yards away are untouched."

"It's dry here, like at your parents' ranch, right?"

"In normal years, we get snow that melts and moistens the soil. Several years of drought has left everything brown and combustible. I'll bet the ranchers around here didn't even bale hay last year. They probably turned their herds loose in the fields all summer and sold off nearly all of them in the fall."

Approaching the town of Sturgis, the interstate was lined with ads for campgrounds and establishments catering to the motorcycle crowds who visited during the annual Sturgis motorcycle rally. Once past town, tiny white dots appeared in the distant prairie. "Are those antelope?" I asked.

"They are. We'll probably see some herds closer to the highway as we get into Wyoming."

Jill stared at the sign announcing the upcoming Spearfish exit and sighed. "I know we need to meet Randy Pannell, but I feel terrible about driving past Spearfish without at least saying a quick hello to my folks."

"There's no quick way to say hello, then leave." I reached out and squeezed Jill's hand. "We'll get back to see them."

Suddenly straightening up, Jill smiled. "It'd be fun to bring the horses over so we could check out areas around where the body was found."

I didn't intend to grimace, but the look I got said I'd telegraphed my negative feelings about riding our horses.

"You react to the subject of horses like I react to discussions about my mother and sex."

"To be clear, we were not discussing your mother and sex with Matt and Mandy. We were discussing sex in your mother's house."

"I don't see the difference. I'd be dealing with my mother if we had sex in her house."

"She was pleased that we were a normal newlywed couple who made the bed springs squeak."

"Moving on..."

"Did the sheriff say anything else interesting when you spoke with him?"

"Not really. He just said Randy had healed from his injuries. They were both looking forward to working with us again." Jill paused. "I think your plan to *provide assistance* with their investigation went over very well. They were accustomed to federal agencies coming in and taking over. Aiding them as we did with the Devils Tower investigation, then stepping back to let them take center stage with the press, made Sheriff Stoddard look like a hero. That move got us a lot of credibility with both Stoddard and Pannell."

"As Park Service Investigative Service Branch employees, we carry sidearms and wear badges, but our role is investigative support. We let the local folks be the cops, and we step back when it's time to handcuff the bad guys and take them to jail."

"It seems strange that our bosses are okay with that approach. Most agencies, like the FBI and DEA, are political, living and dying by their time in front of the news cameras."

"There's nothing strange about it at all. It's like the role of park rangers. They're on site to enhance our visitors' experience and are at their best when they're almost as part of the background. We want people to remember the wonder of Yosemite, not the ranger who explained the park's geology to them." I paused, then added, "And there aren't many investigators, so we don't have the luxury of throwing a large group of agents into an investigation."

Jill thought about that for a moment. "We don't have tactical teams, labs, or even a substantial number of armed people to bring to a confrontation. All we bring to the party are experience and an unbiased eye. We haven't been sucked into the details that sometimes blind the local law enforcement people."

"Being able to step back and see the bigger picture is sometimes what's required to see how the puzzle pieces fit together."

Jill shifted in her seat and nodded to an upcoming sign. "We're crossing into Wyoming. We can take the Beulah exit, or we can turn off at the Wyoming Welcome Center and circle back on Highway 14."

"I'd like to drive past Vore Buffalo Jump on the interstate first to get a sense of the place. After that, we can circle back on the frontage road."

At eighty miles-an-hour, the Vore Buffalo Jump sign on the right side of the interstate whizzed past so quickly that I nearly missed seeing the oversized white teepee sitting next to a rocky hole in the prairie.

"That was it," Jill said.

"Wow. I'm accustomed to national parks that are thousands of acres. That entire site looks like little more than a fenced acre of land."

Jill smiled. "Two acres if you include the parking lot."

* * *

Considering that the site wouldn't officially open until late May, there were a surprising number of vehicles in the parking lot near the teepee-shaped visitor welcome center. I parked next to a white Crook County Sheriff's Department SUV.

Jill walked alongside me to the teepee. "It looks like a party."

"I wonder what's going on. They're not open yet."

The interior space was cramped with ten people gathered around a counter. Most were civilians wearing jeans and tan Carhartt jackets. One of the exceptions was Deputy Randy Pannell, who stepped forward and shook Jill's hand emphatically. "It's really nice to see you guys again." Turning to the group, he introduced us, then explained that the other people were members of the Vore Buffalo Jump Foundation board of directors.

Peggy Landin stepped forward and introduced herself as the foundation's director. "Randy told us about your credentials." Looking at Jill she added, "Randy didn't mention your husband's rugged ranger look."

Jill looked at me. "The emphasis should be on the 'rugged' adjective. We've been in airports and on planes for quite a while and I think Doug forgot to use a sharp razor when he shaved."

A middle-aged woman wearing a US Park Service uniform stepped up. "I'm Nikki Beardsly. I'm an archaeologist by education, currently working as an interpretive ranger at Devils Tower."

"Are you a member of the board?" Jill asked.

"I couldn't pass up the opportunity to be part of one of the most significant archaeological sites in the US. We've found evidence of at least seven different Native American tribes who'd used this site over at least three hundred years."

After we shook hands with everyone gathered in the hut, Peggy suggested we move to the cabin-like structure behind the teepee. "The log cabin is our gift shop. It's also used for our board meetings."

Large enough to seat a small group, the cabin was arranged with a dozen chairs set around the perimeter. Peggy gestured for Jill and me to take seats alongside her. With everyone seated, Peggy nodded toward a man who looked like he could've been in an advertisement for western gear. "Charlie found the body. I'll let him explain the discovery."

Charlie set his Stetson on its crown and stood, his hair looking like it had been molded by the inside of his hat. Although his tan jacket and jeans were worn, they looked like they were fresh out of the washer. The man's graying bushy moustache hinted that he might be about sixty, but his weathered face looked more like he was closer to eighty. "Well, it's like this," he said, leaning forward and placing his hands flat on the table. "We were cleaning up before the first group of schoolchildren arrived for a tour. I was walking around the museum building, picking up trash and checking to make sure no vandals had been around over the winter, when I smelled something rotten, like a dead raccoon or something. I wasn't paying much attention until I saw some camouflage cloth sticking out of a chunk of chokecherry brush behind the building. My first thought was that someone's deer blind had blown away, but when I looked closer, I could see hair and an ear. I got Peggy, who confirmed what I thought I was seeing, then we called the sheriff's department."

Randy nodded. "After I got the call, I confirmed that there was a human body hung up in the bushes on the hill. It had been there for quite a while and no one had messed with it, so I called the coroner's office. Mike came out and we took a bunch of pictures before getting a ladder to pull the body loose from the bushes and lower him down."

Now standing with his arms crossed, Charlie shook his head. "I helped cut brush and lift. Randy and Mike did a nice job of making sure we weren't messing up any evidence around the body. We scooped the debris at the bottom of the hill into buckets so the state crime lab could look for evidence. They took pictures as we removed layers. We handled it like an archaeological dig, taking out layers and looking through twigs, leaves, and debris."

Randy held up a computer memory stick. "I've got a copy of all the pictures we took at the site. Mike added the pictures he took as the body thawed out at the mortuary. It's the darndest thing. Initially, we thought maybe the guy had fallen or been pushed over the rim, like the buffalo fell when they were driven into the hole. But as Mike looked closer, we could see scrapes and bruises that looked more like the guy had been dragged behind a horse. There were ligature marks around his neck, which made us think maybe he'd been hung. But there were scrapes where it looked like he'd dug at the rope around his neck with his fingernails, so we knew he'd been alive awhile after the noose was tightened."

I looked at Peggy. "Was the gate locked when you arrived that day?"

Nodding, she replied, "The lock was intact. We think he must've been dragged under the fence, out of view from the interstate."

Randy nodded. "I was with the coroner when he looked at the thawed body. I told him the guy's clothing was shredded and his head, shoulders, arms, and hips scraped."

Peggy nodded. "It looked like he'd been dragged across the prairie."

Jill smiled at Peggy. "That's a very clinical analysis of the victim's wounds. Are you a doctor?"

Laughing, Peggy shook her head. "No, ma'am, I'm just an old ranch girl who's butchered her share of cattle, antelope, elk, and deer. Trying to figure out what happened to that battered body was more interesting than scary."

"Did you find any identification with the body?"

Peggy shook her head. "There wasn't a cell phone, driver's license, hunting license, charge card, or even a gas receipt in the guy's pockets. I suppose whoever dragged him must've taken them out."

Charlie shook his head. "I think whatever was in his pockets got strewn across the prairie when he was dragged behind a horse. Hell, even his boots came off."

"Did you find any evidence of how the victim got here?" Jill asked.

Randy nodded. "You know how slow grass grows here, and driving a vehicle across the prairie leaves tracks until the prairie grows back. There are still visible four-wheeler tracks down the ditch. After a distance, they come out of the ditch, go through a gate, then cut across the prairie."

"Four-wheeler?" I asked.

"One of those four-wheeled ATVs," Randy explained. "The tires were knobby and the tracks too close together to be a pickup."

Charlie wrinkled his nose. "One of those damn ATVs the newcomers use instead of horses. They're noisy, tear up the prairie, and are generally a pain in the ass."

Peggy chuckled. "Charlie told the game warden they should open a season on them."

"Damn right!" Charlie agreed. "It'd be more of a service to the environment to shoot a couple of them than it is to kill an elk."

I glanced at the other board members who were mostly grinning about Charlie's view of ATV riders. "Is there any chance that one of the local folks with a similar opinion about ATV riders might've thinned the herd?"

Nikki, the Devils Tower ranger, shook her head. "We all complain about the ATV riders, but no one would actually kill one of them."

Charlie snorted. "I've taken the position that they'll be punished in hell rather than on earth."

Randy, the deputy, interrupted. "I followed the back trail about halfway to Aladdin but lost it when the rider went over a rocky area and some depressions that were probably filled with snow."

"I don't suppose you found a boot or some other item that belonged to the victim?" Jill asked.

"He must've lost his boots long before he got near the trail I found."

Peggy looked around the room. "Does anyone else have something to add?" When no one else spoke, she turned to Jill and me. "The reason I asked the board to be here is to provide you with local resources. We're all rattled by this incident, and we're all at your disposal to do whatever you need done."

Charlie nodded. "I've got horses if you'd like to ride the back trail."

Nikki stood. "There are seasonal rangers joining us at Devils Tower for the upcoming busy months. I can call them in to help search or do whatever you need."

"There's a volunteer sheriff's posse who can help with a search too, if you need them," Randy added.

I thought through the information that had just been dumped on us. "Thank you all. At this point, I'd like to see where you found the body. After that, we can speak with the coroner, then check into our room at the Aladdin Motel. If we need your help or if there are more questions that arise, we'll work through Deputy Pannell or Peggy."

The group stood and mingled with Jill while I directed Randy Pannell outside. "I'd like to talk to the coroner about his efforts to identify the victim. If the body is still at the mortuary, I'd like to see him."

"As far as I know, the victim is still in the mortuary cooler. There's no one to claim the body until he's identified."

"After we see where the body was recovered, let's go to the coroner's office," I suggested. "I assume that's in the Sundance courthouse."

Randy chuckled. "Actually, Mike owns a machine shop out toward the Devils Tower cutoff. I'll call to see when he's available to meet us at the mortuary."

"It seems odd that Wyoming still has elected coroners."

Randy's eyes twinkled. "Mike is willing to pick up dead bodies and fill out the paperwork, which is ninety-nine percent of the job. If there's a suspicious death, he ships the body to a pathologist in Rapid City."

"It still seems odd to have a coroner who isn't a doctor."

"It's not that big a deal. Most people die of medical issues which are easily determined. A lot of the rest die in car accidents. Again, the cause of death is easily determined. In the rest of the cases, Mike uses an outside expert." Randy paused, then added, "Most people trust Mike more than they do any doctor."

"Okay, give the coroner a call," I said with a shrug. "Let's meet him at the mortuary later."

Chapter 4

We walked the spiral trail following the inside of the forty-foot-deep Buffalo Jump pit. About a quarter of the way down, Peggy pointed to a steep embankment above us. "This is where the stampeding buffalo jumped into the pit. Some died from the fall, others were crushed when their herd members fell on top of them. The surviving buffalo were speared or shot with arrows from the rim."

At the bottom of the trail was the museum, a structure resembling a steel-sided pole barn. Randy led us aside as we neared the museum entrance. "The body was found over here." He gestured beyond the building.

Charlie had followed along with us to the spot and stepped ahead of the group. "There was still snow here, on the side of the building. He was in those bushes, about halfway down the slope."

We stared at an unremarkable spot of hillside. Aside from the footprints left by the legion of deputies, coroner's assistants, and foundation volunteers who'd looked at or helped remove the body, the location where the body was found looked like all the surrounding brushy hillside except for the trimming that had been done to remove the body.

"Was there anything unusual about the scene?" I asked.

Charlie frowned. "Hell yes, there was something unusual. There was a damned dead body laying there in the bushes. That's not something you see every day."

I heard Jill chuckle but tried to stay focused. "Besides the dead body, was there anything else that was unusual around the body?"

Charlie pulled at his lower lip while considering the question. "I don't know. I was kind of focused on the camo pattern of the jacket. It took a while before I visualized the person."

Randy took over when Charlie had nothing more to add. "I didn't notice anything unusual. If there had been any blood or tissue left on the trail, it had been cleaned up by crows and other scavengers. I couldn't make out any tire tracks inside the fence or evidence of the body being dragged, which makes me think whoever brought him down did it after there was snow on the ground."

I turned to the group. "Do any of the volunteers come down here in the winter?"

Nikki shook her head. "Our tourist season is Memorial Day through Labor Day. We open early for a few school groups, and occasionally we get a fall school group. But the building isn't heated, and no tourists are interested in coming down here after Labor Day."

Charlie nodded. "Aside from mice, there's nothing living down here over the winter."

I looked around at the group of directors. "None of you were here over the winter?"

They shook their heads without responding verbally. I tried to discern any equivocation or delay in their responses, but they seemed equally disturbed by the discovery.

"None of you recognized the victim?"

Charlie spoke up. "At first, he was halfway up the hill in the chokecherry brush, so the lump was barely recognizable as a human being. As the branches were moved away, we realized the man was badly scuffed up. Hell, he could've been my brother and I wouldn't have recognized him in that state."

The others nodded in agreement. Nikki cleared her throat. "I've helped with the recovery of some people who've fallen from Devils Tower. Some of them are pretty badly banged up by the fall, and this guy was even more unrecognizable than some of the climbers we've recovered. I mean, he was a mess."

"Worse than climbers who fell?" I asked.

Nikki cocked her head. "Worse, but in different way. The climbers have compound fractures and impact injuries that leave them deformed. This guy looked more like...like someone had held a coarse belt sander against him. He was scuffed and abraded everywhere." Glancing at the others, Nikki chose her words carefully. "I mean, his nose was gone. It looked like it had been ripped off his face. And so was his left ear."

Peggy stepped forward and gestured toward the museum building. "Let's step inside. I'd like you to see why the museum is here."

The interior of the building featured a walkway around an open archaeological excavation. The soil had been removed, exposing layers of white bones. Farther from the entrance the excavation got deeper and deeper, with each step exposing another layer of bones buried at an even deeper level. Nikki, the archaeologist, stepped between Jill and me. "This site was discovered when surveyors were trying to map a route for I-90 over a solid roadbed. Drilling here, they hit layer after layer of bones. Believing they'd discovered a Native burial ground, they contacted the University of Wyoming archaeology department, which dispatched a professor to examine the core samples drilled by the construction company. He identified the bones as buffalo, rather than human. Apprised of the size and depth of the bone deposits, the professor quickly assessed this as a location where the native tribes stampeded buffalo to kill them. He was astounded by the depth of the deposits and consulted his colleagues. This site was identified as the deepest deposit of buffalo remains ever discovered." Nikki took a breath.

"As you can see, a few layers have been carefully removed. The native people ate or used almost every part of the buffalo. The bones found here represent the portion of the skeleton that wasn't useful, making the depth of this deposit even more incredible. The majority of the skeletal remains here are the small bones located at the base of the buffalo skull. As best we can estimate, this site represents the remains of tens of thousands of animals."

Jill turned in disbelief. "More than ten thousand buffalo died here?"

Nikki nodded. "Yes, we've determined that each drive killed about a hundred buffalo, and the drives were made by multiple family groups or tribes of a hundred or more people. By looking at the depth of the layers, the bones in the core samples, and the types of arrowheads and spears used to kill the trapped and injured animals, we know the site was used for about four hundred years by at least seven different native tribes."

"How can you determine this was accomplished by different tribes?" I asked.

Nikki turned around and pointed to a display on the wall behind us. "As we dug down, we found different types of arrowheads and tools. The type of stone, the style, and the shape of the tools represent the different approaches used to knap and shape the tools by different tribes."

"Knap?" I asked.

"It's the process used to sharpen flint into arrowheads."

"Ah, striking the edge to chip off pieces," I said.

Nikki's knowing smile told me I was off base. She led us to a different portion of the display. "The knapping process is actually more controlled and precise than chipping away at an arrowhead by striking it. The native arrowhead makers gripped a pointed stone in buckskin and pressed it tangentially against the future arrowhead. That process breaks away chips in a more precise and controlled way than striking the arrowhead, which would've broken more tools than were created."

"And you can tell which tribes made different arrowheads and tools?" Jill asked.

Gesturing to another portion of the display, Nikki pointed toward arrowheads mounted in the display. "Some tribes preferred a more rounded shape to their arrowheads. Others made the pointed style that we often see depicted, like in our Park Service uniform patches. The attachment peg also evolved over time from a blunt peg to a more undercut design, giving us a good way of dating the transition of the native tribes who inhabited this area. We also see flint from different sources across North America, which indicates trading between tribes from different regions."

I noticed Randy Pannell tapping his watch. "I think we've got to end our archaeology lesson and visit the coroner."

Chapter 5

Jill and I followed Randy's SUV, backtracking to the Aladdin turn-off, then onto I-90. He led us to Sundance, the next town to the west. We took the second Sundance exit and drove through the southern side of the downtown area.

"I didn't remember Sundance being large enough to justify three I-90 exits," I said as we stopped at Main Street to make a left turn.

A hint of a grin appeared on Jill's face. "You must be getting Alzheimer's. The Sundance population hasn't grown in the past thirty or forty years."

"It's not Alzheimer's. I obviously didn't think we'd ever be back here, so I purged most of the Sundance memories from my mind."

Randy turned into a concrete driveway that circled under the portico of a newer building located on the north side of the street. We parked alongside him in a paved parking lot beyond the mortuary entrance.

"The funeral home must be a profitable business. The building is new, larger, and has a black Cadillac parked in the rear," I said as I unbuckled my seatbelt.

"I assume it's profitable," Jill replied, before opening her door. "On the other hand, appearances are important. I imagine a mortician has to look prosperous but not ostentatious."

Randy met us at the back bumper of his SUV. He nodded toward a dusty Ford pickup and a dark blue SUV with a Wyoming seal on the door parked across the lot. "It looks like Mike and the DCI beat us here. I hope they haven't been waiting long."

Following Randy to the front door, I commented, "You refer to the coroner by his first name, and he drives a dusty pickup instead of a black Suburban with a coroner's logo on the door. I think I've died and gone to heaven."

Randy smiled as he held the door for us. "Things are a bit less formal in Crook County than they are in the big city."

"Tell me he doesn't put corpses in the pickup bed," I said as I walked past Randy.

Randy smiled. "Why not?" He waited a beat, then added, "The pickup is Mike's personal vehicle. The County has a van for corpse recovery."

After we walked through a chapel that seated roughly fifty people, Randy led us to an office door in the back corner of an alcove off the chapel. The two men seated there were dressed in what I'd call *western casual*, with checkered western-cut shirts worn over jeans and boots. A heavyset, freckled red-haired woman wearing a badge was in conversation with the men. They all stood and smiled when we arrived. I recognized Mike Frolander, the coroner, from our Devils Tower investigation. He stepped forward and put out his hand to my partner first. "Jill Fletcher, I'm pleased to see you."

Jill beamed as she shook the coroner's hand. "It's nice to see you too, Mike. Too bad it's under the usual unpleasant circumstances."

Mike shook my hand next. "Well, these are about the only circumstances I get to see anyone these days. Between long days at the shop and too many coroner calls, I don't get to socialize." He stepped aside and introduced the woman. "This is Darcy Cabot, from the Wyoming Department of Criminal Investigation. She'll make arrangements to have our victim taken to the state lab in Cheyenne."

Darcy shook Jill's hand. "Jill Fletcher, I presume. Mike's been bragging about you."

Jill gave the coroner a questioning look. "It's a pleasure to meet you, Darcy," Jill replied.

"I'm Doug, Jill's less well-known partner," I said, shaking Darcy's hand.

She snorted. "You're no well-less-known, Doug. It's just that male cops belong to a much larger fraternity."

The funeral director walked from behind the desk and shook Randy Pannell's hand. "Thanks for coming by, Randy."

Gesturing toward us, Randy introduced Pat Hinzman. "These are the Park Service investigators I told you about, Jill and Doug Fletcher."

Hinzman shook Jill's hand first, his smile warm and sincere. "Nice to meet you, ma'am. Randy and Mike have said a lot of nice things about you."

I assessed the funeral director's smile as well-practiced warmth meant to reassure grieving families. "Nice to meet you, Pat."

Reading my skepticism, Pat's smile broadened as he offered me his hand. "And you're the husband who's comfortable living with a woman who can shoot the eye out of a prairie dog at two hundred yards with a pistol."

"I try to be extra nice to her because I'm a much larger and slower target than a prairie dog's eye."

Hinzman put his left hand on my shoulder. "Hank Stoddard gave you a special introduction when he told me he'd found additional investigative assistance. In Hank's words, you're the most competent and self-deprecating federal law enforcement officer he's ever dealt with. He thinks a lot of you, and that's a high bar."

"All we've ever done is support Randy and the sheriff," I explained. Looking at Darcy, I said, "I hope Randy, the sheriff, and

Mike have been clear about the role that Jill and I play. We're here to assist them. It's their case and we'll gladly step aside if we're causing friction or stepping on toes."

Darcy smirked at Randy. "You were serious when you told me about them."

"Trust me, Darcy. Doug didn't even want to come to the sheriff's news conference after the Devils Tower incident."

We sat in the guest chairs arranged in front of the funeral director's desk. "Randy and Hank solved the mystery. All Jill and I did was help them look differently at the clues."

Randy coughed into his hand, and murmured, "bullshit," muffled in the cough.

Mike slapped Randy on the back. "Got something caught in your throat, Randy?"

"The bullshit is getting so deep in here, it's a good thing we're all wearing boots," he replied.

I redirected the conversation. "We just met with the board from Vore Buffalo Jump Foundation and saw where the body was found. What can you tell us about the victim?"

The coroner leaned forward, putting his forearms on his thighs. "The guy is one hell of a mess. There was no ID found with the body. Randy and I walked the backtrail as far as we could see it without finding anything but tire tracks. I expected to find an occasional clump of cloth that ripped off the guy's clothing caught on a piece of sagebrush. The guy's face is missing." He paused, then added, "Even if I found someone who knew him, I doubt they could identify him given the state he's in."

I looked at the funeral director and DCI agent. "Do either of you have anything to add?"

Pat leaned back in his chair. "I've been in the mortuary business for close to thirty years, and aside from some nasty car wrecks, I've never seen a body in such bad condition." He looked at Jill and drew a breath. "I hate to be crude, but that poor sonofabitch is a disaster. He even lost one testicle somewhere on his trip to the Buffalo Jump."

"Ouch," Jill said.

Mike, the coroner, nodded. "He was dead before the damage was done to his body."

"Did you have a post-mortem exam done?" I asked.

Darcy nodded. "The pathologist in Rapid City did an autopsy. He said all the exterior abrasions were made after he was dead. A rope around his neck killed him before he was ripped to shreds. That being said, the last moments of John Doe's life weren't pleasant. He was choked to death by the rope before being dragged across the prairie. There wasn't anything in the victim's trachea or lungs to indicate he took a breath while being dragged through the sagebrush. It could've been an unpleasant trip, but he wasn't alive for it."

"He was hung, then dragged?" I asked.

The coroner nodded. "Whoever hung him was an amateur. A professional executioner makes careful calculations to make sure the victim's neck breaks, killing him instantly. An amateur just hangs the guy, who slowly dies of strangulation."

Jill sighed. "That's a horse thief's punishment."

"Actually, it's a combination," Mike replied. "Most horse thieves were hung from a tree. Others were dragged behind a horse until the rider figured they were either dead or had learned their lesson."

Jill shook her head. "My Uncle Chet said the lucky ones died. Being left with half your skin scraped off, without water or food was usually a death sentence, too."

I turned to the coroner, changing the gruesome topic. "You haven't been able to identify the victim?"

Mike shook his head. "I was able to get partial fingerprints off four fingers. Darcy ran them through the federal Automated Fingerprint Identification System."

Darcy picked up the conversation, "AFIS didn't get any hits, so he wasn't a criminal, law enforcement officer, military veteran, or anyone who's ever gotten a security clearance. None of the local sheriff's offices have received a missing persons report for a middle-aged guy matching the victim's height and weight."

"How about his dental records?" Jill asked.

Darcy shook her head. "I took dental impressions, but I've got nothing to compare them to until we get a possible ID."

Pat shook his head. "I don't think our John Doe had been to a dentist lately. He'd had a few teeth pulled, and I suspect some of the others were causing him discomfort."

Mike chuckled. "Yeah, I don't think John Doe had enjoyed a steak dinner in awhile."

I looked at Randy. "If he's not someone local, have you found any abandoned vehicles?"

"We found a burned-out hulk of an old car outside Alva, but it was left there after it accidently caught fire. We found the owner."

Darcy shook her head. "Doug, we're on the edge of Black Hills National Forest and surrounded by about another million acres of federal land handled by the Bureau of Land Management. There are remote tracts of land that only elk and deer see. Neither the national forest rangers, nor the BLM folks are particularly concerned about reporting or removing old vehicles they find, and I doubt they see anything more than fifty yards off the single-lane forest roads."

Randy nodded. "There are lots of spots where someone could push a vehicle off the edge of a road, and no one would be too concerned because it would be too far down in a ravine to make salvaging it possible."

Jill nodded. "I've driven the Bear Lodge Pass, and you can see battered vehicles at the bottom of the cliffs below some of the curves."

Frowning, I asked, "They went through the guard rails?"

Mike snorted. "There weren't any guard rails on that road until they rebuilt the highway in the '90s, and some parts still don't have guard rails."

Randy nodded. "You can't put guard rails on a chunk of road only ten feet wide that was blasted out of a cliff face."

I looked at the coroner. "What's your plan, Mike?"

"Darcy is taking the corpse to Cheyenne."

"We'll take his DNA and run it through CODIS, the national database of DNA records." She added, "If he's ever been convicted of a felony, we'll find his identity there."

The coroner raised his eyebrows. "I'm hoping you and Jill can pull a rabbit out of your fancy Smokey Bear hats."

Jill leaned back in her chair. "My magic skills are rusty."

That made Randy laugh. "Well, I'm here to help you two however I can. Hank says it's your show."

"Sure, Randy," I replied. "Right up until it's time for the press conference. Then, Hank will be front and center."

Jill shook her head slightly. "Hank was very generous with his praise of our efforts after the Devils Tower case. Don't lump him in with the glory seekers who've claimed credit for our accomplishments."

Glancing at Randy, I said, "You're right. Hank gave you full credit for saving Randy's butt on the interstate and we were full partners in the final solution, even though it went to hell at the end."

Mike stood. "I imagine you want to take a look at John Doe."

Jill looked less than enthused as she stood. "I assume he's not much to look at."

Darcy shook her head. "No."

Pat stepped from behind his desk, carrying a set of keys. "I cleaned him up as best I could, but anybody that was beat up badly enough to lose his nose and ear ain't pretty."

As we walked out of the office I added, "Don't forget that he lost a testicle, too. That's a lot more difficult than ripping off an ear."

Jill glared at me.

"What? I'm just stating the obvious."

Shaking her head as we walked down the hallway, Darcy said, "You guys are way too hung up on your testicles. They're not essential body parts, like an eye or a limb."

I saw Randy squirm as he took a step. "Speaking personally, I'm kind of attached to my nuts. Just saying..."

The funeral director unlocked a room and led us to a cooler. "Here's John Doe," he said, rolling out a tray with a body covered by a light blue sheet.

As expected, the body was naked, exposing all the abrasions. Coarse stitches closed the Y-incision on the chest and abdomen made during the Rapid City pathologist's autopsy. The coroner shook his head. "There's not much there for me to work with," he observed.

I nodded to the funeral director, signaling that I was through looking at the victim.

Looking at Darcy, I asked, "How long will it take to get results from CODIS?"

"I expect we might hear from the lab in a week if they're not backed up."

Randy Pannell wrinkled his nose, disturbed by the odor of the corpse. "It's not like we expect anything from those results."

"That will include the relatives of missing persons," I added. "If this guy hasn't been reported missing, I doubt CODIS will find a match."

Jill turned to Darcy. "Will you initiate a forensic DNA study if you don't get a CODIS match?"

Darcy drew a breath. "I hadn't planned to. A forensic DNA analysis is expensive, and the only time the state ever paid for one was when we recovered skin under the fingernails of a murder victim." Pausing, she added, "On the other hand, if the Park Service was willing to pay for the study, I certainly wouldn't stop you."

We watched the funeral director return the body to the cooler. "Do you have the victim's clothing here?" I asked.

"I've got them in my SUV," Darcy replied. "There's not much to see. His clothing is pretty well shredded except for his suspenders."

Gesturing to the door, the funeral director ushered us out of the room, locking the door as we left. "I have a couple coming in to discuss prepaid burial arrangements in five minutes."

The coroner nodded. "I think we're through anyway. Thanks, Pat."

We walked to the parking lot and stood near Randy's Crook County SUV. "Now what?" he asked.

"I think Jill and I will check into our Aladdin Motel room and eat supper."

Randy smirked. "You might want to eat in Sundance where there are seven more restaurant options. The food in the Aladdin Café is good, but you might be eating there several times in the coming days."

Jill's look told me she was dead on her feet. "Let's check-in at the motel. I'm too tired to think about food."

Randy shook his head. "You're missing the bull-bites special at the Longhorn Grill."

Grimacing, Jill shook her head. "I don't even want to think about which part of a bull those pieces might be." She nodded toward our rental pickup. "Take me to a bed."

* * *

The Highway 111 exit for Aladdin was fifteen minutes away from Sundance. Jill, asleep with her head leaning against the pickup window, didn't even stir when I turned off of I-90. After half an hour in the truck, I was parked in front of the Aladdin Motel.

The Aladdin General Store looked like it had been built during the town's heyday as a mining town. Beyond the store was a newer L-shaped structure with a couple of matching cabins behind the parking lot. Jill stirred when I turned off the engine. "Are we there yet?" she asked as she stretched her arms.

"We've arrived, although I'm not sure what to expect."

Jill exited the truck and walked toward the office. "I don't care as long as the beds are soft, and they have hot water in the shower."

The office was paneled with tongue-and-groove knotty pine, finished with a coat of urethane which brought out the woodgrain and made the walls look almost wet. The smiling woman who walked out of the back room made us feel welcome without saying a word.

"Do you have reservations for Fletcher?" I asked.

Taking a paper envelope from under the counter, she asked, "Can I see your ID and a charge card, please?" She noticed the badge and gun on my belt as I pulled my jacket aside to reach for my wallet. "Which agency do you work for?"

"We're Park Service investigators," I replied, handing her my Park Service ID and government credit card.

Still smiling, she looked at Jill. "I only have one room reservation, but there are plenty of vacant rooms this time of year. Do you want a connecting room, ma'am?"

Jill removed her ID from a back pocket and slid it across the counter. "We're married. As much as I sometimes want a separate space when he snores, we usually stay in the same room."

Still smiling, the woman slid our IDs back to us. "Would you like a room with a king-size bed or a queen with a hide-a-bed?"

"King-sized would be fine," I replied.

"I'll put you in the Ponderosa Cabin, out back. It's not like there's much going on this time of year, but the cabin will be quieter if business picks up." She slid plastic key cards to us. "By the way, I'm Debbie. The restaurant opens at six o'clock and breakfast is included in your room rate. If there's anything you need, dial 'o' and I'll help you out."

"The general store looks intriguing," Jill said as she took her cards.

The woman's smile broadened. "The general store owner says, 'if the store doesn't have it, you don't need it.'"

Chuckling, Jill nodded. "Thanks, Debbie. We'll have to check it out tomorrow."

"You're registered for a week. Is there something going on at Devils Tower?"

"We're here to help the sheriff's department investigate the body they discovered at Vore Buffalo Jump," I replied.

"That was terrible. Do they have any idea who that poor man was?" I must've seemed surprised by the question because she added, "This is the ultimate small town. The population sign says 'fifteen' but I think they counted the ghosts who haunt the mine. If there's anything going on here, we all know about it."

Jill nodded. "I grew up on a ranch outside of Spearfish. I understand small towns. Unlike my partner who grew up in the city."

Debbie turned to go back to the office, then paused. "You also understand how we all know everything that anyone's said or heard, but we don't know the individuals."

Jill frowned. "I don't understand."

Returning to the front desk, Debbie rested her forearms on the counter. "We delight in hearing and repeating rumors, but everyone is reluctant to share anything personal about themselves."

"Ah," Jill replied, nodding her understanding. "We're all very private. My parents' neighbor was beating his wife, but no one knew because she always wore jeans and long sleeves."

"Yes, ma'am. My maid, Astrid, could be an axe murderer and I'd never know it."

I shook my head. "I'm pretty sure the county would be buzzing if anyone had been killed with an ax."

"Not here. But Astrid drives to Texas every winter after all the hunting seasons close. I don't know where she goes, if she's living alone or with someone, or if she's killing off the local miscreants with an ax while she's there."

I saw a twinkle in Jill's eye. "We're from Port Aransas, Texas. Maybe we should take down Astrid's information. We'll check on her when we get home."

Debbie straightened up, her smile revealing the start of crow's feet in the corners of her eyes. "She's a little wisp of a person. Astrid would tip over if she hefted an ax."

We laughed and walked out the door to our pickup. "Do you buy into what Debbie was saying?"

"About her maid?" Jill asked as she climbed into the truck.

"Not specifically the maid. I mean in general; are the small-town folks really that close-mouthed about themselves?"

Closing the door, Jill weighed my question. "In general, I'd say yes. There are the usual braggarts who tell you how tough they are or how they can break any horse that's ever been brought to a ranch. Most of what they say is bullshit, and everyone knows it. Then, there are the quiet folks. The ones who keep to themselves. You know them well enough to shake hands in church or to greet them in town, but you never get any closer than that to them. Everyone knows about their families, how long they've owned the ranch, and if their accounts are paid up at the store. But you don't know their political views or how they feel about anything but the weather."

I edged the pickup past an RV that appeared to be hooked up to the water and electricity at the general store, then drove a few feet to the second cabin behind the motel. We pulled our suitcases out of the back seat and walked into the building. Like the motel office, the cabin was lined with knotty pine. The tile floor gleamed like it had been polished and I couldn't see a speck of dust anywhere.

Jill set her bag down inside the door and stared at the bed. "That's a handmade quilt. The photos on the walls are all local scenery. I couldn't feel more at home unless someone had placed my childhood teddy bear on the pillow."

"Do you feel bad about not staying with your mom and dad?"

Jill set her suitcase on a cart inside the closet before answering. "Yes, and no. I feel sad that we're not seeing my folks. But I'm dead tired, and I'll sleep a lot better here rather than feeling like I have to help Mom."

"I saw a sign at the other end of the general store that read, 'BAR.'"

Taking her toiletry kit out of the suitcase, Jill walked into the bathroom. "You go ahead and check out the local bar scene. I'm going to bed."

"What if I meet some widow who's got a ranch worth millions and no one to share the money with?"

Apparently unconcerned, Jill closed the bathroom door. "Good luck with that plan," she said through the door before turning on the shower.

After unpacking my suitcase and hanging up my uniform, I turned on the television, expecting to find one channel. Instead, I was offered a full array of cable channels and the option to rent movies on demand. I found a British mystery on a PBS station and was engrossed in the plot when Jill walked out of the bathroom, drying her hair.

"I thought you were going to troll the bar for rich widows."

"I'm already married to a rich ranch owner."

"That's probably a good choice. Anyone you'd meet would probably be land-rich but cash-poor."

I cocked my head. "Explain that."

Jill finished drying her hair and returned the damp towel to the bathroom. "Because of the boom in land prices, a lot of it driven by Californians who don't understand or care about the economics of ranching, land prices have climbed beyond the value they can return by raising cattle. So, if the local folks sold their ranches, they'd make big bucks. The flip side of that coin is that most of the locals are barely eking out enough from cattle sales to pay for groceries and their property taxes. The few exceptions to that are the ranches where oil has been found. If those people own the mineral rights to their land, they're making big bucks."

"Wait a second! What do you mean, 'if they own the mineral rights?'"

"The mineral and water rights aren't connected to the land. They're often separated at the sale, with the mineral rights retained by the original family or being sold off to investor groups."

"Can a rancher stop someone from drilling on his ranch if he owns the land but not the mineral rights?"

"I don't think so. It may depend on the nature of the land ownership. That's not to say the landowner isn't getting something for easement to access the drilling site and pipeline. The big money goes to the owner of the mineral rights, who gets royalties on every gallon of oil that's pumped."

"That's so wrong!"

Jill chuckled. "You say that because you grew up in the Democratic haven Minnesota, where the politicians seem to believe everyone should share in everything. Remember that you're out west where it's every man for himself." Jill wiggled her finger at the television. "Could you find something a little less violent to watch while I try to fall asleep. Somehow sirens and screaming women keep me awake."

"I'm getting into this show."

Jill slid under the covers and pulled the quilt around her neck. "I'd prefer something more restful."

"I think the early news is on."

Jill's head poked out from under the quilt. "Didn't you hear what I said about finding something restful?"

"Maybe *Sesame Street* is on."

My sarcasm backfired. Jill pulled the covers over her head. "I can fall asleep while listening to Elmo."

Chapter 6

After showering and dressing, we walked to the tiny restaurant attached to the motel for breakfast where most of the tables were empty. A sign directed us to seat ourselves. I gestured toward a table in the back corner and Jill nodded, leaving the seat facing the door for me. I was surprised when Debbie, the woman who'd checked us in the night before, walked out of the kitchen carrying two coffee cups and a steaming coffee pot.

"Are you the cook and dishwasher, too?" I asked as she filled our cups.

"When you own a business in a town with a population of 15, you do whatever needs to be done." After filling our cups, she pointed to a chalkboard over the kitchen pass-through shelf. "The specials are on the board and are included with your room. Otherwise, the cook can whip up pretty much anything that's normal western breakfast fare and the prices are reasonable, or negotiable."

Jill chuckled, "Negotiable?"

Debbie shrugged. "You know how it goes. Someone always bitches when their coffee costs more than fifty cents, even though it's five bucks cheaper than at Starbucks."

After considering the rancher's special, which included a steak, hash browns, bacon, eggs, and hash browns, Jill asked, "Can I get a bowl of oatmeal?"

Without writing on a pad, Debbie nodded. "Do you want raisins, cream, and brown sugar with that?"

"Sure, bring me the works."

Debbie looked at me. "And for you, Mr. Fletcher?"

"I'll have the pancake special with my eggs over easy."

Two of the other patrons, who'd all checked us out when we walked in, appeared to be local working folks. Two men wearing hunter camouflage intrigued me. "I think the two guys near the front window arrived in the pickup with the ladders on the side. I'm curious about the guys in camouflage. It's April, not the November deer or elk hunting season."

Jill nodded. "The guy in the other back corner has been staring at us since we walked in. I assume he arrived in that side-by-side ATV parked alongside the building."

I glanced at the man, noting the paper napkin tucked into the neck of his shirt and the dribbles of egg and syrup spilled on the napkin and his shirt. "I wonder if he has Down syndrome?"

Jill smiled at him, and the guy looked away. "I'm not sure if it's that. My dad would say he was slow."

Debbie carried two heaping platters to the men near the door, who'd apparently ordered the rancher's special. Looking over the rim of her coffee mug, Jill watched the food delivery. "Those guys are lean, like ranch hands. If I ate breakfasts like that, I'd weigh three hundred pounds."

"I assume they do something that burns off all those calories."

Jill glanced the other direction. "Our lonely friend seems to be having a conversation with himself. He seems to be getting agitated."

"Try not to make eye contact," I suggested.

"You're the one who taught me to be situationally aware."

"You're already aware of him. Watch him in your peripheral vision."

Debbie went back into the kitchen and returned with the coffee carafe. "Your breakfasts will be up in a couple of minutes. It took John a while to find the oatmeal container. We don't get much call for hot cereal. Most people are more interested in getting the true western breakfast experience, and the locals are more into meat and eggs."

"Why are those two guys dressed in camo?"

Debbie glanced over her shoulder and smiled at the guys I'd mentioned. One of them lifted his coffee cup, gesturing for a refill. Debbie nodded, then turned back to us. "It's the spring turkey hunting season."

"Tell us about your lone customer in the other corner," Jill said without looking toward him.

"That's Barry. He lives on the ranch just east of here with his parents. He's harmless, if you're worried about him."

Jill took a sip from her refreshed coffee. "We're more curious than worried."

Debbie smirked. "Based on my experience, cops aren't ever curious, unless they're worried." She looked toward the corner and called out, "Hey, Barry. Come over here and meet Mr. and Mrs. Fletcher. They're Park Service rangers."

Barry blinked in apparent surprise, then got up from his chair without removing his soiled napkin from the neck of his shirt. He walked over until he was standing next to Debbie. "Mr. and Mrs. Fletcher are staying at the motel for a few nights. Let them know if you see anyone messing around with their pickup."

Barry nodded once, then stood uncomfortably, as if he was about to speak but was unsure of what to say. "Howdy. Nice to meet you." He stared at Jill, looking almost perplexed. "You've got a badge on. Are you a cop?"

Jill put on her polite smile and nodded. "Yes, I'm a Park Service investigator."

"How is an investigator different from a cop?"

"They're pretty much the same thing. We look for bad people, but don't arrest people for speeding or things like that."

Digesting Jill's words, Barry cocked his head. "You're the prettiest cop I've ever seen."

Taken aback by Barry's lack of mental filter, Jill choked on her coffee. "Thank you for the compliment."

Barry nodded. "My mom says it's okay to say things as long as they're the truth."

"What other truthful things have you told people?" Jill asked.

Barry looked at Debbie, then paused. "Debbie sleeps in the same bed with John, but they're not married. Some people think that she'll probably get knocked up because they're sharing a bed."

The comment didn't seem to faze Debbie, who I guessed was on the far side of her getting knocked up years. She smiled. "Would you like another pancake, Barry?"

"I would." Barry was about to return to his table when he paused. "Um, Debbie."

"Yes?"

"My mom says I should say thank you to people who do nice things for me. Thank you."

Debbie winked at Jill. "You're welcome, Barry. I'll tell John to pour another pancake for you."

Barry continued to stand at the table, apparently unsure whether he should return to his table or sit down with us. He turned to me. "Debbie said you were Mr. and Mrs. Fletcher. Are you married?"

I nodded. "We are."

He turned to Jill. "You're very pretty. If you were single and lived around here, men would bother you."

"Do men bother the other pretty single women around here?" Jill asked.

Barry sniffled and wiped his nose on the sleeve of his flannel shirt. "Debbie and Tanya are the only single women in Aladdin. Debbie doesn't take crap off anyone. Tanya is too polite. Mom says Tanya flirts with the cowboys."

"Does Tanya work here, at the café?"

"No, she works at the general store. Sometimes she tends bar and sells stamps in the post office, too."

"It sounds like Tanya is a very busy woman."

Barry frowned. "I don't think she's awfully busy. I think she just does a lot of stuff when it needs doing."

Debbie walked out of the kitchen carrying a platter with our breakfasts and a single pancake on a plate. She set the oatmeal in front of Jill and chastised Barry as she set out a pitcher of cream, a bowl of raisins, and a small cup of brown sugar. "You stop bothering the Fletchers while they eat."

Barry seemed relieved. "Yes, Debbie." He returned to his table.

Setting my platter of food in front of me, Debbie leaned close. "Like I said, Barry is harmless."

"Does he eat breakfast here every day?" I asked.

"During the winter he's here every morning. He helps around the ranch, so once the calving season hits, he's too busy to come down here." Debbie leaned close. "To be honest, I think his parents chase him out of the house, so they have some quiet time. Barry's quite a chatterbox once he gets to know you."

"You let him hang around here?"

"To be honest, we need every dollar anyone spends to make it through until the tourist season. Barry doesn't spend a lot, but he's here every day, he pays for his breakfast in cash, and he leaves a generous tip."

"Does he sit here all day?" Jill asked.

"We shut down after breakfast. Barry checks out the folks at the general store after I run him out, then he takes off on his ATV."

Debbie refilled the coffee for the guys near the window and handed them their bills. They paid her in cash and told her to keep the change.

After finishing off the last spoonful of oatmeal, Jill wiped her mouth. "What's our plan for today?"

Checking my watch, I said, "Randy said he'd meet us here. I thought we should walk the ATV tracks from where the body was found."

Jill snorted. "In your lifetime of cop experiences, have you ever followed a trail across the prairie?"

"I've followed plenty of blood trails."

"Dear, the prairie stretches for miles, and there's no blood trail to follow. If we're going to follow the trail across the prairie, we should ride, not walk."

"I wish Jamie Ballard was here. He followed a trail across the desert for three days."

"I doubt Jamie would hop a plane to Aladdin, Wyoming to help you follow a trail."

Debbie refreshed our coffee again. "Are you looking for a tracker?"

I shrugged. "I was just commenting that I had a partner who tracked a fugitive through the desert for three days until he captured the guy."

"Some of the hunting guides could help you out. This is their off season. I'm sure I could find one or two who would be happy to do something besides whittle toothpicks from pine kindling."

Jill's eyes lit up. "Do any of them have horses?"

"Most of the guys who take people deep into the national forest have riding and pack horses. They haul in tents and gear, then pack out elk and deer on the return trip."

A bell jingled over the door as Randy Pannell walked in. Debbie motioned him over and took an empty mug off a nearby table. She set it in front of an empty chair and poured coffee into it. "I just suggested that Fletchers find an outfitter to follow the trail left by the ATV that hauled that guy to the Buffalo Jump."

Randy sat between us and wrinkled his nose. "I followed that trail as far as I could."

Debbie laughed. "Randy, I love you dearly, but tracking people isn't your strong suit. I was about to suggest Zane McKitt. He's probably bored silly."

Randy raised his eyebrows. "Zane's got a good reputation as a tracker and fair businessman. If the Park Service is willing to pay him, I have no problem hiring him as a tracker."

"I don't suppose he has a spare ATV for a city cop to use?"

The look Randy gave Debbie made me know I'd asked the wrong question. "Tell you what, Doug. Why don't you sit here and drink coffee all day while Jill and I tempt fate by riding bucking broncs into the forest."

"Fine. Maybe he's got a sway-backed gelding that doesn't go any faster than a trot."

Jill snorted. "We're not planning on a wild west posse pursuit. All we're doing is following a trail across the prairie. Your biggest challenge will be not falling asleep and slipping off the horse."

"As you recall, dear, that was the plan in Cottonwood until *you* decided to chase the bad guy on Lightning Bolt."

Intrigued, Randy asked, "Did you fall off the horse, Doug?"

"That damned horse cut under a low branch and knocked me off. I was doing fine until then."

Randy took out his cell phone. "I'll call Zane and see what he's doing."

Chapter 7

Jill and I walked the short distance to the Aladdin General Store while Randy called Zane McKitt. Jill stopped me as we walked past the door marked *Post Office*. "We should call Jack and clear the bill for the outfitter."

"I prefer asking for forgiveness."

Jill sighed. "Jack wasn't pleased about the hay we purchased in Tuzigoot."

"But he signed the voucher."

"Listen, Fletcher, the hay was on *my* expense voucher. I was the one who had to explain it to the auditors."

I stepped up to the store entrance. "No problem. We'll put the outfitter's fee on my voucher. I love arguing with bureaucrats."

"No, you don't! You usually hand the phone to me and expect me to charm whomever you've stirred up."

"If you paid the outfitter with your federal credit card, like a gas purchase, we wouldn't need to enter it on our expense voucher."

Grimacing, she glared at me. "The auditors watch the credit card purchases more closely than the vouchers. People have been fired for buying clothes and jewelry on their federal credit cards."

Smiling, I said, "But you'll have an invoice to back up the purchase."

"That's not good enough. I'd still have to justify the expense as related to our investigation."

"It will be related to our investigation. You'll be able to explain it." I held the general store door open for Jill, the warmth hitting our faces as a hint of woodstove smoke tickled our noses. "Jack says you missed your calling in the diplomatic corps."

Jill leaned close and whispered as we entered. "Fine. I'll call Jack and clear it *before* the charges go on my card."

"Be prepared to hear him refuse."

Jill smiled. "He won't refuse. Like you said, I can be diplomatic and charming."

The interior of the Aladdin General Store was a time capsule. Wallpaper on the wood walls was peeling in places, giving an ambiance to the place that was impossible for any modern structure to create. A stuffed elk head hung in a back corner while the center of the room was taken up by a table covered with antiques and sales items. On closer inspection, I realized the table was actually an old wooden spool for telephone wire. There were groceries, souvenirs, postcards, and big glass jars of bulk candy on the store shelves like I remember from my childhood.

A cute woman, who appeared to be in her thirties, greeted us from behind the counter. "If you need help with anything, just holler."

I approached the counter, which featured an old-fashioned cash register at the far end. "We're killing time while Randy Pannell is making calls."

Glancing at my badge and holster, the woman smiled. "How do you like your Sig pistol?"

"It shoots where I aim it, and it always fires when I pull the trigger. That's about all I can ask for."

She nodded, making her Ruger baseball cap bob. "I prefer my 1911. It's bulky, but I know if I hit something with that big-old .45 caliber bullet, it'll know it's been hit."

I cocked my head, and she lifted her right hand so I could examine the pistol and holster on her hip. "Do you need it often?"

"I think a woman carrying a pistol has a certain deterrent effect."

Jill joined us at the counter. "How do you like that Glock?"

Joining the conversation late, Jill missed the woman's explanation of her pistol. "The Glock is a good piece. It's maintenance free and I like being able to take thirteen shots without having to eject the magazine and reload." She looked at the woman's holster.

"That's a 1911 knock-off, right? You've only got seven shots."

"The guy who taught me how to shoot said you only need to hit someone once with a .45 before they're thoroughly discouraged."

Jill extended her hand. "I'm Jill Fletcher."

"Tanya Armstrong," the woman replied.

I shook her hand and commented, "Barry is quite taken with you."

Tanya's grin widened. "Barry is sweet. He keeps an eye on things around here."

"What kind of things?" I asked.

"He comes in when we're crowded. People see him and immediately underestimate his mental ability. He's stopped several shoplifters."

"Do you need to carry a gun here?" Jill asked.

Tanya shrugged. "Better to have a gun and not need it than to need one and not have it."

Jill nodded toward me. "My partner had a corollary to that. 'When you need a gun, you need it immediately.'"

"Jill, your accent and look say you're from around here."

"I grew up in Spearfish. Doug grew up in a Minneapolis suburb."

"St. Paul," I corrected. "I don't imagine you're from Aladdin."

Tanya laughed. "No one is from Aladdin. The birth rate has been zero here since the prostitutes moved out after the mine shut down."

"Where is home?" I asked. "Your accent has me baffled."

"I've got a news broadcaster's accent. It's kind of Midwestern without the drawn-out Minnesota vowels. I grew up in eastern Washington, near the Idaho border."

"How did you end up in Aladdin?" Jill asked.

"I'm not sure I've *ended up* here. My RV is parked out back with my 4-Star horse trailer. This is a nice place. I've got an okay job with a nice boss who doesn't hit on me. He lets me keep my RV and horse out back. The winters are a little depressing, but a Chinook wind warms things up once in a while. Overall, Aladdin isn't a bad place."

"The quiet life here would drive anyone from the big city crazy," I said.

"Yup. You won't see any southern California girls on roller skates on our boardwalk. On the other hand, the Sturgis 'bike week' packs the store with motorcycle riders for two weeks. Those characters provide a lot of entertainment."

Jill's smile disappeared. "My experiences with bikers haven't been all that positive."

Tanya paused before answering. "They look tough, and a lot of their girlfriends look like they've been ridden hard and put away wet, but for the most part, they're polite and they don't shoplift. I get the impression that things are wilder at their campgrounds when the drinking starts."

A man in striped overalls walked in and marched up to the counter. "Tanya, do you have another box of .22-250 hollow points behind the counter?"

Sliding open a wooden cabinet behind her, Tanya looked through an assortment of ammunition boxes before selecting a silver box. "Are you still having prairie dog problems, Harvey?" she asked as she set the box on the counter.

Harvey pulled a wad of currency out of a wallet chained to a loop in his overalls. "Not so much a problem as an opportunity. If I wanted to get rid of the critters, I'd poison them or buy a few half-sticks of dynamite. Now, I'm charging city slickers $20 a day to come in and shoot at them."

"Shoot *at* them?" I asked.

Harvey smiled, exposing nearly black gums and lips, most likely the result of chewing snuff over his entire lifetime. The outline of the round snuff can was molded into the back pocket of his coveralls. "They shoot up a couple boxes of shells. Sometimes they hit a few. Most times they just kick up bits of dust and scare the buggers."

I nodded to the ammunition he'd just purchased. "Those twenty rounds of ammo won't go far in a prairie dog town."

Harvey snorted. "I don't shoot the prairie dogs. I shoot the damned coyotes who show up the day after the hunters leave.

The coyotes come to eat whatever prairie dogs get shot. I shoot the coyotes.”

“Life’s circles,” I replied.

“Damned straight!” Harvey replied. He accentuated his comment by spitting into a brass spittoon at the end of the counter.

I looked at the spittoon as Harvey left. “I assumed the spittoon was decorative.”

Tanya rolled her eyes and blew out a breath. “I wish.” She waited until the door closed behind Harvey, then blew out a breath. “Those old farts come in here scratching their crotches and spitting toward the spittoon. I’ve got to tell you; I’ve been tempted to sell some of them a bar of soap and send them home to use it. And don’t even get me started on the cleanup around the spittoon. Dumping it out is bad enough, but they only hit it half the time. I spent ten or fifteen minutes a day mopping up spit with bits of tobacco in it.”

Jill chuckled.

Tanya frowned. “It’s not funny.”

“Sorry. I wasn’t laughing at you. I was thinking back to my childhood on the ranch. You described my life during the roundup and branding season. Dad would hire extra cowboys to help, and they were always toothless, smelly, and profane. I learned so much regarding how long a man could go without bathing, along with cuss words I thought were funny, but now choose not to use.”

"I've heard you use some of them," I said.

"Only when you or a horse have pushed me to my limit."

Tanya laughed. "Yeah, I've been known to swear like a sailor when one of those smelly old farts comes in here and hits on me."

Jill nodded. "Sometimes a few cuss words are the only language a cowboy understands." Her cell phone buzzed, and she stepped away from the counter to answer it.

I leaned close to the counter. "What have you heard about the body they found at the Buffalo Jump?"

Tanya leaned her arms on the counter as if she was about to reveal the world's best-kept secret. "I ain't heard nothing."

"Nothing?"

She smiled. "I've heard a thousand different stories and none of them make any sense at all."

"Give me an example," I said.

"Well, one of the ranchers said the guy was a missing hunter from last fall. He probably got lost, starved to death, or froze."

"How did his body get to the Buffalo Jump?"

Tanya's eyes sparkled. "That's the best part. A grizzly bear dragged him there, then hibernated. I guess the bear was planning to eat him in the spring."

"I didn't know there were grizzly bears in the Black Hills."

"A Devils Tower ranger overheard that discussion. She said the last grizzly bear seen in the Black Hills was chased out in 1960."

"What did the rancher say to that?"

"He stiffened up and glared at the ranger before making some comment about the damned folks from the Wyoming Fish and Game department not knowing shit from Shinola. He claims to have seen grizzly bears on his ranch north of Alva."

"Has anyone else seen a grizzly around here?"

"Nikki, the ranger, politely explained that he'd probably seen a cinnamon-colored black bear. They're not common, but it's much more likely to be seen locally than a grizzly."

"Randy Pannell found ATV tracks leading to where the body was found."

Tanya's grin grew wider. "That's much less interesting than having a grizzly bear dragging a body across several miles of open prairie without anyone seeing it."

"What rumors are there that involve an ATV?"

"None of the ATV rumors are very interesting. I kinda like the one where someone found a trucker's body on the interstate. One version of that is that the trucker was changing a tire and a drunk hit him. Being drunk and afraid of being arrested for a DWI, he hauled the body to the

Hwy 111 exit, then dragged it back to the Buffalo Jump Museum."

"That actually sounds plausible, except there wasn't a truck left on the shoulder of the road, no missing trucker reported, and that's a hell of a long way to haul a body when you could just push it into the ditch and drive off."

Tanya snorted. "Ranger Fletcher, I didn't say any of the rumors were plausible. I'm just telling you what I've heard. Don't you think that last one is pretty juicy and nearly plausible?"

"I'm Doug. You don't need to be formal with me. As for plausibility, I'd say that rumor is almost as unlikely as the grizzly bear scenario. But you're right, it is juicy."

Jill returned to the counter, tucking her phone into a back pocket. "You two look like conspirators. What have I missed?"

"Tanya had two great rumors about our dead guy found behind the museum. One involves a grizzly bear and the other involves a drunk trying to dispose of a trucker's body."

Laughing, Jill leaned on the counter looking like the third conspirator. "Those are pretty far-fetched. Do you have any rumors involving an ATV?"

Tanya shrugged. "People drive ATVs all over the prairie during hunting season, and others just drive them around to be idiots. Have you considered that the ATV tracks have nothing to do with the dead guy?"

Jill looked at me. "We've assumed there's a connection."

"Why?" Tanya asked.

"Because the dead guy was found at the end of an ATV track trail," I replied.

Tanya's eyes sparkled again. "None of the cops have discussed that. I suppose that's one of those close-kept secrets during an ongoing investigation. Did you just spill the beans to me?"

Jill snorted. "You know more about this investigation than we do."

Smiling, Tanya replied, "Maybe I do! I certainly have heard more rumors than you have."

Jill nodded toward the door. "Is that your horse trailer parked behind the store?"

Tanya's demeanor immediately softened. "Yeah, that's for hauling Bill."

"Do you keep him here or is he boarded?"

"There's a shed with a stall behind the store. Rex lets me keep him here for free. I just have to pay for hay and keep his stall clean." She paused, then asked, "Are you a horse person, Ms. Fletcher?"

"Please call me Jill. Yes, I grew up on a ranch outside of Spearfish."

"I didn't start riding until I was almost a teen, but I fell in love with horses."

"What breed is Bill?" Jill asked.

"He's a sorrel overo registered Paint."

Jill nodded, apparently understanding Tanya's horse language.

"I've heard of sorrels, they're a reddish breed," I said. "What's an overo?"

Tanya gave Jill a look, then spoke with me patiently. "Paint is a horse breed. Sorrel is a color. Overo and tobiano are coat patterns or markings."

I nodded, pretending to understand while Jill changed the subject. "Is there a nearby place to ride?" Jill asked.

Gesturing toward the back of the store, Tanya said, "There's the whole Black Hills National Forest behind us. As long as I keep track of which direction is south, we never get lost. If we ride south, we always hit Highway 24."

A middle-aged man with graying temples walked through a door behind the elk's head mount. "Excuse me folks," he said to Jill and me. "Tanya, I need a count on the Black Hills logo merchandise for my order."

Tanya stood and nodded. "I was just briefing our Park Service customers on the dead guy found at the Buffalo Jump."

The man nodded. "I appreciate that, but we don't know anything except rumors. I need to submit my shirt, sweatshirt, and cap orders this afternoon or we won't have them before the tourist season starts."

Tanya held up a sheet of paper. "I'm nearly done. I'll finish it up right now." Excusing herself, Tanya turned and walked toward a clothing rack near the back of the store.

We walked outside and stood on the boardwalk by the door. "What do you think about Tanya's rumors?" Jill asked.

"I suppose they're like rumors everywhere. There may be a thread of truth stitched in that quilt, but it's hard to find."

"Like *Where's Waldo*."

"Who's Waldo?"

Jill cocked her head. "Really? You've never heard of the *Where's Waldo* books?"

"Nope."

"They're complicated picture books with hundreds of faces and things on the pages. There's a character wearing a striped stocking cap, named Waldo, and his image is hidden in each page. It's for little kids. They search the scenes looking for Waldo."

"Huh. And it keeps them occupied by spending time looking for this Waldo character?"

"I babysat for some neighbor kids, and it kept them amused for hours. Of course, they had it figured out the first time through the book, so it was too easy for them to whip through it the second time."

"What did Jack say about using an outfitter?"

"I explained that was the most expedient way to find the ATV trail, and using horses would be much faster than walking the trail on foot."

Smiling, I nodded. "You charmed him into accepting your proposal?"

"You make it sound sleazy. All I did was share my local knowledge of the terrain, the capabilities of a good tracker, and the advantages of horseback versus foot searches."

"Yeah. Call it whatever you want. I call it charming the boss."

Randy, who was walking toward us from his SUV, apparently overheard the exchange. "Doug, you are so cynical. You consider normal people doing normal things to be charming. There's nothing underhanded about just being nice to other people."

"That's right, Doug. Some people are nice to others without having an agenda."

I shook my head. "I've been around too many sleazy people who are trying to take advantage of others. I tend to err on the side of caution until proven wrong."

Randy snorted and looked at Jill. "Did you hear that? Your husband doesn't feel that you've proven him wrong about having ulterior motives."

I raised my hand, stopping Jill's reply. "In her case, I'm not being suspicious. I *know* Jill has ulterior motives. I've seen her in action."

Trying to change the topic, Jill asked, "What did the outfitter say?"

"Well, I seem to have caught him in a weak moment. Zane is so bored that he's helping his wife paint the bedroom. I got the impression he might pay *us* for an excuse to get out of the house and exercise the horses."

Chapter 8

At Randy's suggestion, we ate lunch at Cowgirl Pizza and Laundromat. Jill ordered a spinach salad with smoked chicken but stole pieces off the supreme pizza Randy and I split. Wiping pizza sauce from her fingers, Jill commented, "Combining a laundromat with a pizza place seems so unusual."

Randy shrugged. "Sundance needs a laundromat, and the owners already had the pizza place going next to an empty storefront. Why not combine them?"

"It makes sense to me," I added. "I haven't used a laundromat in years, but I remember getting tired of reading outdated women's magazines while I waited for my loads to wash and dry. It seems like eating a pizza while I was sitting around would've been a big step up."

Grimacing, Jill shook her head. "Greasy fingers and clean clothes don't mix."

Randy slid a package with a wet wipe across the table. "That's why they have the wet wipes."

Jill ripped open the package but wrinkled her nose. "Your pizza is dripping with grease. I don't think ten packages of wet wipes would be enough to clean your fingers enough to fold a white t-shirt."

Checking his watch, Randy eyed the remaining two pieces of pizza. "I hate to see that pizza go to waste but Zane said he'd meet us at the visitor's center at one o'clock."

Jill handed our waitress a charge card. "You could ask for a to-go box."

Randy stood as our waitress handed a pen and charge slip to Jill. "Nah. It'd probably just get left in the back seat of my SUV until it started to smell. Better to leave it behind."

Jill signed the slip and looked at me. "It could be your breakfast."

"Breakfast is included with our room. There's no point in bringing pizza back to the motel."

* * *

In the "Welcome to Wyoming" visitor center parking lot, a slender guy was leaning against the fender of a heavy-duty Chevy pickup attached to a stock trailer. We parked alongside Randy's SUV. As we walked toward them, Jill whispered, "I think Zane's picture is next to the word 'cowboy' in the dictionary."

I nodded. From his scarred cowboy boots to his faded jeans, sheepskin jacket, and sweat-stained Stetson, Zane looked western. His two-day beard growth made it appear he'd just come in from a cattle drive.

His smile was genuine, and his handshake firm.

"We heard you were painting the bedroom," I said as we shook hands.

"Yeah, well, it wasn't quite that bad," Zane said with a chuckle. "But my wife was starting a honey-do list, and that's never a good start to a day."

Jill shook Zane's hand, then looked at me out of the corner of her eye. "My husband has mastered the ability to mess up every project I ask him to do. I'm sure it's a strategy to get him out of honey-do projects."

Randy shook his head. "That doesn't work with Zane. He's a cabinetmaker. Every builder in the county wants him to make cabinets for their construction projects."

Zane put up his finger to stop the conversation. "I'm a guide first and a cabinetmaker second. Nothing takes priority over scouting for game in the summer. I turn down all the cabinet projects once hunting seasons start."

We followed Zane to the back of the stock trailer and watched him release the latches and open the doors. "What game do you guide?" I asked,

Patting the rump of the left horse, Zane replied. "I guide everything from antelope to elk." Responding to Zane's touch the horse backed out of the trailer.

Jill stepped forward and took the horse's lead rope. "This is a beautiful animal," she said as she led the gelding to the grass alongside the parking lot.

"Rascal is a good old boy," Zane said as the second horse backed out of the trailer. "So is Hercules. They're the horses I can put novice riders on and not have to worry about them getting spooked by a shadow in the underbrush and dancing out from under some city slicker."

"Your other horses are more skittish?" I asked as Randy led Hercules toward Jill.

"Puma is my ride. He's not skittish, but I have to let him know who's in charge or he'll take off on his own."

"Jill grew up on a ranch, so she might be able to handle Puma. I'm hoping for Buttermilk or Daisy."

Zane chuckled. "You're not a rider?"

"My history with horses is checkered. I either slide off, get knocked off, or end up hanging on by my teeth."

"You'd best lead Thunder over to Jill and swap her for Rascal."

"Thunder is more spirited?"

Zane smiled. "It's not that he's spirited as much as he responds better to a person who knows how to be easy on the reins, but firm in the saddle."

Thunder jerked his head to the side, nearly pulling the lead rope out of my hands. "Yeah, this one is better suited to Jill's firm touch." Feeling the need to act like I had a clue about what was going on, I reached out and stroked Thunder's neck. "Easy boy. I'm just leading you to the horse person. Try not to hurt me as we walk over to the other horses." The pained expression on Jill's face made me defensive. "Hey, I'm talking softly to him, sounding reassuring. He doesn't know what I'm saying."

"You're walking like you expect him to rear up and kick you."

"Isn't that what horses do?" I asked, handing her Thunder's lead rope.

She took Thunder's lead rope and gave me Rascal's lead. She held her hand up to Thunder's muzzle. He eyed her suspiciously for a second, then rubbed his nose against her hand. "Hi, Thunder. You and I are going to be best buddies."

Thunder took a small step forward and let Jill rub his ears. "My wife, the horse whisperer."

Zane walked up with Puma. "You two are married?"

I nodded as I put my hand out to Rascal, trying to mimic what Jill had done with Thunder. "We're life partners and work partners." Rather than nuzzling my hand, Rascal turned his head away and looked at Jill. When he turned back toward me, he snorted, spraying me with horse snot.

Gasping in frustration, I took a half step back, and wiped the snot off my face. "See! The horse hates me."

Zane patted Rascal's neck. "I'm sure that was a gesture of admiration and friendship."

Jill reached over and picked some hay seeds and litter off my jacket. "I think this hay was irritating his nose. He was just clearing his nostrils."

I stared at Rascal. "Next time you need to sneeze, turn your head the other way." *I knew horses don't understand English, but he stuck out his tongue as if telling me that wasn't going to happen.*

Zane helped me bridle Rascal while Jill did the same with Thunder. Our guide checked both Puma and Rascal's cinches before mounting. "Jill, how did you ever get teamed up with a city slicker who doesn't know how to ride?"

"Aside from not riding and being a cynical cop, Doug's a pretty nice guy." Jill gave me a leg up into the saddle. "Try not to fall off and embarrass yourself," she whispered.

"Whatever happens is up to Rascal. I'm just a passenger." As if hearing my uneasy words, Rascal swung his butt to the side when Jill walked to Thunder and rechecked his cinch for the final time before mounting.

Jill swung into the saddle like a gymnast and Thunder spun around, ready to follow Zane and Puma.

Randy, who had already bridled and mounted Hercules, pointed at a spot roughly a half mile away from the interstate. "I followed the ATV trails until about there."

Zane spurred Puma, and they started in the direction Randy pointed. "You said 'trails' as in plural?"

"Yeah, I assume it was one ATV driving out to the Buffalo Jump, then following the same track back again. The tires went over the same tracks most of the way, although it veered off a bit from time to time."

On horseback, it only took us about twenty minutes to cover the open prairie between the visitor center and the end of the ATV trail. Zane reined Puma in and studied the ATV tracks. "So, these go to the Buffalo Jump, end there, then come back on the same path as they took going in?"

"They definitely end at the Buffalo Jump. Unless two ATVs drove in together and were lifted out by helicopter, I'm pretty sure it's the same one coming and going."

Zane slipped down from the saddle with practiced ease, then knelt beside the tracks. "There was no helicopter involved. It was the same ATV coming and going. It has a nick in one of the tires on the right side, so I can easily say it's the same ATV." Zane remounted his horse and spurred him away from the interstate. I didn't have to do anything. Rascal was happy to follow the other horses without my intervention.

"How far were you able to follow the trail?" Zane asked Randy.

"The trail kind of comes and goes. I assume there were patches of snow or packed ground. I followed the tracks about halfway to Aladdin before I lost them in the open prairie."

"Show me where you lost the trail," Zane said.

Randy spurred his horse, and suddenly Rascal and I were trotting along behind the other three horses. I held the saddle horn with one hand and the reins in the other, trying not to look like I was about to fall off, which was exactly what I was trying not to do.

After another fifteen minutes of riding, Randy reined Hercules to a stop. "I don't see the tire tracks anymore. I think this is where I lost the trail last time, too."

Zane started zigzagging ahead of us, making Rascal restless. He stopped a few yards ahead and turned to us. "Stay put there while I try to find the trail."

Zane worked back and forth, much like I'd seen hunting dogs casting for a scent. His eyes continuously studied the ground, and Puma seemed to be one with him as they moved. About a hundred yards ahead of us, he motioned for us to move ahead.

Randy rode next to me as we followed. "I told you he was good."

Zane walked, occasionally pointing to something on the ground invisible to me. After about twenty minutes of following the trail, the red cupola of the Aladdin General Store came into sight. The trail we were following seemed to be headed generally to a spot somewhere west of the general store and motel.

Reining in Puma, Zane jumped down and knelt, staring at a spot on the ground. "Randy, you'd better look at this."

We all dismounted and led our horses to Zane, who was crouched next to one of the many clumps of ground-hugging sagebrush. Randy tilted his head to look under the branch Zane lifted. "Well, I'll be..."

"What is it?" I asked.

"A boot," Randy replied.

I held Thunder's reins so Jill could get a closer look. "How do we know if that came from our victim?" she asked.

Zane reached out with his left hand and picked a bit of brown and black cloth no larger than a dime from a broken branch stub. "I've been following intermittent tire tracks, broken sagebrush, and bits of cloth for the last couple of miles." Examining the cloth closely, he asked, "Was your guy wearing camo?"

Randy removed a blue plastic glove from his pocket and pulled it onto his right hand. Reaching under the bush, he pulled the boot free from the branches. "What was left of the victim's clothes was camo," Randy replied as he examined the boot.

Zane stood and stretched. "Were both of his boots missing?"

Jill held an evidence bag open for Randy, who placed the boot inside of it. "Yeah, both boots were missing, as were any other apparel like his hat and gloves."

Randy chuckled as he sealed and marked the evidence bag. "Along with his face and one of his nuts."

"Ouch," Zane replied, feigning pain, but grinning.

"I don't suppose you've spotted a nose or ear along the way?" I asked.

Zane wrinkled his nose, "Nah, the critters do a good job of cleaning up tissue and blood. Hell, I've had to chase magpies off a quartered deer carcass before I can load it on my pack horses."

I looked toward the west where the sun was starting to dip toward the horizon. "How much longer can we go on before we need to ride back to the trailer?"

Zane looked back, then ahead. "We're closer to Aladdin than we are to our starting point. I'm sure Randy or I can find someone who'll give us a ride from Aladdin to the trailer. You all can have a sarsaparilla while I fetch the trailer."

"I think a cold beer might be in order," I replied.

Zane smiled. "You'll be off duty then?"

Jill took Thunder's reins and mounted. "'Off duty' is a relative term. Technically, we're required to have our sidearms and cell phones with us at all times."

Zane looked at me. "Does that mean you can't ever drink alcohol?"

After three tries and the help of an anthill, I managed to pull myself onto my saddle. "Let's say we take off our badges once in a while." I looked at Jill. "Right, dear?"

"What my smartass husband is trying to say is that we enjoy a drink after the horses are put away and the holsters are hung up."

Zane adjusted his Stetson, then nodded to Jill. "Those are the same rules we use in hunting camp. Some of the East Coast city slickers think I'm their lackey who will take care of everything while they get drunk. I disabuse them of that fallacy the first night in camp. Everyone carries their load."

"Disabuse?" I asked.

Randy chuckled. "I've got a degree in English literature. Not much call for that in Alva, Wyoming."

"I'll bet you're happier here than you would be in a city newsroom or teaching," I replied.

Zane turned Puma toward Aladdin, then said over his shoulder, "I'm immensely happier."

* * *

Ten minutes later Zane raised his hand, using the Army signal for stop. "I've got another boot, Randy."

Randy and Hercules trotted ahead. Zane held the reins while Randy bagged the second boot. Randy was ready to remount the horse when Zane nodded ahead. "Unless

102

I'm mistaken, there's a glove about twenty yards ahead."

"I see something shiny, up there," I said as we neared the road past the Aladdin General Store.

Zane nodded. "I've been watching that for a while. It looks like the sun reflecting off a rifle scope lens."

"I wonder if our victim dropped his rifle?" Jill asked.

Zane shook his head. "I think it's something else. Maybe binoculars?"

Randy was the first person to dismount and examine the reflective glass. "It's a camera." Using a gloved hand, he picked up the camera with a telephoto lens.

"I wonder if the photos on the memory card are recoverable?" I asked.

Zane glanced at me. "I assume that's a rhetorical question."

"More like thinking out loud," I replied. A car drove past, the road less than thirty yards away. "Why isn't there a fence here? Isn't this someone's pasture?"

"It's open range. There's a sign at the last cattle guard warning people that cattle have the right of way."

"You're shitting me," I said, looking around for a cow or steer.

"No, sir," Randy replied. "It takes so many acres to feed a steer here, it doesn't pay to be putting up a fence every quarter mile."

Randy pushed all the buttons on the camera, then gave up. "I think the batteries are dead." He dropped the camera into another evidence bag, then looked toward the store. "If you guys want to stay on the trail, I'll call the dispatcher and arrange for someone to give me a ride back to the trailer."

"Before you go, you might want to bag up the plastic holster that's lying over there." Zane pointed at something black stuck in a clump of sagebrush.

Randy walked over and pulled it loose. After examining it, he looked up. "It's one of the kinds you jam into your waistband rather than hook onto your belt." He looked around the bush, then the entire surrounding area. "I don't see the pistol anywhere."

Zane looked deep in thought. "What's going through your head?" I asked.

"Most of those polymer holsters have an internal locking mechanism. It keeps the pistol from falling out, or from someone pulling it out. It takes a little inward twist on the butt to release the pistol from the holster."

"You'd expect the pistol to still be in the holster?"

"Yup."

Jill looked around. "I suppose someone found it and took the pistol."

Zane shook his head. "Why leave a fifty-dollar holster behind if you're stealing the pistol?"

I considered what we knew about the last minutes of the victim's life. "I wonder if he pulled his gun and got a shot off at the guy who roped and dragged him."

Randy joined us as he dropped the holster into an evidence bag. "I suppose that's as likely as anything."

Zane nodded and tossed his keyring to Randy. "I'm curious. The strap on that camera and the holster wouldn't last very long if the victim was being dragged behind the ATV. I think we're closer to the beginning of the trail than the end."

Jill and I followed Zane. The terrain changed from prairie to open timber as we moved behind the store. The gentle rise of the prairie got steeper, and the sagebrush disappeared, replaced by junipers, cedar, and ponderosa pines. Zane stopped again barely past the timber line. "I think you two could follow the trail from here." He nodded toward the ground. Evident in the thin grass and pine needles was a path where something had been dragged. The randomly dropped pine needles on most of the forest floor were aligned along the line where the victim had been dragged. The random pinecones that littered the area had been pushed aside.

"Let's see wherever this goes," I said.

Zane turned Puma and followed alongside the trail that went up the hill, then turned abruptly to the right. Within twenty yards, we were behind the store and motel and the dragging trail ended. Next to the start of the trail were a pair of binoculars. A camouflage glove was caught in the branches of a deadfall pine tree a few yards away. A green folding three-legged camp stool was tipped over under the branches of a juniper tree, partially covered by pine needles and forest litter.

"Huh," I said, looking at the stool under a juniper. "I'm amazed this didn't blow away over the winter."

Dismounting, Zane looked around. "This little hiding spot is sheltered from the wind. If I was going to spy on the store, this is where I'd sit. I'd be out of the wind, wearing camouflage clothing, and be nearly invisible."

"I wonder why a guy with binoculars and a camera with a telephoto lens would be hiding behind the general store?"

Zane stared at the store, then back to the gear on the ground. "Maybe a better question would be, 'who would be so upset with a guy watching the back of the store that he'd drag him across the prairie and dump his body at the Buffalo Jump?'"

"I don't see a pistol here," I said, walking a circle around the victim's hiding spot.

Zane nodded. "Most folks aren't going to leave a perfectly good shooting iron lying on the ground. I'm sure either the killer, or someone who wandered by later, picked it up and added it to their personal collection." Seeing my skepticism, he added, "Finders, keepers."

Jill dismounted and knelt near the overturned camp stool. Staring at the back of the store, she shook her head. "I guess we've got a pile of mysteries. Who was John Doe? Was he strangled before he was dragged? When did this happen? Why was he hiding up here dressed in camouflage? Why was he taking pictures of the back of the store and motel? Who caught him? Why did they kill him?"

Zane cleared his throat and tugged at his collar. "I don't know about you two, but I'm getting a little parched. I'd think better with a cold long-neck beer in my hand."

Laughing, I reined Rascal and turned toward the back corner of the store. "Is there really a bar at the end of the store?"

Zane and Puma were beside me before we'd gone five yards. "The last time I checked, there was a bar. And they serve more than sarsaparilla."

"Hey," Jill called from behind us. "Gentlemen would wait until I'd mounted my horse before riding off."

Zane turned to me and smiled. "Jill seems to be under the mistaken impression that we're some sort of gentlemen."

I reined in Rascal and stopped. "You might get away with rushing to the bar without her, but I have to live with Jill after you've gone."

Puma stopped and Zane tipped his hat back. "Yeah, I suppose the lady might take issue and retaliate in unpleasant ways."

"You're married, right?"

"Yep."

"So, you get it?"

"Of course, I do. I was just being...what was it that Jill called you? A smartass?"

"We should go back and bag the evidence."

Zane looked at Jill as she approached. "Doug, that gear has been sitting there for months. Months. You don't have evidence bags, and you really need Randy to bag and tag it."

"Aw shit," I said. "I'll keep watch on the site. Send Randy back with bags and a camera."

Zane chuckled. "So, you really are a cop, and you know the cop and evidence rules."

"Sometimes I hate to admit it, but yes."

Chapter 9

Sitting alone gave me time to reflect on what we'd seen and found. Jill's questions kept rolling through my mind. Mostly, I kept going back to, *why were you sitting here with binoculars and a camera?* The answer to that question could well lead us to the *Who were you?* question.

Looking down the hill, I had an unobstructed view of the general store and the four hookups for RVs. To the left of that, I had a view of the motel through some scraggly oak underbrush growing in a shallow ravine. The rear door of the store opened, and Tanya walked out carrying two garbage bags. She walked past the RV spots to a dumpster. Setting down one of the bags, she lifted the dumpster lid, threw in the two bags, and then let the lid fall with a metallic clang that echoed up the hill.

Although I was wearing blue jeans and my Park Service green jacket and sat next to a horse, Tanya never looked up the hill. She studied the ground ahead of her and the back of the building. But she never looked up the hill. *I'm invisible to her. A man in camouflage, tucked into a juniper bush, would be invisible to the world. Invisible to anyone except whoever found him. Who would be wandering these hills? Did the sun reflect off his binoculars or camera lens to reveal his hiding spot?*

The lengthening shadows cast the timbered hillside in darkness. My mind was wandering when another thought popped into my head. *The killer dragged the victim from this spot and within a hundred yards of the store. Then his ATV drove across a state highway and miles of open prairie. Why didn't someone see him?*

My thoughts were interrupted when Randy walked around the back corner of the store with a bunch of evidence bags in his hand. He paused, looking up the hill. Seeing me, he waved and trudged up through the timber. Standing, I brushed the pine needles off my pants and untied Rascal's reins from the tree I'd been leaning against.

"Did you wait until all the beer was gone before you came to rescue me?" I asked as Randy approached.

"There's beer?"

"Zane and Jill were headed for the bar."

Arriving at my spot, Randy took a second to catch his breath after the uphill climb. "Their horses were tied up outside the bar, but I never went in. Jill said you needed evidence bags for stuff that you'd found up here."

I pointed to the glove, camp stool, and binoculars. "The dragging trail started here.

It appears our victim may have been hiding under this juniper and spying on the store and motel."

After pulling on blue gloves, Randy folded the camp stool and slipped it into an evidence bag. "Why would someone sit up here and watch the store?" he asked as he picked up the binoculars and glove, then put them into bags.

"A while back, I was watching a show about illegal Appalachian moonshine operations. The police and feds from the Bureau of Alcohol Tobacco and Firearms spent a lot of time walking the woods, then camped out watching stills to see who showed up to collect the moonshine."

"Do you think our victim was an ATF agent watching for a moonshine operation?"

"Has the sheriff's office had any calls about missing ATF agents?" I asked.

"The feds aren't particularly forthcoming with information," Randy replied after marking the evidence bags. He nodded toward the store. "We should head down the hill before it gets seriously dark."

I led Rascal down the hill, walking alongside Randy. "The feds aren't forthcoming when it comes to sharing information, but I think the sheriff would get a call if they were missing an agent." A new thought flashed in my mind. "Have you found an abandoned car or pickup in this area?"

"Not that I recall."

"How would a guy get here without leaving a vehicle somewhere?"

Randy shrugged. "On horseback?"

"Where's the horse?"

"I don't know. Maybe the guy on the ATV came back and got the horse."

"If he brought the horse in by trailer, we're asking the same question about an abandoned vehicle, but with a stock trailer."

"Maybe he hiked in."

I looked around. "What's the nearest town? Sundance? Beulah? They're both a long hike from here."

"To the north there's nothing but Bureau of Land Management and national forest land."

"How far would someone have to hike from the north to get here?"

Randy thought as he walked. "I can't think of a real road for probably fifty or sixty miles. I suppose there are tracks through the timber, but nobody walked here from that direction."

"How else would he get here?" I asked as we neared the back corner of the general store.

"ATVs are everywhere. Nobody even notices them anymore."

I stopped. "Speaking of that, why didn't anyone see the killer drag our victim across the road while driving his ATV?"

"Like I said, ATVs are everywhere, and nobody notices them anymore. Unless he dragged the body across the road and was almost hit by a pickup, nobody would've given it a second look."

"You don't think someone would question the sight of an ATV dragging a body across the prairie?"

Randy gestured for me to keep walking. "If I saw an ATV dragging something across the prairie, I'd assume he was getting rid of a roadkill deer or a dead calf. It'd never occur to me that it was someone dragging a body, and I'm a cynical cop."

"We should ask around," I replied as we neared the hitching rail in front of the bar.

"You are joking."

"What?"

"Doug, we can probably interview all of the residents of Aladdin in about two minutes."

"Ah, all fifteen of them," I said, glancing at the population sign in front of the general store.

"I really think they counted the family of skunks that were living under the dumpster when they did the census. I've counted four people."

"I thought maybe there was a nearby ranch with a bunch of kids."

"No. There are four. Well, five if you count Tanya who's only been here for a few months."

"Did you interview all of them?"

After watching me start a square knot, Randy took Rascal's reins from me and tied the lead rope to the hitching rail. "I don't usually interview skunks."

I let Randy grin for a second before clarifying, "Did you interview Tanya and the other humans working at the store and motel?"

"I haven't interviewed *any* of them. We only determined that the drag trail started here about an hour ago. I've been focused on the Buffalo Jump and the visitor center located near the interstate. It seemed more likely that the killer had arrived and departed from that area than him coming from Aladdin. The store is like ten miles from there."

"But the tracks you found were going toward Aladdin."

"To be honest, they were going west, along the road. Not north, toward Aladdin." Randy held the bar door open for me. "Doug, there's nothing in Aladdin. Why in hell would I think the killer or victim had anything to do with this hole in the wall?"

Tanya looked up from behind the bar. "Hey, this hole in the wall is where I live."

Jill, with a can of Coke in her hand, looked at us. "What are you two arguing about?"

"I asked why Randy hadn't interviewed the people who live in Aladdin about the body that was found at the Buffalo Jump."

Randy sat next to Zane and pointed at the beer in his hand. "I'll have one of those."

Then he leaned back and replied, "Because I didn't know the guy had been here."

Tanya twisted the cap off a beer bottle and handed it to Randy. "What guy was here?"

I sat next to Jill and gestured for a beer. "The dead guy who was found at the Buffalo Jump was dragged from behind the store."

Tanya hesitated for just a fraction of a second before touching the pistol on her hip. "A dead guy was behind the store?" she asked as she twisted the cap off a beer and set it in front of me.

Jill watched Tanya intently.

Zane took a swig of beer. "Yeah, I followed the trail from the Buffalo Jump to a hunting blind up the hill from the store. It appears the guy was sitting up the hill."

Tanya took a step back and leaned against the cooler behind the bar. "He was hunting behind the store, and someone dragged him away?"

Zane shrugged. "It's hard to say when he got dragged away. It's been a while, probably sometime last fall or winter."

"Did you notice an ATV dragging a body across the highway?" Randy asked.

Tanya crossed her arms. "Not recently." Then she paused. "I mean, it's something that would've stuck in my mind if I'd seen it."

Jill's voice was soft and even. "Have you noticed anyone sitting in the timber behind the store?"

Tanya opened her mouth but hesitated. "I don't often look up the hill. I mean, it's just trees and stuff. I'm usually focused on doing something for the store or dealing with Bill when I'm in the back."

Jill nodded toward Tanya's pistol. "I used to carry a 9mm when I was younger. I could never handle the recoil of a .45."

Tanya relaxed a bit. "I'm not concerned about the recoil because I only plan on shooting once. When you shoot something with a .45, it stays shot."

Randy leaned forward to look past Zane. "Unlike the well driller, you shot thirteen times with your 9mm before he stopped running."

Zane's eyes went wide, and he turned toward Jill. "That was you in the Hulett shootout?"

I gestured for Randy to zip his lips. He saw Jill look away, then made a circle on the bar top with his beer bottle. "I might've spoken out of school. Sorry, Jill."

Seeing Jill's remorse, Zane turned toward her. "I'm sorry. I get it. I really do. I take no joy in shooting an animal. I can't imagine how I'd feel if I shot another person."

Jill nodded. "Thank you. Can we talk about something else?"

"So," Tanya said, "who was this guy who was sitting behind the store?"

Randy finished his beer and gestured for another round. "We don't know. At this point, he's John Doe in the Sundance funeral home."

Tanya pulled out three beer bottles and twisted off the tops before handing them to Randy, Zane, and me. She looked at Jill and asked, "Are you still nursing that soda pop, or are you ready to move on to something stronger?"

"I don't suppose you have a bottle of chardonnay in the cooler?"

"There aren't many wine drinkers this time of year. I've got wine on the shelf, and I could put an ice cube in it, or I could put a shot of rum in your Coke."

Grimacing at the prospect of an ice cube in her wine, Jill paused. "Could I have a glass of room temperature red wine?"

Tanya walked to the end of the bar and pulled a wine bottle out of a carton. "This California red is scrumptious." She unscrewed the cap and poured a generous glassful.

Sipping it, Jill's eyes lit up. "This is good. Since you think it's scrumptious, could I buy you a glass?"

Tanya glanced at the door into the general store, then at her watch. "What the hell, if not for you guys drinking in here, I'd be off the clock anyway."

Zane glanced at Randy. "Not that I'm in any rush to get home, but is someone coming with my truck and trailer? I should unsaddle the horses, feed them, and brush them down."

"Keith, the night deputy, is driving over from Gillette. He should be here pretty soon."

Zane looked at Jill and me. "Does this slow pace of life drive you guys crazy?"

"Police work is always hours of boredom and moments of terror," I replied. "I've got nothing against this pace."

"Bullshit," Randy replied. "You were just reaming me because I hadn't interviewed the entire population of Aladdin."

Jill choked on a swallow of wine. Tanya handed her a stack of bar napkins as she coughed. Finally catching her breath, Jill looked at me. "You're mad because Randy hasn't interviewed all fifteen people in Aladdin?"

I leaned back. "In my defense, there are only five residents, including Tanya."

"I've been interviewed now," she said, grinning. "You'd better get after the other four, Randy."

Zane held up his beer bottle. "No one said the body was dragged across the highway in the daylight."

Jill looked at Tanya. "Have you ever heard ATVs around here at night?"

She snorted. "Like, all the time. The walls of my RV are paper thin, and I hear ATVs, arguing cowboys, and loud pickups. All. The. Time."

Randy raised his eyebrows. "See, Doug. I told you, there are ATVs running around this country day and night."

Zane nodded. "They've become ubiquitous."

Jill shook her head. "Just because you've got a degree in English doesn't mean you need to impress us with twenty-five cent words."

"I think ubiquitous is a fifty-cent word," Zane replied.

Tanya took the wine bottle off the back counter. Before Jill could stop her, she'd topped off both of their glasses. "No one else is going to drink this stuff. We might as well finish off the bottle."

Zane smiled. "I guess that means it's time to take off your badge and shut off your cell phone."

Randy stood as a sheriff's department cruiser appeared across the street from the bar. "It looks like Keith made it over from Gillette. I'll fetch the pickup and stock trailer and be back in a bit."

"I can get it," Zane replied.

Randy waved him off. "Finish your beer and regale the Fletchers with stories about Wyoming hunting."

Zane tossed his keyring to Randy. I turned to Zane. "What hunting tales do you have?"

Randy took another drink of beer. "Most of them are about the stupid flat landers who come out here." Realizing that Jill and I fit that description, he backtracked. "Not everyone who comes here for a hunt is stupid. I mean, there are people who are downright smart and well-prepared. On the other hand, I get people who show up in a brand-new outfit, with a brand-new rifle they've never shot, and new boots they haven't worn anywhere except to try them on in the store."

"And that's a problem?" I asked.

"They're not prepared, physically or mentally, and they're not ready for the rigors of a big game hunt. I make sure they know how to be safe with their rifles, and that the guns are properly sighted in, but I can't prepare them for their first heart-pounding sighting of an elk."

"You pack everything in by horse," Jill countered. "They shouldn't be too physically stressed out by the hunt."

"We pack into a base camp, but we walk from there. I've got guys whining about blisters before we've walked half a mile."

Zane set down his beer and stared at me in the mirror. "Tell me about your John Doe. Was he in shape or was he a butterball?"

"Butterball?"

"That's what I call the overweight, out-of-shape hunters who show up in camp. They're huffing and puffing as we walk up a slight incline and ready to quit hunting by noon of the first day."

I looked at Jill. "John Doe was pretty banged up, but I had the impression he was a middle-aged guy with a paunch."

Jill stared into the corner, trying to visualize our viewing of the corpse. "There were suspenders with his clothes. You know, the kind you button into your waistband. I've only seen fat ranchers wear suspenders to keep their pants up."

Zane frowned. "His suspenders weren't ripped off?"

A light went on in my brain. "His pants were shredded, but the suspenders were protected by his coat."

Zane leaned his elbows on the bar. "There you go. How many city slickers have you seen wearing suspenders? Your John Doe was a middle-aged, fat, local guy with binoculars and a camera. He didn't just happen to wander through, because he brought one of those three-legged camp stools to sit on."

I nodded. "That sounds reasonable. The only problem with that scenario is there's nobody missing. If he was a local guy, someone would've called the sheriff's department to report that he hadn't shown up when he was expected home."

Zane shrugged. "So, he was either divorced or a single guy, living alone. There's an empty house or trailer somewhere."

I frowned. "I think his neighbors would've noticed that someone hadn't been taking care of his cattle or horses."

Zane looked at Jill. "You grew up out here. If you had an odd neighbor, would your family go and check on him?"

"Our nearest neighbor was Uncle Chet, who lived a mile away. We relied on each other for help during the busy seasons."

"How about your other neighbors? Were there any hermits who kept to themselves?"

Reflecting on something humorous, Jill chuckled. "There was 'Crazy Willy' who lived by himself. The only time we saw him was when we passed each other driving our pickups down the road."

"Would you have gone to check on him if you hadn't seen him in a while?" Zane asked.

"Hell no! I wouldn't go near his place under any circumstances."

"There you go! Your John Doe is a crazy old loner who shuns interaction with his neighbors and is unmarried or divorced."

"Why would someone like that be sitting behind the store?" I asked.

Zane leaned back, deep in thought. Then he jerked forward and looked at Tanya. "You're living in the RV behind the store. Do you keep your shades drawn?"

Tanya's mouth fell open. "I don't need to close them. There's nothing back there but..." She paused. "That dirty old sonofabitch was a window peeper?"

I laughed. "That seems unlikely. I mean, it's not like he walked over from the ranch next door. He must've had a vehicle of some kind."

Zane raised his eyebrows. "Like I said, ATVs are ubiquitous. They're everywhere. If someone left an ATV sitting for a few days with the keys in it, there are folks who might see that as an invitation to borrow it."

Jill shook her head. "They're licensed, like cars and snowmobiles."

Zane shook his head. "No one is going to drive into a ranch to check the registration on an ATV. Hell, I bet a quarter of the ATVs in the county have never been registered. Ranchers buy them and keep them around their own property. I'm sure they don't see the need to register them if they never plan to ride them off their own land."

Zane's pickup and trailer arrived. He finished his beer and stood. "I'm off."

Jill got up too quickly and caught her balance on the edge of the bar. "We've got to help you with the horses."

"Ms. Fletcher, I think you might've had a bit too much wine to be of much help. Randy can help me get the bridles off and get the horses into the trailer. I'll take them home, unsaddle them, and turn them out into the pasture."

"You're sure we can't help?" I asked.

Zane looked at me and smiled. "Thanks, I've got this."

"You can give us an invoice for your guide service," I said as Zane walked out.

"Nah. You got me out of the house to do something interesting. Randy helped me put up hay last summer. I think we're even."

Tanya was clearing the bottles and wine glasses from the bar. I took out my credit card and handed it to her. "I'm paying the bar tab."

She took my card and ran it through the machine, then handed me the charge slip and a pen. The total was $28. "You didn't charge us for the wine."

Smiling, she shook her head. "That was on the house."

I added a $10 tip to the charge slip and returned it to her. "Keep your shades down."

Tanya blushed. "I never thought…"

Jill leaned on the bar and whispered, "Never underestimate the creativity of a pervert."

* * *

Zane was pulling away when we walked out. We waved then started walking down the boardwalk running the length of the general store toward the motel. We'd hardly gone ten feet when Jill stopped. "Aw, geez!"

Looking around in confusion, I asked, "What? Did you forget something?"

Pointing toward the vehicles parked in front of the motel, Jill snorted. "That's Uncle Chet's pickup."

Looking at the three vehicles in front of the motel, I was at a loss. "What makes you think that's Chet's pickup? Did you see him?"

"Look at it. The side is scraped where he ran off the road and we rode the horses out to rescue him."

"There have to be a hundred dusty brown pickups with scraped sides in Wyoming."

"Trust me. It has South Dakota plates. It's Chet's."

"It's okay. We'll say, 'hi', and have supper with them. Then they'll drive back to Spearfish." I quickly realized the mistake in my reasoning. "Oh, hell. It's dark and neither Chet nor my mother will drive in the dark anymore. They're here for the night."

Jill straightened up and drew a breath. "I've had two giant glasses of wine. There's the issue, '*In vino veritas.*'"

"Isn't that a line from one of the Eagles' songs?"

"It's Latin for 'in wine there's truth'. I tend to speak too openly about things after a couple glasses of wine."

"Smile and let me do the talking."

Nodding, Jill agreed. "For the next two hours, until my wine headache kicks in."

I reached down and took her hand. "You usually get amorous after two glasses of wine."

"You can kiss that plan goodbye." Jill let go of my hand and waved as we approached the motel. "Smile and wave, dear. Your mom just walked out of the motel office."

Chet walked out of the office after my mother. Behind him were Jill's parents.

Through clenched teeth Jill smiled and said, "This just keeps getting better."

My mother hugged Jill first, showing her deep love for my wife and her thanks for continuing to put me. While hugging me, Mom whispered, "I thought you two were investigating a murder? You two have been drinking."

"We had one beer with the tracker who helped us today."

After releasing her hug, Mom gave me a look reserved for the times she'd caught me telling her a white lie. Ignoring the look, I hugged Jill's mom, Molly. Then, I shook hands with Chet and Jill's father, Al. "We're surprised to see you."

Al smiled. "Well, the women decided that we needed to take a road trip."

I nodded. "If we weren't coming to Spearfish, they decided to see us one way or another."

Chet pumped my hand like a long-lost brother. "Aladdin isn't that far from Spearfish. You could've stayed with us and commuted back and forth."

"Our jobs aren't nine-to-five, and as you know, Molly likes us to be home when supper is ready."

Molly smiled. "Doug, you know I'm happy to see you no matter what ungodly time of the night you finally wander in to eat reheated leftovers."

Al laughed and slapped my back. "Help me haul our suitcases out of the pickup."

Chet, Al, and I walked to the pickup and pulled four small overnight bags out of the covered bed. Carefully wiping the dust off his hands after closing the tailgate, Chet glanced at Molly, Jill, and my mother, who were deep in conversation. "The women had things to discuss with Jill. They didn't want to wait until your investigation was over."

Picking up two of the suitcases, I leaned close and asked, "Do I even want to know which topic was so important?"

Al nudged my shoulder, urging me toward the motel. "No, you don't want to know."

"Let me guess, it either involves female issues or bodily functions."

Al laughed. "It might be both."

Chet removed a motel key from his pocket and unlocked the first unit. "Your mom and I are in here." Realizing that he'd admitted he was sharing a motel room with my mother, Chet stammered, "We've got two queen-sized beds."

"Chet, I don't care if you got the room with the Jacuzzi tub and a mirror on the ceiling. You're both adults and I'm glad that you're enjoying each others' company."

"I'm a bit old-fashioned," he said, holding the door open while I carried the suitcases inside.

Al looked around the small room with two beds, a nightstand, and a small table with two chairs. "Looks like I'll have to bring a chair over from our room if we're going to play cribbage."

Setting the bags on the bed, I shook my head. "We're working. I won't have time for cribbage."

"Damn," Al replied. "I could almost taste that fine whiskey you were going to buy for me when you lost."

Chet stiffened. "I forgot to pack the cribbage board and cards."

Nodding toward the door, Al gestured for me to follow him to another room. As we walked down the boardwalk, he whispered, "Chet's getting more forgetful."

"Is that what the women are discussing?" I asked as Al unlocked the door two rooms down from Chet's."

Al shook his head as he held the door for me. "Molly's got osteoporosis. The doctor wants her to start taking some expensive medicine. He's afraid she's getting more unstable, and each fall might lead to a broken bone."

I set the suitcase on the nearest bed. "That seems like a reasonable plan."

Al tossed the other suitcase on the farthest bed. "You grew up seeing doctors and being treated for ailments. We've never been the doctoring kind of people."

I drew a breath and stared at Al. "It's about time for you to face up to your age and the things that modern medicine can do to make these upcoming years more comfortable."

"But the doctor is twenty miles away."

I put up my hand. "You're retired, so the time isn't an issue. You have reliable vehicles, and you can afford the gas. Besides, you can make a day of the trip and eat out. Maybe you can even go shopping while you're in town."

"Shh. Don't say shopping. I don't shop. I go into the store to buy something when I need it. The store sells it to me, and I leave. I don't shop."

"Fine, don't shop. But eat lunch in a restaurant and buy groceries. Make a trip to town an adventure instead of a chore. Besides, it'll get you out of the house."

"What's the matter with our house?"

"There's nothing wrong with your house. Your house is lovely. But you need to get your butt out of the recliner once in a while to do something other than move to the kitchen table to eat."

"You're pushing the limits of my patience, Fletcher."

I shook my head. "No, Al, I'm trying to tell you that we love you and want you to be healthy and live for a long time. That means going to the doctor when you need to, taking the medicine the doctor prescribes, and enjoying life by doing more than reading the paper, watching the news, and playing cribbage with Chet." I paused. "Has Chet won a game of cribbage since I was last here?"

"I think he won a game in February. Yep, it was right after Valentine's Day."

I gestured toward the door. "We should meet up with the others before they think we fell asleep."

Al stood close to me as we walked away from their room. "I liked it better when you were scared of me."

"I was never scared of you."

"You acted like you were."

"I have always treated you with respect, but I haven't ever been scared of you."

Al laughed as we met Chet on the boardwalk. "You never thought I might shoot you if you mistreated Jill?"

Chuckling, I said, "I've seen you shoot. I haven't been worried about being hit by any of your shots."

Chet snorted and slapped my shoulder. "You'd better be careful. He does make a lucky shot once in a while."

Jill's look of concern was alarming. Hearing Chet's comments, she collected herself and asked, "Who's getting shot?"

"No one," I replied. "Let's get supper before Debbie closes the kitchen."

The café was empty when we arrived. I pointed toward a table for six in the far corner and stuck my head into the kitchen where Debbie and John were eating. "Can you feed six of us?" I asked.

Debbie immediately smiled and gestured for John to prepare. "The menu is limited this time of night, but we can certainly whip up something." She picked up menus from the counter and followed me to the table. "The special is meatloaf and mashed potatoes."

Jill rocked her head while studying the menu. "I'm undecided. What do you recommend?"

"The meatloaf and mashed potatoes are your best bet."

Handing Debbie the menu, Jill nodded. "I guess I'll have the meatloaf."

Al and Chet both handed their menus to Debbie. "I'll have the meatloaf," Al said.

Chet hesitated. "I'm torn between a cattleman's steak or the meatloaf."

Without hesitation, Debbie replied, "Meatloaf."

Mom and Molly both ordered the meatloaf special. Then, Debbie looked at me. "For you?"

"Could I get hash browns with meatloaf?"

"Nope."

The abrupt answer surprised me. "No?"

"John shut the grill down. I suggest mashed potatoes, which are currently staying nicely warm in a big pot next to the gravy."

"Mashed potatoes for me, then."

Debbie smiled. "Good choice. What would you all like to drink? I have coffee, milk, and soda pop."

Al smacked his lips. "I'd like a taste of whiskey."

"You'd have to get that from the bar on the other side of the general store." Seeing Al's reaction, Debbie explained, "We're a café, we don't serve hard liquor."

"Wine?" Jill asked.

Debbie smiled. "You are the first person who's ever asked me for a glass of wine."

Jill nodded. "So, there's no dusty bottle under the counter?"

"If there was, it'd be so old it would probably have turned to vinegar."

Jill laughed. "I'll have water."

The rest of us chose decaf coffee and Debbie left.

"I like her," Molly said. "She's professional but decisive. No beating around the bush trying to act like she's trying to make us happy."

"I think that's the only way she can survive here," Jill replied. "They don't have a lot of business in the off-season, and they're swamped during the summer. Debbie has developed her coping mechanism."

Our dinner discussion centered on the miserable, too-cold, and snowy winter, the late thaw, and the prospect of a good hay crop because of the moisture from the snowmelt. At some point, Al asked about our investigation and Jill responded that it wasn't a suitable dinner conversation.

After departing to our rooms/cabin after dinner, Jill took my hand. "You're dealing with our surprise visitors very well."

"What's to deal with? They're here and we can only make the best of it."

"I expected you to be edgier. You're deep into the investigation and all of a sudden, we're talking hay, snow, and cattle prices."

"I was ready for a diversion."

I unlocked the door and held it open for Jill. "How's your wine headache?"

Slipping off her coat, Jill shrugged. "It's there. I'll take a couple of Tylenol, and hopefully, it'll be better by the time I get ready to fall asleep."

"I don't suppose..."

Jill frowned. "How can you even think of romance after supper with our parents?"

I pulled Jill close and kissed the top of her head. "I think it's all the fresh mountain air."

She snuggled into my arms and then chirped, "Ouch."

"What?"

"Your holster stuck me in the ribs."

"Why don't you unbuckle my belt?"

She pushed me back. "You have got to be kidding. That sounded like a line from some pornographic movie."

"How would you know what a pornographic movie line sounds like?"

Jill spun away and slipped into the bathroom. "I don't live in a convent," she said through the door.

I twisted the deadbolt on the cabin door and set my holster on the nightstand. Hearing the shower, I decided to turn on the television. The meteorologist was gesturing toward a high-pressure system centered over Nebraska that was going to keep the skies sunny for at least the next three days. Further west, a storm was brewing over the Pacific Ocean that would pull moisture over the Cascade Mountains but would probably be dry once it passed the Rockies.

I stripped off my clothes and put on a fresh t-shirt and boxers before slipping under the covers. I turned off the lights, so the only illumination came from the television. After a brief flash of light as Jill opened the bathroom door, she switched off the bathroom light and stood still.

"Aren't you coming to bed?"

"My eyes haven't adjusted to the darkness, and I don't want to stub my toe." A moment later she slipped under the covers and snuggled against my side. "You *do* know I still have a headache."

"How can you do this to me?"

"What?"

"You climb into bed, push yourself against me, then tell me you have a headache. That's borderline sociopathic behavior."

She kissed me gently. "I can snuggle with a headache."

Chapter 10

There were half a dozen people in the café when Jill and I arrived for breakfast. Randy waved at us from a table in the back corner. We were apparently less of an oddity today, either because it was our second day there, or because Randy had fulfilled everyone's need to check out the person who didn't seem to belong.

Debbie delivered mugs of steaming coffee without being asked. I noticed Barry in the opposite corner trying hard to pretend he wasn't looking at us. "Barry has asked me several times if you were going to be back," Debbie said.

I nodded at Barry, then asked what the breakfast specials were.

She pointed to the board behind the counter. "There's a theme. I only erase the board to change the specials when the seasons change. The specials are the same as they were yesterday. They'll be the same tomorrow."

Jill looked at the board. "How long will we have to stay here until they change?"

"You missed the equinox. Will you be here for the summer solstice?" Debbie asked with a smile.

"I'll have the Denver omelette," I said.

"Oatmeal for me," Jill replied. "We'll both have whole wheat toast."

"Wait a second," I protested. "The pancakes look great."

"I'm concerned about your fiber intake."

Debbie looked back and forth between the two of us. "Okay, which is it?"

I sighed. "Whole wheat toast."

Randy sat quietly sipping his coffee through the whole exchange. "Is this what married life is like?"

Jill smiled. "I'm looking out for his health because I love him and want him to be with me for a long time."

"Oh, I respond to enough domestic calls to know about the other side," he replied.

I had my cup halfway to my mouth when a gunshot rang out. Randy was past me before I could push my chair back. His pistol was in his hand as he rushed out the front door. I was a step behind. Jill was at my heels.

We all paused outside the door, trying to determine where the shot had originated. "I'll check the store's front door," Randy said. "Jill, go to the motel desk. Doug, cover the store's back door."

I cut between the café and the general store, pistol in my right hand, and my left hand holding my coat open, so my badge was visible. I had just turned the corner when I startled Tanya, who was standing just outside her RV, peeking around the edge and looking toward the hill.

"Is he gone?" she asked as I trotted toward her.

"Please holster your gun, Tanya."

"Hell, no. Is he gone?"

"Is who gone?" I asked, raising my gun and preparing to shoot at a threat on the hillside behind the store.

"The BEAR! Is the bear gone?"

I drew a breath and lowered my gun. "I don't see a bear. Did you shoot him?"

Tanya shook her head. "No. He was trying to open the dumpster, so I took a shot over his head. He took off up the hill."

I focused on the hill but didn't see anything. "I think he's gone."

Randy burst through the store's back door, gripping his gun with both hands, ready to defend himself against whatever gun-wielding threat he found outside. "What's happening?"

"Tanya scared off a bear," I replied.

"It was a damned big bear," she said, taking a step from behind her RV so Randy could see her. I realized her feet were bare, showing how unprepared she was to deal with the bear. She was wearing flannel pajama pants and was braless under her white tank top. The scooped tank top exposed a bright pink scar along her collarbone.

Randy returned his pistol to its holster and drew a breath. "Jesus, Tanya. The bear wasn't the only thing you scared." Jill ran up behind me.

I holstered my gun and raised my hands. "The excitement is over. Tanya scared off a bear."

Her adrenaline rush fading, Tanya looked down, realized her tank top was translucent, and gasped, quickly crossing her arms over her breasts. "Um, sorry. I didn't mean to get everyone stirred up by shooting."

Barry sauntered out of the café with a napkin still tucked into the neck of his shirt. His gaze went to Tanya's exposed cleavage, making her even more uncomfortable.

"I'm going to finish getting dressed," she said as she blushed and walked to her RV.

Randy stopped her. "Did you hit him? The bear?"

Tanya shook her head. "I shot over his head. If I'd been aiming at him, he'd be dead." Then she rushed into her RV, slamming the door behind her.

Jill was beside me. "Do you believe her?"

"Which part? You mean, about seeing a bear?"

"I'm sure she saw a bear. I was thinking about her comment that the bear would be dead if she had aimed *at* him."

Randy inspected the dumpster and the surrounding ground. "There are fresh claw marks in the paint and bear tracks all around. There was definitely a bear here."

Walking back to the café, I asked Randy if shooting over a bear's head was the normal Wyoming bear deterrent.

"It depends on how hungry the bear is."

"What if he's really hungry?"

Randy sniffled as he thought. "If he's really hungry, a shot over his head wouldn't chase him off. He might growl at the shooter and keep rooting around in the garbage."

I held the café door for Jill and Randy, then asked, "What if he was starving?"

"If he was starving, he probably would've been really irritated by the shot and might've charged Tanya. She would've had to empty her gun into him and hope the bear died before he covered the ten or fifteen yards between them. I prefer to have a shotgun with slugs when I'm dealing with a bear. An ounce of lead is much more lethal than Tanya's pistol."

Seeing us return, Debbie carried our breakfasts to the table. "Don't worry, they haven't been sitting under a heat lamp. John remade them after the bear left."

"That wasn't really necessary," Jill protested.

Debbie nodded to the corner where Barry sat at a table covered with plates. "It's not like they went to waste. Barry just got more than he'd ordered, and that didn't hurt his feelings."

"We'll pay for them," Jill said.

"Don't worry about it. Barry pays for everything he eats. We're all happy."

"Could I get a couple of flapjacks?" Randy asked. "Chasing the bear around kinda gave me an appetite."

"They'll be up in no time."

"Did you check the camera for pictures?" I asked Randy as I turned to my breakfast.

"The batteries were dead, and we didn't have the right charger around the sheriff's office."

"You didn't have the right kind of batteries?" Jill asked.

"Nah, it's some square rechargeable lithium battery pack. I just need the right charger cord."

"What's your plan?"

"The general store has all kinds of tourist stuff because people are forgetting their charger cords all the time. I thought I'd check with them after breakfast."

Jill spread grape jelly on a slice of toast. "What's Plan B if they don't have the right adaptor next door?"

Randy chuckled. "Amazon can deliver a replacement in two days if I pay for express shipping."

* * *

After breakfast we paid our bill, leaving a generous tip. As we stood, Chet and Mom walked into the café. Spying us, they walked to our table. Mom hugged Jill, "We heard an explosion. What happened?"

"The woman who works at the store scared off a bear that was trying to get into their garbage," Jill replied.

Mom's eyes got wide. "A bear?"

Chet chuckled. "I thought it sounded more like a gunshot than an explosion."

Jill waved off Mom's concern. "The gunshot scared the bear away."

Looking at our dirty plates and empty cups, Mom sighed. "You've already eaten."

I nodded and gestured to Randy. "Deputy Pannell and I were just going over to the store to see if they have a power adapter for a camera we found. Randy, this is my mother, Ronnie, and Jill's Uncle Chet."

Randy shook hands, smiling politely. "I hate to be rude, ma'am, but we need to find that adapter."

"Jill, why don't you have a cup of coffee with Mom and Chet while Randy and I look for an adapter. We'll probably be back in a couple of minutes."

Jill motioned for Debbie to come over. "We'll need a bigger table so there's room for Mom and Dad. I assume they'll be here shortly."

I heard Debbie explaining the breakfast specials as we walked out of the door. Randy gave me a sly look. "So, your mother and Jill's uncle are an item?"

"Mom came out for a visit, and Chet got sick. She fell for the old guy and stayed on to nurse him back to health."

"I thought you were a city kid?"

"Mom considers this an adventure. She kept her place back in Minnesota for a while, but eventually accepted the fact that the Black Hills are now home."

"Are you comfortable with the old guy sponging off your mom?"

I snorted. "Chet owns a couple sections of land. If anyone is the gold digger in that relationship, it's Mom."

"Huh. I suppose it's hard to get your head around your mom moving in with a guy."

I held the door for Randy as he walked into the store. "I'm happy for her."

"You're a better man than me. If I found out someone was...bedding my mom, I'd tell him where to get off."

"Randy, at their age, I doubt they're doing much but snuggle under the covers. It's not like Mom's going to get pregnant."

"How do Chet's kids feel about the arrangement?"

"He's never been married. I'm the only *kid* involved, and I'm happy for them."

Tanya looked up from an inventory sheet. "Who are you happy for?"

Having changed out of her flannel pants and tank top into her usual uniform of Ruger ball cap, baggy jeans, and an oversized sweatshirt, Tanya looked like a different person. "My mom moved in with Jill's uncle. They're both happy."

Tanya smiled. "That's nice. Did you guys need something, or did you just pop in to chit-chat?"

Randy held up the evidence bag with the camera we'd found while tracking with Zane. "I need a power cord or an adapter for this camera."

Tanya cocked her head. "Are you sure that's going to be enough to get that camera going? I mean, it looks like someone took a hammer to it."

"We'll try charging the battery. If that doesn't work, we'll have to try something else."

Tanya led us to a rack covered with a variety of power cords and cell phone accessories. "I don't know if any of these will work on a camera. I'm not an electronics expert, but I think most of the stuff here is for charging iPhones and Android cell phones."

Randy examined the charging port on the Nikon camera, then looked at the cables. "Well, it's definitely not a full-sized USB or an iPhone connector." He held up others as he checked out the options. "Not a USB-C either, because it's nearly square."

I went farther down the selections, passing all the iPhone options until I found a cord with a USB plug on one end and a mini-3 USB plug. "This looks promising," I said, holding up the plastic clamshell container.

Tanya was amused by our analysis. "Guys, I have a razor blade behind the counter. I can slice open the clamshell so you can try the plug in the camera. If it's not the right one, I'll just tape it shut. No harm. No foul."

We walked to the counter next to the cash register where Tanya found a box cutter in a drawer. She made a careful cut in the clear plastic, then shook the cord until the plug peeked through the cut. Handing the container to Randy she said, "Give it a try."

Opening the evidence bag, Randy removed the camera and tried the plug in the camera. He smiled. "It looks like we have a winner."

I handed Tanya my credit card. "I'll pay for the cord."

Randy sliced open the plastic clamshell and removed the cord. "Hang on, Doug. We need a plugin for the USB on the other end."

"I've got a USB plug in our cabin."

Tanya handed me the receipt. "Dang, I wanted to see what pictures were on the window peeper's camera."

"What if there's a picture of the killer?" I said as I signed the receipt and returned the credit card to my wallet.

Her eyes lit up as she smiled. "I know! That's what I was hoping to see."

Randy put the camera back into the evidence bag. "I think a judge would frown on us showing a civilian the pictures on a camera before the cops looked at them."

"It wouldn't be *before* you see them. It'd be *as* you see them."

Randy handed Tanya the packaging for disposal. "That's the same thing."

Sighing, Tanya put the plastic into a waste basket. "There are probably just birthday parties or sunset pictures."

I led Randy to the door. "That sounds like sour grapes."

"I haven't thought about Aesop's fables in a long time," she said as we left.

Randy stopped me on the boardwalk outside the door. "Tanya's a bit of a mystery, isn't she."

"How old do you think she is?"

Randy stared at me, deep in thought. "Yesterday, I would've guessed thirty-five. Having seen her in a tank top and now noticing the crow's feet at the corners of her eyes when she smiles, I'd add ten or more years to that guess."

I nodded toward the motel and led Randy to our cabin. "Why's a smart, attractive, forty-five-year-old woman living in a trailer behind the Aladdin General Store?"

"I'm more curious about her wearing over-sized clothes and carrying a .45, that she obviously knows how to shoot."

"She's been a victim of something, somewhere, sometime," I replied as we rounded the corner.

"Still on the run."

I nodded as I took the cabin key out of my pocket. "She's hiding her appearance, her location, and she's prepared if her pursuer finds her."

"Do you think she's in a witness protection program?"

Laughing, I unplugged my phone charger. "The US Marshals would never put someone in a place this obscure."

"I thought that was the point of witness protection."

I attached the new cable to the plug, then handed the other end of the cord to Randy. "The Marshals want people in places where they will blend in. Tanya is more like a neon sign than in camouflage."

Randy plugged the camera in and waited until a red light started blinking. "I hope a flashing red light means the battery is charging and not that I've activated the timer on a bomb."

"You've got to quit watching spy shows on television. Nobody in Aladdin, Wyoming is going to hide a bomb in a camera."

"You're just a Debbie Downer. You tell Tanya there are probably birthday party pictures on the camera. You tell me that Tanya isn't in witness protection. Then, you kill my *bomb-in-the-camera* theory."

"I won't tell you about Santa and the Easter Bunny." I pointed at the camera. "Push the on button and see if the camera fires up."

Sitting on the nearest bed, Randy searched the camera, then pushed a button on the top. The LCD screen on the back lit up. "This looks promising." He pushed arrow buttons on the back of the camera, then an image appeared. "Well, look at that."

"What is it?" I asked as I walked around to look over his shoulder.

Paging through screens, we looked at photos of Tanya's trailer, the rear of the motel, the back of the store, then a series featuring Tanya as she carried bags of garbage to the dumpster. The photos before that showed a couple walking out of a motel room. The earlier pictures showed them walking into the room, preceded by photos of them walking out of a restaurant.

Stopping, Randy looked at me. "That woman isn't Tanya."

"Do you recognize the restaurant?"

Randy paged back and studied the restaurant picture. "I think that's a steakhouse in Gillette."

"Page back to earlier photos."

There were photos of the same woman in the motel pictures walking out of a house wearing medical scrubs. Another showed her entering a dental office, preceded by pictures of the man, wearing a suit, walking into the same office. "What do you make of that?"

"I think our guy was spying on that couple. I think he was trying to catch the man and woman in an affair," I stated.

"A jealous husband?" Randy speculated as he paged through more pictures of the same couple.

"Maybe he was a private investigator. Those earlier pictures showed a man playing golf and racing across the prairie in an ATV. They look more like insurance fraud evidence than vacation pictures," I replied.

The cabin door opened, and Jill walked in. "Whose vacation pictures are you looking at?"

"Randy is looking at the pictures stored in John Doe's camera." I leaned close to Randy and pointed to the picture of a golfer for Jill. "I bet he's being investigated for insurance fraud. That guy is probably collecting disability from a job injury or car accident."

Randy paused and looked up at me. "Wouldn't someone notice if a private investigator was missing?"

Jill cleared her throat. "By the way, our parents are on their way back to Spearfish."

"Good."

"Good? They weren't pleased that we're too busy to entertain them."

"We are. Thank you for clarifying that with them." I pointed to the camera. "Randy, show Jill the last pictures on the camera."

Jill watched in silence until Randy stopped scrolling. "John Doe was watching the store?"

"Randy, see if you can remove the camera's memory card. We might be able to look at the pictures on Jill's laptop computer."

Randy searched for the location of the memory card while Jill booted up her laptop computer. With the XD card out of the camera, Jill slipped it into a slot on the side of her computer. Images popped up on her computer screen and she scrolled through them as we watched over her shoulder.

"These are much crisper than the images on that little LCD screen," Randy commented.

"Yes," Jill agreed. "We can see much more detail of the store and the campground."

"Enlarge the pictures of the couple going in and out of the dental office, restaurant, and motel," I suggested.

Enlarging the images lost some of the clarity, but Randy immediately blew out a breath. "I recognize him. That's one of the Gillette dentists with his assistant."

Jill paused the computer slideshow. "Is he married?"

Randy shrugged. "I think so. But I'm not sure."

Restarting the slideshow, Jill said, "If he's not divorced yet, I bet the papers have been filed."

"Don't jump to conclusions," I replied. "It may be the woman's husband who took the pictures."

We got to the Aladdin pictures and watched them flash up and disappear. "Why was our victim watching the back of the store?" Jill asked.

"I think he was watching Tanya. Enlarge the picture of her carrying out the trash."

With the enlarged picture in front of us, Randy pointed at the screen. "She's always dressed in baggy clothes. In this picture, she's wearing a baseball cap that obscures her face. It's almost as if she's trying to hide her identity from a security camera."

I stood, slowly arching my back to stretch it out after being hunched over the computer. "Maybe Tanya's got more to hide than we know about."

Chapter 11

We followed Randy's SUV into Sundance and parked near the family restaurant which Randy described as a few blocks from the courthouse. Hank Stoddard waved to us from a table in back, near the restrooms. Standing, he shook Jill's hand. "How's my favorite Park Service Investigator?"

Jill laughed as she sat across from the sheriff, "I'm fine. How are you, Hank?"

"I'm fair to middlin', depending on the day."

The sheriff handed me a menu. "How's my second most favorite investigator?"

I chuckled. "Just because my wife is cuter, you move me into second place?"

"Well, Jill is easier on the eyes than you are."

"That's it?" Jill replied. "I'm only easier on your eyes?"

Hank laughed. "You endeared yourself to Randy and me a long time ago, Jill. It'll be hard to displace you from the top spot." Randy nodded his agreement as he sat in the fourth chair.

The waitress approached our table and took our beverage orders. "Are you ready to order, or do you need a couple more minutes?"

The sheriff looked up from the menu. "What's the lunch special?"

"The special is a barbecue burger with steak fries. We've also got chuck wagon stew."

Stoddard nodded. "Give us a minute, Jade."

The young waitress nodded. "No problem. I'll get your drinks."

The sheriff set his menu aside and leaned forward. "Anything new to report?"

Randy made sure no one was listening, then said, "We got the photos off the victim's camera. He was taking pictures of the back of the general store, and possibly spying on their female employee. There were also pictures of a Gillette dentist sneaking in and out of a motel with his female assistant."

Stoddard looked at me. "What does that tell you?"

After taking a moment to consider my answer, I replied, "I think it's likely our victim was a private investigator. Someone hired him to spy on the dentist and/or his assistant. After that job, someone else hired the PI to poke around Aladdin. He had several pictures of Tanya, who works at the store. She's a little elusive about her past, carries a .45 on her hip, and wears baggy clothing that hides her figure."

"Back up to the private investigator angle," the sheriff said just as the waitress arrived with our drinks.

After setting the glasses of soda and iced tea on the table, she took out her order pad. "Are you folks ready to order?"

Randy and I ordered the barbecue burger special. The sheriff ordered the stew. Jill waffled, then decided on a BLT with a side salad.

After watching the waitress leave, I leaned forward. "The pictures look like the kind of candid photos a private investigator would take using a telephoto lens."

The sheriff looked at Randy. "Have you ever heard of a PI in these parts?"

"Someone said there's a guy who hung out his shingle in Moorcroft. I've never run across him."

"Can't you pull up his license?" I asked.

The sheriff shook his head. "Wyoming doesn't license PIs. There aren't many of them, and anyone can open an office and print up a bunch of business cards."

Jill looked unhappy. "Wouldn't someone report the disappearance of a businessman?"

Stoddard leaned back. "In general, I'd say yes. But, if the guy wasn't married and lived on his own, who would report him missing?"

Randy nodded. "Yup. If you've got an old bachelor living outside of town, there's a chance that none of his neighbors will report him missing."

"You're kidding," I replied.

Randy looked surprised. "I think you lived in the city too long. Wyoming and South Dakota folks are independent. We don't spend a lot of time worrying about what our neighbors are or aren't doing. We like to let people do their own thing if they're not hurting anyone else."

Stoddard smiled. "The people who want to hang out with others go to a bar or to church and rub elbows as much as they want. There are a lot of folks who prefer to be left on their own, and we're fine with that."

"There was an old, widowed rancher who lived outside Spearfish," Jill added. "He died over the winter, and no one noticed he was dead until the Jehovah's Witnesses knocked on his door in the spring. They called the sheriff because of a terrible smell coming from his house."

"I'll be darned," I said. "The Jehovah's Witnesses do serve a purpose."

"Shush," Jill chided me. "They're just..." She stalled, trying to come up with an appropriate adjective.

"See! You can't come up with a good purpose for their door knocking." I turned to the sheriff. "Who else would notice that someone was missing?"

"Normally, I'd say a neighbor, or maybe the electric or cable companies if someone isn't paying their bill."

"I think most everyone pays those bills automatically," I said.

"If he was living outside of town, he'd heat with propane. The Co-op might notice if someone didn't call for a fill," Randy suggested.

The sheriff leaned away from the table and gestured to a woman at a nearby table. "Excuse me, Sandi. Have you got a second?" He pulled an empty chair over from a nearby table and slid himself over so the woman could sit next to him. After introducing Jill and me to the bookkeeper from the local Co-op, he asked, "How would you know if one of your propane customers was missing?"

"It's hard to say," she replied. "I suppose I'd be suspicious if someone didn't order over the winter."

"Would you call them or send someone out to check on them?" I asked.

"Probably not. I'd assume they'd signed on with Jack's Propane out of Gillette or moved."

"Would you check your records to see if one of your rural male customers stopped calling for deliveries?" Stoddard asked.

"I don't need to. Everyone got their regular deliveries. I had one family whose propane was paid for by the Hulett Free Church, but everyone else got their propane and paid for it by the end of the heating season."

I shrugged. "I suppose it would be the same with the electric company?"

"They don't shut off anyone's electricity until spring. They might have records of someone who stopped paying."

The sheriff nodded. "Thanks, Sandi."

She pushed her chair back and was about to stand when she paused. "There is one odd thing that came up. We had a customer who prepaid for his winter propane and has an autofill contract, so the driver fills his bulk propane tank every two months. The driver told me that one of the customer's tanks was only down by twenty percent. He knocked on the door, but no one was around. I called the house and never got an answer. I expect it was someone who moved and didn't tell us."

"Isn't it odd for someone to prepay for enough propane for the winter, then leave without asking for a refund?" Jill asked.

"It is a little odd," Sandi replied, "which is why I brought it up."

"Who was that?" Randy asked.

"His name is Jake Foster."

"What do you know about him?" Randy asked.

"He's got a hobby ranch outside of Moorcroft. Rumor has it that he's a bit of a shyster who's divorced. Last I heard, he was driving an over-the-road truck. I figure he got stranded somewhere without a load or found himself a girlfriend living somewhere warmer than here."

"Is there any chance he's been working as a private investigator?"

Sandi snorted. "I don't know who'd trust him enough to do PI work. He's got a bit of a reputation, locally." She said goodbye and returned to her table.

Jill had her phone out and was typing information in before Sandi returned to her table. "I've found a business listing for Jake Foster Investigations, in Moorcroft."

Stoddard nodded to Randy. "Call the Department of Criminal Investigation and give them Foster's name. They can track down his dentist and compare John Doe's dental impressions with Foster's."

Randy chuckled as he looked up Darcy Cabot's DCI phone number. "I'll have our new friend Darcy at DCI ask the dentist if he's getting a divorce."

Stoddard frowned. "Why?"

Jill explained the pictures of the dentist and his assistant that we'd found on the victim's camera.

* * *

After the sheriff paid for our lunches, we shook hands and talked with Randy just outside the restaurant. He stared down the street as a truck pulling a trailer with a tractor drove past. "Well, the sheriff is going to get a search warrant for Foster's Moorcroft office. I suppose we can do a wellness check at Jake Foster's house."

"I think a wellness check is in order," I replied.

"Do you want to ride with me, or follow in your rental truck?"

Jill sighed. "We should drive separately. We'll probably get a call from one of our parents with a request to drive to Spearfish for something."

"Yeah," Randy replied. "I might be dispatched to something that could tie me up at the Montana border for the rest of my shift."

Following Randy onto I-90, we drove west from Sundance. Jill stared out of the passenger's window, obviously deep in thought about something. "What's bugging you?" I asked.

"Mom and Dad are getting old. So are your mom and Chet."

"That's kind of inevitable and preferable to the alternative."

"The alternative?" Jill asked.

"Dying and not getting older."

"Let's not go there," she replied. "What do you think we'll find at Foster's house?"

"I expect to find an empty house. The door won't be locked, so we'll go inside to make sure he's not lying dead on the kitchen floor."

"But we think he's the victim found at the Buffalo Jump."

"We suspect he is. Until Darcy Cabot gets word that the victim's dental records have been matched by a forensic odontologist, it's only a suspicion."

"I feel ninety-nine percent sure we'll have a match."

"I agree, but until we get the final word, it's only a suspicion."

"What does your gut say about his motive for sitting behind the Aladdin store?"

I mulled the question as we passed a herd of antelope grazing by the interstate. "Tanya is an enigma. Women don't *just show up* in an RV and stay in a tiny town. She is toting a gun and wearing clothes that hide her figure." I paused. "Something about her story is just off."

"She's running away from something or someone." Jill stared out the side window. "Did you notice her blonde roots?"

"What?"

"Her hair is dyed brown."

"Lots of women dye their hair when they start turning gray," I replied.

Jill shook her head. "Tanya's roots are blonde, not gray. She's also had some cosmetic surgery. I think her lack of facial wrinkles is due to Botox."

"I didn't notice that."

Smiling, Jill replied, "Men are clueless about the little tricks women use to look younger."

"What else have you noticed about Tanya that I missed?"

"When she ran out to shoot at the bear, she was wearing a tank top. I think she has breast implants and had liposuction on her tummy. Wherever Tanya was before, her appearance was important to her."

"Breast implants?"

"Women's breasts sag by the time they reach Tanya's age. Hers were right out there."

"And the tummy tuck?"

"A little of her abdomen was exposed below her tank top. She had some little scars, like the ones left by liposuction."

"You're thinking she's a California movie starlet?"

Pausing to consider the question, Jill stared out of the windshield. "I don't think movie people know how to shoot like Tanya. I'm thinking she was a realtor who was paranoid about showing houses alone. Or maybe she was the night manager at a bar or restaurant and felt the need to carry a gun when closing up and making the night bank deposit."

"Interesting. Why would a realtor run away to Aladdin, Wyoming?"

"I don't have a theory. I don't think many realtors get into situations so bad they need to hide from a customer."

"Maybe she was married to some Las Vegas mobster and felt like she needed to keep up her looks, so he wasn't tempted to upgrade to a young dancer."

Jill smirked and shook her head. "I think you're really reaching with that scenario."

"True, that may be a little out there. What other jobs would require you to look young, yet leave you feeling the need to carry a .45 when you're gone?"

"Lots of women want to maintain the appearance of youth. Anyone who is climbing the corporate ladder might want to look younger than they are. There's this whole issue of people over 50 being 'aged out' of the job market. Bosses don't want to train someone who they think will retire in a few years."

When I chuckled, Jill glared at me. "They should come to work for the Park Service. I swear some of our rangers are eighty years old."

"Some of them *are* eighty. Their knowledge is irreplaceable. No recent college graduate is able to recite natural history and ecological facts like someone who's lived through them."

"I understand that. I like my pilots and doctors to have a little gray in their hair. They know more and have experience dealing with the unexpected."

"True," Jill replied. "Tanya was doing something that required her to look younger than she is. We can rule out her having been a pilot or doctor."

"This is fun. It's like looking at someone in a restaurant and trying to guess their occupation. I've rarely felt like I've correctly identified the person's true background."

"On the other hand, everyone knows you're a cop when they see you," Jill said, her eyes twinkling. "No one thinks I'm a cop."

"You're not cynical enough to be a cop."

"I hope I'm never as jaded as you are. You've dragged me as far as I care to travel into your universal distrust of the human race."

"Not everyone is a dirtbag. I just assume they are until they prove otherwise."

"It appears we've reached Moorcroft," Jill said as Randy turned on his blinker.

We drove through town, which had the normal array of cafés, motels, bars, and churches you'd expect in a burg with a population a shade over 1,000. Randy turned north and continued out of town a few miles. Then he turned onto a gravel road with no marker indicating a road name or number. Although the area was rural by most standards, there was a driveway and a house every quarter mile. Most of Wyoming was divided into larger parcels.

"Hobby farms," Jill said as we passed the third house with a small barn and a single horse in the pasture.

Randy turned into a driveway marked only by a fire number. "Foster didn't have a horse. His pasture is overgrown." I hung back, letting some of the dust cloud settle as Randy drove ahead of us down Foster's gravel driveway.

Jake Foster's house was a single-wide trailer house with aluminum skirting enclosing the area between the trailer and the ground. A small pole barn behind the house had two garage doors. The barn's metal siding appeared new, and the garage doors were stark white against the red of the siding.

Decades older than the barn, the trailer's blue paint had oxidized, and the aluminum window frames looked like they'd rattle in a strong wind. Randy got out of his SUV and stared at the trailer.

We joined him and Jill asked, "What do you think?"

Randy wrinkled his nose. "Nothing but the propane truck has been down that driveway in weeks." He looked toward the barn. "I'm seeing crushed weeds and others that are starting to grow in the driveway in front of the barn. Nobody's driven in and out of there since last summer."

We walked down a cracked concrete sidewalk to the wooden steps leading to the trailer's entry door. Randy climbed the steps and knocked on the aluminum storm door, causing it to rattle in its frame. "Sheriff's department. Is anyone home?" Not getting an answer, he opened the storm door and knocked on the interior door, repeating his announcement.

"Try the doorknob," I suggested.

Randy rattled the knob but shook his head. "It's locked."

"Hang on," I replied. "Jill, check under the rocks on the right side to see if he's hidden a key. I'll check the left side."

Randy watched me turning over some brick pavers. "Be careful, there might be a rattler under one of them."

I dropped the paver I'd just lifted and glared at him. "Not funny, Randy."

"I found a key," Jill announced. She reached up and handed it to Randy, who unlocked the door.

We stood inside the tiny living/dining room. The place smelled musty, with a slight odor of garbage so old it had molded, then crusted over. The sink was full of dishes with dried-on food, and the cups contained dried remnants of coffee.

"No one's been in here for months," Randy announced as he handed us pairs of blue Nitrile gloves.

I leafed through the pile of mail on a coffee table noting Jake's name and the mailing address. "Jake has a PO box in Moorcroft. I bet it's overflowing." Further down in the pile, I found an envelope addressed to Foster Investigations with an address on Bighorn Avenue in Moorcroft. "And here's his business address."

Jill was in the kitchen. She groaned and quickly opened and closed the refrigerator door. "There's a Styrofoam take-out container evolving into a new life form, and a carton of coffee creamer that I don't even want to think about."

Randy glanced at the breakfast bar. "Here's a check he never deposited. Unless I miss my guess, I think it's signed by the dentist's wife."

I perked up. "Are there any other checks or invoices there?"

Randy quickly ran through the items strewn across the breakfast bar. "Not that I see."

Jill squatted next to a plastic wastebasket and peered inside. "This is mostly junk mail. The item on top is a Christmas decoration catalog from the hardware store. Do you think this place has been empty since December?"

Randy paused. "That would make sense. I don't think any Wyoming resident would sit outside during hunting season without wearing some item of orange clothing. It appeared the victim was dressed in camouflage."

Jill glanced at the short hallway beyond the living room. "I'll check the bathroom if you guys check the bedroom."

Randy grinned. "You don't want to look in the bedroom of a dirty old man who may have been spying on Tanya?"

Jill walked past and turned into the bathroom. "I don't want to look either place. Single men tend to live in pig sties. I'll take a chance that there's not a body in the bathtub and that the bathroom will be less disgusting than the bedroom."

I was walking into the bedroom when I felt a hand on my shoulder. Turning, I found Jill behind me. "I thought you were checking the bathroom?"

"He hasn't cleaned the tub or toilet in months."

"He hasn't been here in months."

"Let me rephrase that," she said, stopping at the bedroom door. "I don't think Jake owned a toilet brush or bathtub scrubber. If I had to clean his tub, I'd start with a putty knife."

The bedding was piled on the mattress. The white sheets had turned gray from poor laundry detergent or infrequent washing.

"Now that we know Foster isn't here, we need to leave everything in place. Randy, call the sheriff and ask him to expand the search warrant to include Foster's home and garage."

Randy took out his phone and dialed. "I'll have him include any vehicles, just in case there's something in the garage."

"Good thought," I replied. "Let's step outside and lock the door. We'll look in the garage windows while we wait for the search warrant."

Chapter 12

We stood next to Randy's SUV while waiting to hear from the sheriff. Jill seemed deep in thought as she studied the area. "What's on your mind?" I asked.

"I've seen developments like this outside of Spearfish. They're marketed as hobby farms to city people who want to feel like cowboys."

Sensing there was more to that thought, I asked Randy, "What do the locals call these developments?"

"One of our neighbors called them Gunsel plots."

Randy chuckled, which made me ask, "What's a Gunsel?"

Jill looked at Randy who replied, "It's a derogatory term for a wannabe cowboy. We can say it around the Gunsels and tell them it's Spanish for 'accomplished rider.' They puff up and take it as a compliment."

Jill wrinkled her nose. "My dad says they're trying to 'yuppify' the ranches. They've got no expectation or need to make money off the land. They're just rich city folks pretending to be ranchers."

Randy's cell phone rang, and we waited quietly while he nodded and said, "Okay," several times. His phone chimed as he disconnected the call, and he touched the screen. "The judge's clerk just emailed me a copy of the search warrant. We're good to go."

Jill led us back to the house and opened the door. "Where should we start?" she asked as we pulled on gloves.

"Let's go through the bedroom first," I suggested. Choosing to ignore the pile of bedding, I opened the nightstand drawer while Jill looked in the closet. Randy opened drawers in the dresser.

"I've got a handgun in the nightstand," I said. Pushing it aside, I found a medicine bottle containing a medication name I didn't recognize and a stack of pornographic magazines.

"There's a shotgun and rifle in the closet," Jill said. "Also a few dress shirts and a couple of fall and winter coats. That's it."

I looked at Randy who was kneeling as he inspected the bottom dresser drawer. "The upper drawers are clothes. He stored his ammo, a hunting knife, and some family photo albums in this drawer." He stood and stretched, then opened a small box on top of the dresser. "At some point, he needed a tie bar and cuff links. There's also a man's wedding ring and a high school class ring."

"What year did he graduate?" Jill asked as she stepped out of the closet.

Holding the ring up to catch the light, Randy replied, "Hulett High School, class of 1980."

Doing the math in my head, I said, "That would make him about sixty-three."

Randy shrugged. "There's nothing about his body that would reveal his age."

"Except his suspenders," Jill replied. "He's got the kind that buttons onto your waistband. I can't imagine anyone younger than sixty wearing anything like that."

Randy lifted a pair of gray work pants out of a laundry hamper. He rolled the waistband inside out and held it out for us to inspect. "Buttons for his suspenders. They have a 48-inch waist and a 28-inch inseam. I'd say he was chunky."

Jill snorted. "The medical term is obese."

I closed the nightstand drawer. "Which means he probably didn't walk a few miles, from wherever he parked or was dropped off, to the Aladdin store."

Jill turned abruptly toward the living room. "Did you see a computer, tablet, or cell phone?"

Randy followed. "There's a charging cord on the breakfast bar that probably fits a cell phone."

Jill was looking under the couch and chair when I walked into the living room. Spying an electrical cord running to the recliner, I slipped my hand in alongside the cushion. "Here's a laptop that's still plugged in." I pulled it out, then pulled on a cord that eventually released a computer mouse from the cushion.

Jill accepted it from me and sat on the couch, placing the mouse on the end table at her elbow. "I don't recognize this Apple computer model. Based on the letters being nearly worn off the keys, I'm guessing it's really old." She sat with her fingers poised over the keyboard. "Numerical security code. What do you think? His birthday? His phone number? The fire number?"

Randy leaned against the counter. "Looking at this pigsty, I'm thinking this guy was no rocket scientist. Type in 1234."

Jill thought for a second, then typed in the numbers and waited. "I'll be darned. That was it!"

"What do you see?" I asked, sitting next to her.

"I'm not familiar with these programs. I assume they're free things he downloaded from the internet." Jill moved the mouse on the table, then frowned as she ran her fingers along the edges of the computer. Pushing a button, a tray the size of a drink holder popped out exposing a shiny CD with handwritten notes on top. "This computer has a CD-ROM slot."

"Is there a .jpg file?" Randy asked.

Reinserting the CD, Jill replied, "There is, along with a bunch of .pdf files and a spreadsheet."

"Open the latest .pdf," I suggested.

"It's a bill he created for twenty-three hours of work, plus mileage and meals."

"Who did he bill?" Randy asked.

"Bridget Thomas, on Roundup Circle in Gillette. The notes say, 'adultery investigation.'"

"Can't say I've met her," Randy replied. "She must not be a speeder, drunk, or miscreant."

I chuckled. "Miscreant?"

Randy wrinkled his forehead. "It's an all-around term for lawbreakers."

"I know," I replied. "I've just never heard anyone use the term in a sentence before."

Randy thought for a second, then said, "I wonder if Bridget Thomas is the dentist's wife?"

"What's the date of the bill?" I asked.

"The bill is dated November twenty-fourth."

Randy cocked his head, thinking. "I think the uncashed check on the breakfast bar was dated in December."

"I think we're narrowing down the window of Foster's death," I replied.

Jill straightened up. "Listen to this. Here's a bill to Patrick Streed of Portland, Oregon for forty hours of investigation, mileage, and meals. In the notes, it says, 'missing wife.'"

"What's the date on that bill?" I asked.

"December 1st."

I looked at Randy. "Why would someone from Oregon hire a PI from Moorcroft to search for a missing wife?"

Randy just shook his head.

Jill leaned back. "Was that a rhetorical question or do you really want some thoughts?"

"Either way," I replied.

"This Oregon guy suspects his wife is in northeastern Wyoming because of something in her past, or he doesn't have a clue where she is, and he's hired people all over the region."

"Why don't you call him and ask that question?" Randy replied, giving the obvious solution.

"I think it's too early to call Streed. Let's get more information before we tell him that the PI he hired to find his wife was killed." I turned to Jill. "Can you take a picture of that invoice, so we have the guy's address and phone number?"

Jill hit a few computer keys and smiled. "I just emailed it to myself."

"Are there other recent invoices?" I asked.

Clicking through lines on the computer, Jill shook her head. "Offhand, I'd say Foster's business was pretty slow. The most recent billing before the adultery bill was last August. It was to that insurance company with the duck sponsor. The note says, 'disability claim.'"

Randy nodded. "The golfer and ATV rider, no doubt."

Looking around the living room and kitchen, I saw little to be learned by searching the small area with most everything clearly in view. "Let's take a look in the garage."

The path from the house to the barn/garage was bare dirt and weedy, like it hadn't been used often. The windows in the garage doors were covered with dust and wiping them with the edge of my hand did little to provide visibility inside the unlit building. Randy, having local knowledge, walked to the side door and opened it.

"It's not locked." He held the door open for Jill, who found a light switch within reach after stepping inside.

I was right behind Jill when she froze. Because Jill was blocking most of the doorway, Randy and I stood outside the garage waiting for her next move.

When nothing happened, I whispered, "What's up?"

"There's something, or someone, in the back of the garage."

Randy, being slimmer than I was, slipped past Jill. "Since there aren't any footprints to the big doors or the side door, I'm inclined to think it's a *something* rather than a *someone*."

"That's not the answer I was hoping to hear, Randy," Jill replied.

"Sorry, but that's the reality."

I nudged Jill ahead and stood alongside Randy. "When you say *something*, what options come to mind?"

Jill let out her breath like she'd been holding it. "Well, we've already encountered a hungry bear today. Since they're just coming out of hibernation and are starving, I see a freezer in here and it's possible that Mr. Bear is chowing down."

"I doubt it's a bear. They need a darned big hole to get inside." Randy replied. "I'm more inclined to think of skunks or raccoons."

"Not rats or mice?" I asked as I looked at a variety of dusty junk piled haphazardly around the walls of the building.

Jill reached over to the wall, flipping more light switches, bathing the interior of the building in nearly blinding bright light.

"What the hell?" I asked, shielding my eyes until they adjusted to the overwhelming brightness.

"Those are grow-lights," Randy said, moving further into the building. Pointing to the opposite wall he added, "And those are pots for growing something large. Since this doesn't look like a landscaper's operation, I'm inclined to think Mr. Foster was supplementing his PI income by growing marijuana."

I walked to a shelf lined with fertilizers and plant growth supplements. "I suppose the PI business wasn't providing enough income to support him, so Foster started his own little marijuana operation. I take it Foster hasn't been on your radar as a drug dealer?"

"We tend to focus on the meth and oxycodone sales," Randy said, walking to the far side of the barn and lifting tarps that exposed bags of potting soil and additional stacks of large plastic containers. "There's a little marijuana around all the time, but nobody's dying from that or burglarizing farms to support their addiction."

Jill hung back. "Randy, having grown up on a ranch where we regularly found critters hiding under things, I'd appreciate it if you'd stop pulling tarps off the piles. I don't want to run you to Sundance for an antivenin shot or to the Moorcroft grocery store to buy a case of tomato juice to wash the skunk stink off of you. I really don't like dealing with people who've been bitten by a rattlesnake or sprayed by a skunk."

"Yeah," I agreed as I stepped away from a pile of pots.

Randy's eyes lit up as he dropped the corner of the tarp he'd been looking under. "Perfect! I'll call Darcy and tell her we've uncovered a possible marijuana-growing operation. We'll need the DCI resources to investigate the scene. I'll wait here for her. You guys don't need to hang around if you've got other things to pursue."

As Randy walked away, Jill looked at me. "Are we really going to call the guy in

Oregon, or are we going to keep that card up our sleeves for later?"

"I'm reluctant to let him know we're onto him. Let's determine where he lives. Then we can contact the local police to get a better sense of who he is and why he's looking for his wife."

"Ah, the value of local knowledge," she replied as we walked to the pickup.

Jill flipped through search pages on her phone as I drove back through Moorcroft. I stopped at a gas station in the tiny downtown area to top off the tank. While paying for gas inside the station, I bought two bottles of iced tea and handed one to Jill when I returned to the truck. "Do you remember Foster's business address?"

Tipping her head back, she stared at the truck's ceiling. "It was on Bighorn Avenue, but I can't recall the street address."

I drove one block and saw the sign for Bighorn Avenue. The street was one block long to the left, so I turned and passed a bar, beauty salon, then a row of deserted storefronts. Jill pointed to a building to our left. "I bet that's it. The one with the brick façade and Venetian blinds drawn shut. There's a faded sign taped to the glass."

Making a U-turn around a memorial at the end of the block, I drove back. "That's it. The sign looks like it was made on his desktop printer. I think we can assume the building is locked and we can't see inside through the blinds. I'm surprised the landlord hasn't been after Foster to pay the rent."

Jill looked up and down the short block. "There are at least two other empty stores in this block. I bet the landlord is happy to hold onto the chance that he'll get rent whenever Foster shows up."

Shifting the pickup, I drove away from Foster's office. "We can leave the office and the mail that's probably piled inside the door for the Wyoming DCI crew."

"Don't drive off yet," Jill said, holding her phone out to me.

"What am I looking at?" I asked, idling at the curb in front of Foster's office.

"That's a satellite view of Patrick Streed's address."

"It's rural," I said, noting the thick forest with a few open spaces.

Jill took the phone back and enlarged one of the open spaces. "What do you see?"

"That looks like a trap shooting range."

"Next to it, there are a couple of longer clearings that look like a rifle range with setups for several different distances. I wonder if there's a pistol range in this pole building?"

"That could explain where Tanya learned to shoot her .45."

"And gained the knowledge to understand how lethal it is." Jill took the phone back and moved to a different screen. "Streed's mailing address is Portland,

Oregon but he lives in a rural area that's actually a township outside of the city."

"Can you determine which police department serves his community?"

Jill smiled and handed the phone back to me. "It's the Portland PD."

I touched the phone icon and was speaking with a dispatcher after one ring. I identified myself and asked to speak with a patrol sergeant. After being on hold for two minutes, a male voice answered, "This is Sergeant Stonebridge. My caller ID says I'm speaking with J. Fletcher, USPS. I assume that's the Park Service and not the Post Office."

I touched the speaker function, "Sergeant, this is Doug Fletcher, I'm with my partner, Jill. I have you on speaker. We're Park Service investigators, not postal inspectors."

"What can I do for the US Park Service?"

"We're investigating the death of a private investigator whose body was found on a Park Service property. In the course of our investigation, we discovered an invoice to Patrick Streed, who lives in a rural area outside of Portland. Is he familiar to you?"

"Sure, Pat Streed runs the local gun range. It's where all the local law enforcement officers go to requalify."

I hesitated, looking at Jill while I considered my words. "Sergeant, I'd like to get some background on Mr. Streed without the request getting back to him. Can we be discreet?"

"Before we go any further, can you give me your badge number and the name of your supervisor?"

I provided both Jill and my ID information, and Jack Pardee's name and phone number. "We work for the National Park Service Investigative Services Branch. It's an unfamiliar acronym, NPSISB. We work out of Texas and investigate crimes on National Park Service properties across the United States."

"Is this a good number to call you back?"

"Yes. Please verify our identities and the nature of our assignment, then get back to us."

I disconnected the call and handed the phone to Jill. "I hope he's not one of Patrick Streed's close personal friends." Starting the truck, I drove away from the stop sign at the end of Bighorn Avenue and turned onto I-90.

"I feel like we need to talk to Tanya," Jill said, holding the phone on her lap. "If she's connected to Streed, we may have provided a pathway to locating her."

"She is probably our prime murder suspect. I think a quiet conversation might be more informational."

Jill's phone rang and she quickly switched it over to speaker. "Jill Fletcher, NPSISB."

The caller chuckled. "That acronym is a mouthful. I just got off the phone with your boss. He says Jill and Doug Fletcher are the real deal. What do you know about Pat Streed?"

Jill looked at me, unsure how to answer the question. "At this point, all we know is that a PI billed him for services, and the invoice said, 'missing wife.' We're following up on all of the PI's customers, trying to find someone who had a motive to kill him."

"Was your dead PI shot?"

"No. He was strangled."

Stonebridge laughed. "You can eliminate Pat from your investigation."

"Why do you say that?"

"Pat owns a gun range. If he was going to kill someone, I'm pretty sure that person would be dead from a single shot to the head. He can outshoot any of my officers with a pistol, and I've seen him break 100 straight clay pigeons on the trap range."

"Is Mrs. Streed still missing?"

"She cleaned out their joint checking and savings accounts last October and disappeared. Pat filed a missing persons report, but every indication is that she left voluntarily and doesn't want to be found. Given that she's an adult and not wanted for any crimes, we aren't actively pursuing the investigation."

Jill leaned close to the phone. "Was there some event that triggered her departure?"

"Not that I know of. I mean, Pat runs hot and cold. He has a temper, and he might've gotten into it with her."

Jill was about to ask another question, but I cut her off, not wanting to give out more information about what may have been an abused wife. "Sergeant, do you know why Streed hired a PI from rural Wyoming?"

"I think Pat hired people all over the northwest US and Southwestern Canada. He thinks she is hiding out somewhere. She'll probably come back when the money runs out. Do you know where Sarah is?"

Jill's eyes went wide, but I answered. "We haven't run across Sarah Streed anywhere in our investigation. To be honest, we have a number of the PI's customers to follow up with and this seems to be another cold lead."

"Fair enough," Stonebridge replied. "Let me know if she shows up on your radar. Like I said, we've still got an open missing persons investigation."

"Thanks, Sergeant." I paused as if I'd just had a thought. "Give us a description of Sarah Streed and we'll check with the local coroners to see if they have any Jane Does who match her description."

"I've met Sarah a couple of times. She's blonde, about forty-five years old, five-six, maybe a hundred and ten pounds. Any time I saw her, she was wearing makeup that made her look twenty." Stonebridge chuckled. "I don't mean to be crude, but she was a looker. Heads turned when Sarah Streed walked into a room.”

“I’ve met the type,” I replied. “I had an ex-wife who always tried to look half her age. She wore makeup like Tammy Faye Baker and her plastic surgeon was on retainer.”

Jill frowned, not realizing where I was going.

Stonebridge chuckled, “Sarah Streed had a little work done. Pat joked that she’d gone from a 34A to a 38D in one day.” He paused. “Good luck with your murder investigation. Let me know if you find a blonde Jane Doe with breast implants and who’s had a nose job and tummy tuck.”

Jill ended the call, glaring at me. “You didn’t have to disparage Sherry to get that information about Sarah Streed.”

“If I’d poked around, asking more questions about Mrs. Streed’s physical description, he would’ve gotten suspicious. This way, I was just another divorced cop grumbling about his ex-wife.”

Jill wasn’t entirely bought into that line of thought and sat back with her arms crossed. “Did Sherry really wear heavy makeup and have a boob job?”

“You’ve met her. Sherry was a born-again flower child. She never even wore lipstick and wouldn’t dirty the temple of her body by putting bags of silicone in her breasts.”

Relaxing slightly, Jill looked at me. "What do you say about me when it's just the guys talking?"

"I tell them you're the best thing that's ever happened to me."

"Smartass. What do you really say?"

"That's God's honest truth. You're the best thing in my life and I'm not afraid to tell people that."

Jill reached across the seat and rubbed my thigh. "Have I told you today how much I love you?"

I reached down and put my hand on top of hers. "You haven't said it today, but I know." I paused, lifting her hand off my thigh. "Keep your hands to yourself, or we're going to need a motel room."

Laughing, Jill said, "I forget that men respond to sexual stimulation like a microwave oven." She sat up and became serious. "We're driving to Aladdin to talk to Tanya, right?"

"That was my plan."

"How are you planning to approach her?"

"I plan to approach her from the front."

Jill sighed. "Smartass. What are you going to say to her?"

"Can I see your driver's license, Mrs. Streed?"

"Whoa! You're not going to beat around the bush?"

"I want to see the look on her face. We'll know instantly if the woman we know as Tanya is Sarah Streed."

Chapter 13

Tanya was ringing up the sale of an Aladdin General Store t-shirt when we walked in. She acknowledged us with a nod, then continued chatting up the buyer as she put the shirt and receipt into a shopping bag.

Smiling, she asked, "How are my favorite rangers?"

I smiled back and put a pack of sugarless gum on the counter while reaching for my wallet. "We're good. How are you today, Sarah?"

Tanya froze for just one second, then continued ringing up my gum. "You've forgotten my name between this morning's bear incident and now?"

"Actually, I'd like to see Sarah Streed's driver's license."

I could only describe the look on Tanya's face as desperation. She leaned close and whispered, "God, how many people have you told?"

I spoke softly. "I haven't told anyone, and I don't plan to, if you'll be honest with me."

Sarah stepped back from the counter until her back was against the wall. "I have to leave."

"Actually, you have to stay. You need to answer some questions about Jake Foster."

"I don't know anyone named Jake Foster."

Jill's focus had been on Tanya/Sarah's gun. Somewhat reassured that Sarah hadn't reached for her pistol, she said, "Pat Streed hired Jake Foster to find his wife."

Sarah's lips went dry, and she licked them. "Does Pat know I'm here? He'll kill me."

"We think Jake was close to connecting the dots, but we don't believe he ever passed his suspicions to your husband."

"How can you be certain?"

"We think Jake's been dead for four or five months and your husband hasn't come to pick you up."

I let that information sink in while I unwrapped the package of gum and popped a piece into my mouth. "I'm more interested in Jake Foster's death and the connection between you and Foster."

"I told you! I've never heard of Jake Foster before you mentioned his name."

"When did you arrive in Aladdin, Sarah?"

"I don't know. I suppose it was September." She paused. "Yes, it was after Labor Day. I asked for a job at the café and

Debbie said their business dried up after Labor Day. She told me to ask at the store.”

“You never ran into Jake Foster at the store? He was a chunky guy, in his sixties. He wore suspenders.”

“What makes you think I’d have met him here?”

“He’d taken pictures of you carrying garbage to the dumpster. You didn’t see him sitting on the hill behind the store?” Jill asked.

“No. When?”

“It must’ve happened in late November or early December,” I replied.

“No. I’ve never seen anyone on the hill...” Sarah paused. “There were deer and elk hunters who walked up there in November and some turkey hunters have been up there since the spring season opened. Other than them, the only person I’ve ever seen up there is Barry. He rides his ATV all over.”

Jill looked at me as soon as Sarah mentioned Barry.

“Have you ever seen Barry riding up there with another person?” I asked.

Sarah shook her head. “He’s offered me a ride, but I’ve never seen him with another person.”

Jill leaned on the counter, putting on her most non-threatening look. “Sarah, we’re not going to tell anyone who you are, or that you’re here. I know you’re anxious, but nothing has changed since yesterday or the day before. Okay?"

"It's not okay! How did you identify me? You must've spoken with someone who knew I was missing."

"I spoke with a Portland police sergeant. I told him we had a dead private investigator who'd been hired by your husband to locate you. Sergeant Stonebridge told us that Pat Streed hired PIs all over the Northwest to find you. We specifically told him that we had *not* found Sarah Streed but were only following up on all of the PI's customers."

"Corey Stonebridge is one of Pat's buddies. I'm sure they'll talk about your call."

"Take it easy," I said. "I didn't say where we were. Even if your husband figures out which PI we are investigating, he'll be looking at all of northeastern Wyoming, southeastern Montana, and southwest South Dakota. That's a million square miles."

Sarah became more agitated. "That's a lot of acreage, but there aren't that many towns and people here. He'll have his people scouring the area."

Jill gestured for Sarah to settle down. "Take a breath. You've been on the move. There's no reason for him to spend a lot of money scouring the region."

"You don't know Pat. He's a vindictive sonofabitch. He told me he'd kill me if I ever left him." Sarah pulled down the neck of her sweatshirt, exposing a pink scar with crude stitching running along her collarbone. "Pat did this."

"He's had months to cool off since you left. Your husband has probably moved on with different PIs, in other parts of the country."

Sarah shook her head. "You don't understand. He did this with a box cutter while I was tied to the bed. He didn't slash me. He cut me slowly, right down to the bone. He told me if I ever left him the next cut would be six inches higher, across my throat."

"What did you tell the people in the ER?" Jill asked.

Sarah's laugh was sharp. "He sewed me up with a needle and thread. 'No need to get a doctor involved,' he said."

I nodded. "I'll talk to Sheriff Stoddard. We'll get you protection."

Sarah shook her head and took a keyring from her back pocket. "I'll just disconnect from the store's water and power and put Bill in my trailer. I can be hundreds of miles from here tomorrow."

Jill shook her head. "Give us two days. I'll stay in the RV with you. Okay?"

"What will you do against pure evil?"

I took a breath. "Jill put thirteen shots into a running guy who was firing at the Crook County deputies. And I'll be in the cabin twenty yards away."

Something that had been nibbling at the back of my mind surfaced. "If you cleaned out your joint bank accounts, where has Pat found the money to hire all these investigators to find you?"

Sarah shook her head and put up her hands defensively. "I can't..."

"He's laundering money through his gun range," I guessed.

"I never told you that, and I'll never testify." She paused, gripping the RV keys so hard they cut into her hand. "I'd never live to testify, and Pat would never live to go on trial."

"Listen to me," I said. "I'll call an FBI friend, and they'll put you in protective custody."

"No. I'm putting Bill into his trailer and we're leaving." Blood dripped from Sarah's fingers as the RV keys dug into her palm. "Just let me drive away."

She took a step toward the door, and I moved down the other side of the counter across from her. "Stop, Sarah."

With Sarah focused on me, Jill slipped around the far end of the counter and tiptoed up behind Sarah as I moved to block the door.

Sarah stopped a few feet away and put her hand on the butt of her gun. "Get out of my way."

I raised my hands, as if surrendering and spoke loud enough to cover the sound of Jill's approach. "I won't shoot you, Sarah. I need you to stay here and talk to the FBI. There's no way I can let you drive away before you tell them about the money laundering.”

Jill put her hand on top of Sarah’s gun hand. “You’re not going to do anything stupid. Okay?”

Sarah sobbed, “I need my gun to keep Pat from killing me.”

I removed Sarah’s pistol from her holster and slipped it into my waistband. “Trust me, we won’t let anyone hurt you.”

“You don’t know Pat.”

“Pat won’t get near you. I promise.” Jill put her arm over Sarah’s shoulder. “We’re all going to our cabin until we can sort out a plan.”

Chapter 14

I stood behind the store and dialed the number for the Rapid City FBI office stored in my phonebook while Jill walked Sarah to our cabin. A cheerful young woman answered, "FBI Rapid City field office, how may I be of assistance?"

Forgetting, or ignoring, the proper professional jargon I asked, "Is Jess Pond around?"

After a pause, the woman replied, "May I ask who is calling for FBI Special Agent in Charge Pond?"

"Sure, tell him Park Service Investigator Fletcher is calling."

After a minute or two on hold, the woman was back. "Um, Special Agent in Charge Pond would like to know which Investigator Fletcher is calling."

"Tell SAC Pond that he'd better answer the damned phone no matter which one of the Fletchers is calling."

My abruptness startled the woman who was apparently accustomed to callers with greater decorum. "I take it this is Inspector

Doug Fletcher. Jess said Inspector Jill Fletcher would be extremely polite."

"Yes, this is Doug Fletcher. May I speak with his holiness?"

The woman chuckled. "I've never heard anyone refer to the SAC as 'his holiness' before. Hang on."

"What is it this time, Fletcher?"

"Good afternoon to you Mr. Special Agent in Charge. I take it you have a new receptionist screening your calls."

"Shaundra is an intern who happened to pick up the phone before I got to it. What's up?"

"I have a woman in protective custody who informed us that her husband is laundering money through his business. I thought you'd like to talk to her."

I heard Jess' office chair creak, then he closed his door. "Where the hell are you? Is this something local?"

"I'm in Aladdin, Wyoming, investigating a murder victim found at Vore Buffalo Jump."

"Someone's laundering money through a tourist site?"

"Get serious, Jess. The woman has been in Aladdin under an assumed identity while hiding from her abusive, money-laundering husband."

"How did you stumble across her?"

"Our dead victim was a Moorcroft private investigator who'd been hired to locate the woman."

"Did she kill the PI?"

"She claims she didn't. At this point, I'd say it's unlikely she was the murderer."

"And she wants us to go after her husband, who's laundering money?"

"Actually, she wants to run away, hoping her husband, who threatened to kill her if she ever left him, can't find her."

"Dammit, Fletcher. Where do you come up with these crazy crimes? Hang on while I open a file on this. Where is the husband's business?"

"He runs a gun range outside Portland, Oregon."

"And the wife is in Aladdin? Holy shit. She really found an out-of-the-way spot."

"The wife says her husband is buddies with the Portland PD sergeant I spoke with while checking out the PI's recent business. You probably shouldn't call the Portland PD to ask for the files on Patrick Streed."

"Hang on." I heard computer keys clacking while Jess searched. "Where are you holding this woman?"

"Right now, we're at the Aladdin Motel."

"Shit. Shit. Shit. I assume you're holding Sarah Streed."

"Right."

"Do not take her to the county jail. I don't want her to show up on anyone's arrest log. Portland PD has her on a nationwide hold. They'll be notified if she's pulled over for a traffic violation or is arrested."

"Oh, shit. I was trying to be sly with my questions, but the cop I spoke with is her husband's buddy. I've really stepped in it."

"Do you think your contact in the Portland PD was really close to Streed?"

"He's close enough to know that the wife has silicone breast implants."

"Do they know exactly where you are?"

"They'll figure out that the dead PI lived in Moorcroft and they'll narrow the search to northeastern Wyoming real quickly."

"How well do you know the local sheriff? What is his name?"

"I know Hank Stoddard very well."

"Call him as soon as you get off the phone. Explain that you just stuck your foot in a hornet's nest and in 24-48 hours the swarm will be all over you."

"Have you got somewhere in Rapid City where you can stash the wife?"

"It'll take a couple of hours to get set up. But yes, I can put her in a safe house."

"We'll be there in about ninety minutes."

"What? You're driving her over right now?"

"That's my plan. Jill's parents want us to spend some time on the ranch. We'll drop off Sarah Streed, then pop over to see my in-laws."

"Someone has to be in Aladdin when the Oregon folks come poking around."

"Someone?"

"All right. You and Jill need to be in Aladdin when the husband or his cronies show up."

"Why us? You're the one with all the hostage rescue teams and firepower. We're just lowly park rangers." The pause was so long I thought the call had been dropped. "Are you still there?"

"Sorry. I muted the phone while I laughed."

"This is not funny, Jess. This place is really exposed and we kind of stick out like neon lights."

"I know. I've been to Aladdin. What's going to stick out worse in Aladdin? Your father-in-law's dusty pickup, or a bright shiny FBI SUV?"

"We're driving a rental pickup, not Al Rickowski's rig."

"Swap with him. Tell him some cock and bull story about enjoying the feel of the road in a real ranch pickup."

"We'll figure out something. You've got to have some forfeited vehicles in the FBI fleet for undercover work."

"I might be able to find a rusty Camry in the back. But, holy shit, Doug, there is not a place near Aladdin to set up a backup team without them looking like cops setting up an arrest."

"You could bring in a sniper and spotter in camouflage to sit on the hill behind the Aladdin store. It's the spring turkey hunting season so they wouldn't look out of place.

The motel isn't busy, so you could put a couple of people wearing western-style clothing in one of the rooms. They could hang out in the café, looking like early season tourists."

"Let me mull it over. I'll see who I can pull off anything else without compromising ongoing investigations. I'll see you in a couple of hours."

"Where are we meeting?"

Jess chuckled. "How about the Spearfish truck stop where the prostitute tried to undress you during the sting operation."

"She did *not* undress me. At least not entirely." I waited for Jess to stop laughing. "We were in the motel next to the truck stop, not the actual truck stop."

Pond caught his breath. "Meet me behind the truck stop."

* * *

Jill helped Sarah pack some clothes and toiletries into a bag while I parked the pickup next to her RV. I stood by the pickup's fender, studying the hillside behind the store, trying to identify the spot where Jake Foster had been hiding, then scanning the rest of the hillside, looking for any signs that we were under surveillance. Not seeing anyone, a light reflecting off binoculars, or anything suspicious, I returned to the pickup and opened the back door.

Watching the parking lot in front of the motel with my hand on the butt of my pistol, I heard the RV door close. I stepped away from the pickup, so I was between anyone in the parking lot and Sarah. Jill hustled Sarah from the RV into the pickup's back seat. Closing the door, she patted my shoulder. "Go!"

I backed up to turn around, then drove to the road past the store. I looked for the non-existent traffic, then prepared to turn right.

"Turn left. That'll take us into Belle Fourche."

Hesitating, I looked both ways but saw no other traffic. "I'm torn between taking the smaller, untraveled highway to Belle versus getting onto the interstate where there will be a lot of traffic around."

"If someone unfamiliar with the area is driving here from the east or west," Jill said, "they'll drive up from the interstate. No visitor is going to take a roundabout route here through Belle and Highway 85 into Spearfish."

Turning left, I looked at the open expanse of the two-lane road ahead of me. As a city kid, I felt more secure in crowds. Jill felt comfortable in the open spaces.

"Can I have my .45 back?" Sarah asked from the back seat.

Jill turned around and put her arm on the seat back. "You'll have to trust us. Okay?"

"If we get run off the road, I'd feel more comfortable looking out for myself."

I glanced at Sarah's worried face in the rearview mirror. "If we're approached by a car with Oregon plates, I'll gladly hand you the .45."

Sarah's look was skeptical, but she didn't argue. She looked at Jill. "You *will* take care of Bill until I get back, right?"

"As I said when we first met, I grew up on a ranch. Bill will be treated as if he was my own horse."

"If you ride him, he's got a soft mouth."

"We never put up with cowboys who were hard on a horse's mouth. I'll be gentle."

Sarah nodded, accepting Jill's reassurance.

We encountered a total of three pickups, a semi, and a dusty old Mercury on the trip from Aladdin across the border into South Dakota. The vehicles were outnumbered about ten to one by the antelope who were eating the freshly sprouting prairie grass.

There was more traffic once we turned south on Highway 85. The scariest vehicle was a semi loaded with giant round bales of hay. One of them looked precariously unsecure, so I passed the truck and stayed ahead of it all the way to Spearfish.

A clean, black SUV was idling behind the truck stop. I pulled up next to it and Jess Pond stepped out of the driver's door. A woman wearing an FBI bulletproof vest got out of the other door and approached us.

Jess smiled and shook my hand as Jill helped Sarah get her suitcase out of the backseat.

"Jess Pond, this is Sarah Streed."

The female FBI agent was watchful of the area around us. Looking stern, she held out a bulletproof vest. "This is for your passenger."

I passed the vest to Sarah. "Please put this on."

Jill held the suitcase while the female FBI agent helped Sarah pull the vest over her head. Together, they fastened the Velcro straps under the arms. "Is that comfortable?" the agent asked.

Sarah squirmed and tugged at the bottom of the vest. "I don't suppose you have one in pink."

One corner of the female agent's mouth curled into a smile. "Sorry, I left the pink and plaid vests at the office."

Sarah sighed. "What happens now?"

"We have a safe house in the hills overlooking Rapid City," Jess explained. "You and Special Agent Weyer are going to be BBFs for the next week."

Sarah looked at Special Agent Weyer. "I hope you don't snore."

"Call me Andrea. You'll have your own bedroom, so snoring won't be an issue."

Jess became serious. "Please don't try to run away. The house is secure. You'll be safer there than anywhere you've been since you left Portland."

"I don't have a cell phone, and I haven't spent anything but cash for months. I've left no trail of crumbs for anyone to follow."

Jess glanced at me. "That's very smart. How about the RV?"

"I paid cash to a private party, and I've never transferred the title."

I tried to visualize the RV and license plates. "But the RV has Oregon license plates."

Sarah closed her eyes and sighed. "Yeah, but it's parked out of sight, behind the store."

I looked at Jess. "The Wyoming Department of Criminal Investigations is searching the PI's home, computer, barn, and office tomorrow. They should be able to access any correspondence he had with Patrick Streed. In a couple of hours, we should know if the PI passed on his suspicions about Sarah's alter ego, Tanya, to Streed or not."

"What's your gut telling you?" Jess asked.

"My gut says that the PI has been dead for months. If he'd given Streed any information about Sarah's suspected location, someone would have been poking around long ago."

"What about your phone call to the Portland PD?"

I blew out a breath. "I was very oblique, saying that we were following up on all the PI's customers. I suppose the sergeant might've been suspicious."

Sarah glared at me. "My husband and Corey Stonebridge are buddies. I'm sure Pat got a call last night that piqued his interest."

Jess stared at Sarah. "I need to know what your husband was into, and how much he's worried about what you might tell us. That'll help me with my risk assessment and response."

"I want immunity," Sarah said. "Get the US Attorney for whatever state we're in on the phone."

Jess glanced at me, then spoke to Sarah. "What would I tell the US Attorney? She's not going to give you blanket immunity from anything until she has a sense of what you know."

"You can tell her to talk to her counterpart in Oregon about human trafficking and prostitutes being shipped in from the Philippines and Indonesia and arms dealing. The money is being laundered through Pat's shooting range and gun sales."

"You know the details?"

Sarah snorted. "I'm the dumb blonde who didn't have to leave the room when 'the boys' discussed business. You see, I'm not smart enough to understand how the girls, guns, and money moved around."

Jess nodded to Special Agent Weyer, who helped Sarah into the back seat of the SUV while Jill put the suitcase on the other side. He stepped close to me. "If she knows all that, someone's going to be very interested in either bringing her home or silencing her.”

“It’s only a matter of time for someone with a lot of money and resources to find the woman who showed up out of nowhere and lives out of an RV hidden behind a store in Aladdin.”

“I’m struggling to figure out how this all ties into my dead PI. Aladdin, population 15, is way too small for those to be unrelated incidents.”

“Maybe the people who show up looking for Sarah will be able to answer that question.”

I shook my head. “The PI was spying on her months ago. If the husband or his cronies knew she was in Aladdin, they would’ve acted before now.”

“Maybe your phone call will be the catalyst to get things moving.”

I was struck with a thought that was so obvious that I was embarrassed to bring it up. “Maybe he’s had dozens of PIs scouring the country, trying to find Sarah. He might’ve gotten so many leads to follow that he hasn’t worked far enough down the list to check out Aladdin. Is there some way your people can start calling PIs to see if they’ve been passing possible sightings of Sarah on to Streed?”

“I can’t pull resources off other investigations based on your gut. On the other hand, if the US Attorney gets excited about Sarah’s information, priorities could change. She might be very excited about catching a couple of Streed's people who might want to flip on him rather than spend decades in prison. After I talk to the US Attorney, I'll call our Cheyenne office and alert them to the DCI search." Jess paused, thinking. "You'd better notify the sheriff of your suspicions, then dust off your bulletproof vests."

Frowning, I said, "We're doing a cold case suspicious death. We didn't pack any vests."

"I suggest you make friends with someone who'll loan you a couple of vests."

"You're unwilling to loan fellow federal law enforcement officers bulletproof vests?" I kidded.

"All our vests are stenciled 'FBI'. There are rules against loaning them out to other agencies who might misrepresent themselves as FBI agents. It's in the manual."

I snorted. "I think your manual had a picture of J. Edgar Hoover on the back, and you lost or threw it away the week after you graduated from Quantico."

Jess smirked. "I still pull it out to refresh my memory every time I spit polish my shoes."

I looked at Jess' scarred boots. "Right."

"I'll throw in a couple of vests when I bring my team to Aladdin. In the meanwhile, contact Hank Stoddard and ask to borrow a couple of his."

Chapter 15

After calling her mother, Jill drove to her family ranch from the truck stop. I called the sheriff's office from the pickup.

"Hi Hank, I thought I'd give you an update."

"Randy's been keeping me informed. He's at the Foster place with the DCI. It sounds like finding that place through the Co-op was a lucky catch."

"Jill found Foster's billing statements on his computer. He's only had three recent customers and we narrowed the field to a guy in Oregon who's searching for his missing wife."

"You think you've found the missing wife?"

"We confirmed that the single woman working at the Aladdin store is the person the PI was searching for. Her name is Sarah Streed and we just turned her over to the FBI."

"Why turn her over to them?"

"She says her husband is mixed up in money laundering, human trafficking, and illegal arms deals. The FBI will talk to the US Attorney about getting her immunity in return for filling in the blanks about her husband's business dealings."

"How about the PI murder? Isn't she your prime suspect?"

"We don't think so."

"Well, shit the bed. This is one screwed-up mess."

"It's going to get even messier if the husband figures out his wife is in Aladdin."

"He's had months to find her. Why would he make that connection now?"

I blew out a breath. "I spoke with the local police in Portland. The sergeant I spoke with is her husband's buddy and we think they'll be on the scent pretty quickly."

"Then what?"

"Considering how much the wife knows, someone's going to show up planning to either retrieve or eliminate her."

"From Aladdin?"

"I think we need to be prepared for that," I said.

The sheriff paused. "What do you need from my department?"

"The FBI may be able to provide some agents to watch the motel and store. Jill and I are staying there, so we'll be part of whatever happens. Neither the FBI, nor Jill and I have any local knowledge. We need Randy and anyone else you can spare to help us scope out the area and set a trap."

Jill tugged at the front of her shirt. "Vests."

"Jill and I weren't planning to get involved in any shooting situations, so we didn't bring our bulletproof vests. Do you have a couple we could borrow?"

The sheriff chuckled. "I think we've got a couple spares in the back room. I do have to warn you that none of them are tailored for a woman's figure, and at a few thousand dollars apiece, I'll be billing the Park Service for a replacement if you get shot."

"Fair enough. But rest assured, getting shot is not a part of any plan."

Stoddard laughed. "It never is, until it happens."

"I'll keep you posted as soon as I hear anything from the FBI."

"Doug, keep in mind that I'm one deputy down. I can pull in some people on overtime, but I don't have the resources to assign people to 24/7 Aladdin surveillance."

"I understand, Hank. We hope whatever happens will occur in the next forty-eight hours. If it drags on longer than that, everyone will be stretched to cover Aladdin."

"I assume you don't want any of our marked vehicles parked in front of the store."

"Good point. We definitely don't want to spook anyone who's looking for Sarah. Do you have any vehicles that you've seized?"

"Any of them usually go to the state. I can have my folks in their personal pickups and cars with handheld radios."

After caring for Bill, we drove to Spearfish. Chet's pickup was parked in Rickowskis' driveway when Jill and I pulled in.

"Oh boy. We get to talk to the whole family, again."

Jill glared at me. "No one appreciates your sarcasm."

"I'm sorry. Did I say that out loud?"

Jill parked the pickup and we walked to the house. "Be nice, okay?"

"I'm always nice," I said.

"You're cynical and sarcastic way too often when dealing with issues involving our parents."

I stopped with my hand on the doorknob and smiled. "There. I'm happy and on my best behavior."

Jill laughed. "Really? You can turn it on and off that quickly?"

I opened the door and whispered, "I can, but usually choose not to."

The kitchen was filled with the aroma of frying chicken, sage, and onions. Al and Chet were at the table playing cribbage with lowball glasses of dark liquor near their hands. Molly and my mom were talking near the stove.

Chet looked up, a smile spreading across his face. "It's about time another cribbage player showed up. I'm out of quarters and was about to start writing IOUs."

Al's sly smile hinted that was indeed the case. He picked up his drink and sipped it without comment.

Mom swept across the kitchen with her apron flowing. She hugged Jill as if they hadn't seen each other in years. "Has Doug been treating you okay?"

"He always treats me well."

Mom pecked my cheek. "Have you shot anyone today?"

I sighed and looked at Jill, who mimed a smile, reminding me that I'd agreed to be nice. "Not today, Mom. Tomorrow is another day."

Chet had been halfway through a sip of whiskey when I made the comment. He choked, then snorted and coughed. When he caught his breath, he shook his head. "You need to warn me when you're going to say something that tickles my funny bone."

I couldn't help but smile. "Sorry, Chet." I walked behind him as he picked up his cribbage hand. With all even numbered cards, there was no way for him to make a count of fifteen, or to make a run.

I walked behind Jill's father, who held a hand containing only fives and face cards. He looked up at me as he threw a five and a jack into his own crib. "If I'm lucky, I'll get a cut."

I pulled the pegs out of the cribbage board and put them into the slot on the back side. "Time for supper," I said.

"Hey!" Al protested, "I was just about to skunk him!"

"You were probably cheating…again. It's suppertime."

Chet happily surrendered his hopeless hand to me. "It's about time. My stomach was leaning against my spine."

Mom shook her head. "Chet, if you gain one more pound, you'll have to move the pickup seat so the steering wheel doesn't rub your belly."

Chet leaned back and patted his ample belly. "I guess that's what will happen after this meal. I love Molly's fried chicken and stuffing with gravy."

Al finished his drink and smacked his lips. "Chet, when did you last have a meal of Molly's that you didn't love?"

Jill carried plates to the table as Al considered the question. "I'm not sure. But my memory isn't what it used to be."

I set trivets on the table for the cast iron skillet and the pan of stuffing coming out of the oven. Jill rushed to help her mother, who was struggling to lift the giant cast iron skillet filled with fried chicken.

Mom looked at the kitchen door like she was expecting someone else to arrive. "You didn't bring in your overnight bags."

Setting the chicken on the table, Jill shook her head. "We kind of rushed out of Aladdin. We didn't have time to pack anything."

Chet raised his eyebrows. "I guess you'll be sleeping naked on those cold sheets."

"Or we'll be driving back to Aladdin where our clothes are," Jill replied.

Molly sat as I carried the pan of stuffing to the table. "Maybe you can sleep in your father's t-shirt, like you did when you were little."

Jill looked at me, obviously not taken with the suggestion. When I didn't respond, she spread a napkin on her lap and smiled. "Mom, that was when dad's t-shirts hung down to my knees. I'm not sure they'd cover my backside anymore."

Al smiled at me. "Doug might find that look appealing."

Molly frowned, "Shush. Don't embarrass your daughter."

Al forked two pieces of chicken onto his plate, then waited for me to pass the stuffing to him. Jill handed me the bowl of gravy. Leaning close she whispered, "We're driving back to Aladdin."

Al looked at me. "You didn't respond to my comment."

"I love the sight of my wife's cute backside, but we need to be in Aladdin early tomorrow morning."

Placing a chicken breast on my plate, Jill whispered, "Nice recovery."

Molly waited until everyone else had chicken before taking a single chicken leg for herself. "I'll give you the Big Ben alarm clock, Jill. It'll wake you."

"Mom, the Big Ben alarm clock ticks so loudly that I can't fall asleep."

"Well, you could put it under a pillow, I suppose."

Jill sighed as she cut off a piece of chicken breast. "I think that would defeat the purpose of having the alarm clock in the room. We'll be fine driving back to Aladdin tonight."

Chet peeked out of the window. "It'd be nice to be young and able to drive in the dark."

Al licked the crumbs from his fingers. "I don't think it's as much about seeing in the dark as it is being smart enough not to drive around in the dark when there are deer, antelope, and cattle on the road."

"That's why you have insurance," Chet countered.

Al was unconvinced. "I'd rather not take my rig to the shop for a week, then fight with the insurance company afterwards. I'm perfectly happy to sit home and watch television after sunset."

Jill, having finished her half chicken breast, candied carrots, and small scoop of stuffing, pushed herself back from the table. "I remember a few times when you and the cowboys closed the bars after roundup."

"That's what I mean," Al replied. "I'm smarter than I was back then. I don't need to run into a steer on the road, and I don't need a DUI either."

Chet slapped the table, startling all of us. "It's not that. You're a damned cheapskate and you'd rather drink at home than pay what the bar charges!"

With expectation in his eyes, Al looked at me. "That's especially true when my son-in-law brings me bottles of expensive booze. I don't suppose you have a bottle in your suitcase?"

Shaking my head, I replied, "Darn it all. We left our suitcases in Aladdin." I twisted to look at Jill, who was removing dessert from the oven. "What kind of booze was it that we bought for Chet and your dad?"

"You don't have any booze in your suitcase. You said you'd pick something up after we got to South Dakota."

I snapped my fingers. "It must've slipped my mind."

Chet's grin was priceless. "You didn't bring any booze because you weren't planning to play cribbage this trip."

I stood and went to help Jill, who was dishing up some kind of cobbler made with red fruit. "There's vanilla ice cream in the freezer and the ice cream scoop is in the drawer next to the stove."

By the time I found the ice cream and scoop, Jill had already passed around bowls of cobbler. Chet looked at me expectantly. "Are you planning to stand there holding that carton until it melts or are you serving it?"

Laughing, I removed the lid and stepped next to him. "I'll scoop until you tell me to stop."

Mother grabbed my arm after the second scoop. "Stop now or there won't be any ice cream left for the rest of us."

Chet looked up at me. "How about just another dab?"

I worked my way around the table, dishing up ice cream for everyone. As expected, Jill only wanted one scoop on her half-piece of cobbler. I scraped the bottom of the carton to get a full scoop for myself.

Mother waved her spoon at me. "See! If I hadn't stopped you, neither you nor Jill would've had any ice cream at all."

We all laughed, and Chet dug into his dessert as if he was starving.

Jill paused halfway through her dessert and wiped her mouth on a paper napkin. "Dad, can we swap pickups with you for a couple of days?"

"Is there something wrong with your rental? I could drive it to the airport and swap it out for a different truck."

"The brand-new rental stands out among the ranch trucks at the motel."

Molly paused. "Why do you care, dear?"

Jill looked at me, not sure of how best to answer. "We need to be less obvious *out-of-town* folks for a couple of days."

Al knew what I was getting at but decided to yank my chain. "Aw hell, if you're trying to be less obvious, you need to get some trail dust on your clothes and maybe a little horse manure on your boots." He leaned over, lifted the tablecloth, and stared at my shoes. "For that matter, you might want to find a pair of boots instead of those damned yuppie hiking shoes."

Chet nodded his chin toward the door. "See if my Stetson fits you. Nothing says you're local better than a scarred pair of boots and a sweat-stained Stetson."

Molly was about to say something when she stopped abruptly with tears filling her eyes.

Jill put her hand on Molly's arm. "What's wrong?"

Molly pointed to the hallway. "Junior's closet."

I frowned. "I don't understand."

Al's smile disappeared, but he nodded. "See if Junior's boots and hat fit you. They're still in his closet."

"I don't know if we need to go that far."

Jill stood and patted my shoulder. "Come on."

In her late brother's bedroom, Jill opened the closet. "Junior was slender, so his clothes won't fit you." She pulled a sweat-stained hat from the shelf and gently wiped the dust off of it. "See if this fits you."

Gently setting the hat on my head, I realized the fit was nearly perfect.

Jill handed me a pair of scarred cowboy boots that were sitting in the closet. "I have no idea what shoe size Junior wore."

"I don't think this is necessary."

Jill knelt down and untied my hiking boots as I sat on the bed.

Pulling on the right boot, I said, "I feel like Cinderella."

"I've got news for you, Cowboy. I'm not Princess Charming."

The boot fit, although feeling the impressions left by Junior's feet seemed creepy.

"Does it fit?"

"I'm not sure I want to do this."

"Put on the other one and try walking in them."

I walked into the hallway. Unaccustomed to the undercut heels, I felt like a woman must feel when trying on high heels for the first time. I walked into the dining area.

"Find the man a sheepskin coat and hand him a set of reins," Chet exclaimed. "We're ready for the round-up."

Molly still looked weepy, but she nodded.

Al leaned back and frowned. "Now all you need is a two-day beard and a little horse scent."

Jill stepped back and shook her head. "Your jeans are too new, your shirt is the wrong cut, and your belt looks like it came from J.C. Penney's. Other than that, you look just like an ad for Marlboro cigarettes."

Al struggled out of his chair. "Hang on." He disappeared down the hallway and reappeared with a belt that looked like it had been in a war. "Try this on."

I pulled off my own belt and threaded Al's belt through my belt loops. "We use different holes, but the length is right."

Chet shook his head. "Al, how many pants sizes ago did that belt fit you?"

Al was solid but had grown a bit of a barrel chest since he stopped working the ranch. He glared at Chet. "I wear the same length pants I did when I was eighteen."

Molly broke out laughing. "The length isn't what's changed."

"How about Jill?" Mom asked.

Jill smiled. "I wear the same size jeans I wore when I started college."

I glanced at Jill's chest but got the *don't you dare go there* look. Getting the message, and having learned to sometimes keep my mouth shut, I didn't say anything.

"There are probably a couple of shirts in my closet. My boots and hat fit the same."

Chet glanced at my holster. "You might want to swap out that government-issued pistol for a six-shooter. And Jill's cheap piece of crap plastic gun doesn't look like it belongs here."

"I have to draw the line at our weapons," I said. "We need to carry familiar pistols we know how to shoot. I'm not swapping out my Sig for a Colt."

Al waved that off. "People carry all kinds of guns these days. Nobody knows Doug's gun from anything else men carry. I see quite a few women carrying Glocks, and I expect there are more in handbags that I don't see. Their guns aren't a problem."

Chet shrugged. "I thought we were going for an Old West look."

Jill, who'd emerged from the bedroom with several shirts on hangers, shook her head. "We're trying for a *we belong here* look. Dad and Doug are right. Our weapons won't stand out because of the open carry laws here, and we're going to carry the guns we know how to shoot."

"Attagirl," Mom said, surprising all of us. "Try to stay out of the line of fire."

Jill took the Stetson off my head and hung it with her shirts and hat on pegs near the door. "We're not the main show here. Our role is to support the other agencies involved and to be their backup. No one is getting shot or hurt."

"What other agencies?" Al asked.

Jill bit her tongue, realizing she'd said too much. "We're helping the Crook County Sheriff's Department."

Al glared at me. "Jill said 'agencies.' That's more than one. Who else is involved in whatever you're up to?"

"We've spoken with the FBI. They're probably going to supply some agents."

"Whoa," Chet said. "If the FBI is involved, this is some serious shit you're digging into."

"It could all be nothing," Jill replied, sitting down. "We're going to hang around

Aladdin for a couple of days, continuing our murder investigation. We hope that the rest of the things we're investigating will be dealt with on the West Coast."

Mom leaned on her elbows. "You two are using so many weasel words. It *might* be dealt with on the West Coast. It *might* involve the FBI. We're *assisting* the sheriff." She paused. "The last time you 'assisted' the sheriff, Jill was almost run over by a semi, and you got into a gunfight that hasn't been seen since the OK Corral."

Molly nodded. "You're working hard to blend in with the locals like you're undercover."

Chet's eyebrows rose. "Are you undercover? Will it be like the last time when that hooker had her way with Doug in the Spearfish motel?"

"No hooker has had her way with me. Not in Spearfish, or anywhere else."

Chet started laughing. "I like my version of it better."

Laughing, Jill pointed her finger at Chet. "Don't you ever tell that story to anyone. Do you understand me?"

"You're too late! I told Harvey Koski that Doug caught VD from the hooker and had to be treated with antibiotics!"

Mother punched Chet's arm. "You did no such thing!"

Chet rubbed his arm. "Like I said, I like my version of the story better than what we've been told. And that whole thing about

Doug yelling, 'Mickey Mouse' out of the window to bring in the backup cops. That's just not believable."

I glanced out the window at the setting sun. "We need to get going so we don't run into any cattle in the dark. Al, can we borrow your pickup?"

A set of keys slid across the table and bumped into my hand. I looked up at Chet. "Take mine. It's way less noticeable than Al's truck. Besides, I'd like to try driving something less than ten years old."

I looked at Jill, who shrugged. "It's dustier, scraped up, and older than Dad's truck. I think it'll work."

We stood, getting hugs from Mom and Molly, then handshakes from Chet and Al. They all walked us outside, stopping on the back step.

"Never-ending food and wit at the Rickowski ranch."

Jill took Chet's keys from me. "You're just jealous because your mother isn't as colorful as my family."

"I can't argue that. Compared to Al and Chet, my mother is a model of decorum."

The driver's door of the pickup creaked as Jill pulled it open. "Yup, this is a perfect undercover vehicle. No cop would be caught dead driving this."

I sat on the cracked vinyl seat and buckled the seatbelt. "On the other hand, we're not going to be chasing down any bad guys in this."

"Chases are off the table when we're driving Chet's truck." Jill turned around and we waved as we drove down the driveway. "Weren't you the cop who commandeered an aging Oldsmobile for a chase in the Grand Canyon?"

"Trust me, I've learned that lesson."

"You're trainable?" Jill asked.

"Listen, smartass. I'm entirely trainable. I did not make a comment about your bra size being the same as it was in high school."

"If you were entirely trainable, you wouldn't have brought it up now, either."

We rode in silence for a while until I thought I had come up with the right words. "I'm sorry. You're perfect."

"Thank you."

"Are you okay with me wearing Junior's hat and boots?"

Jill didn't respond for so long, I thought she hadn't heard me or misunderstood my question. "It's eerie, seeing another person I love wearing my brother's clothes. I really thought Mom had burned all of Junior's stuff."

"I'll throw them away after this week."

"No, hang on to them."

"I'll buy some different clothes if we have to go undercover again."

"It's not that. By wearing them, it's like you're bringing a bit of him with us. I feel good about that. It's like a sign from heaven. This is going to turn out okay because Junior is watching over us."

I reached out and touched her shoulder. "It'll be okay no matter what."

"I wasn't sure of that before. But now I am."

"How does Junior feel about you and me?"

Jill glanced at me. "You don't know?"

I shook my head.

"You're the one wearing Cinderella's slippers. Don't you think that's a sign?"

Chapter 16

Barry was the only other diner when we walked into the café for breakfast. Today's aroma was fresh cinnamon rolls. Inhaling deeply, I reveled in the childhood memory of Mom's baking in the days before my father died. Jill gave me a funny *what's up* look.

"The smell of cinnamon rolls brought back good memories of my mom's kitchen when I was a child."

Debbie brought the coffee carafe to our table as we sat down. "Where is everyone?" Jill asked.

"You two slept in. The rush was at seven. I've already fed the hunters, the carpenters, and two hungry cowboys. I still have half a dozen cinnamon rolls if that appeals to you."

Jill glanced at the menu board and sighed. "Is there any chance I could get a bowl of oatmeal with some raisins?"

"Sure. It'll take a few minutes, but John can whip up a bowlful for you." Debbie looked at me.

"Two eggs, over easy, bacon, and one of the cinnamon rolls."

Debbie nodded. "Do you want John to cook yours up right away? Or are you going to be a gentleman and wait until Jill's oatmeal is cooked?"

I didn't even glance at Jill. "I'm fully housebroken. I'll wait and eat with Jill."

"Are you sure you don't want the cinnamon roll right away?"

Jill smiled. "Bring the cinnamon roll now. I might steal a bite of it to tide me over until the oatmeal is ready."

Debbie laughed. "You two seem to have struck a balance in your relationship. That's a good thing, because the nearest divorce lawyer is in Gillette."

Jill frowned. "There won't be a divorce."

"You don't believe in divorce?" Debbie asked.

"Not really. I'd kill him before I'd divorce him."

Debbie seemed shocked before she said, "There is a third option. I made mine so miserable that he packed up his shit and left. After seven years, I can have him declared dead and I get everything."

Debbie disappeared into the kitchen and Jill leaned close. "Do you think her husband really packed up and left?"

I stared at the kitchen door for a moment, thinking about Debbie and the local culture. "I saw a NO TRESPASSING sign on a ranch entrance while we were driving to Belle. It said, 'I have a shotgun and a backhoe, leave now.'"

Jill shivered. "That's way too close to the sign we saw on the dead-end road in Florida.

I don't even want to think about that experience."

"Are you still having nightmares?"

Jill looked at me. "Aren't you? Or was being nearly killed just another day in the office for you?"

"I have nightmares, but most of them involve children, thinking I should've or could've done something differently to protect or save them." I paused, then added, "There's still the one nightmare about forgetting I had an English paper due. In my nightmare, Mrs. Nelson made me write out my paper on the board while the whole class watched."

"Mrs. Nelson terrorized you?"

"When you're in eighth grade, it's easy to be intimidated by a tough talking teacher who looked like she could kick your butt."

"You are kidding me."

"Nope. I can still see her blue eyes boring into me because I was talking to the kid next to me while she was explaining the proper conjugation of verbs."

Leaning close, Jill whispered, "Barry is staring at us."

I waved at him. "Hi Barry. How are you doing?"

"What did he do?" Jill whispered.

"He got very interested in whatever is on his plate."

Debbie walked back to top off our coffee. "You're in luck, Jill. John found another carton of oatmeal on the shelf, and it wasn't past its expiration date. At least not after John used his Sharpie to mark it as oatmeal so there'd be no future confusion about the contents."

"There was confusion about the contents?" I asked.

"Not unless you missed the picture of the fat guy wearing a black suit on the carton. Hmm. The label might've said oatmeal right above his head. Dang, John probably didn't need to obliterate that date...I mean identify it as oatmeal."

Jill rolled her eyes. "First of all, I don't believe your story. Secondly, even if it is true, how would dry oatmeal go bad?"

Debbie's eyes twinkled. "That's what I told John!" She walked to Barry's table and cleared most of the dishes while speaking softly to him.

A moment later, Barry walked over and stood next to Jill. "Your husband looks like a cowboy today."

Looking up at him, Jill said, "We found some boots and a hat for him to wear. Do you think it's an improvement?"

Barry was confused by the question. "I don't know. He looked okay before. Now he just looks more like the rest of us instead of looking like a cop."

"Do you think I look like a cop?"

Barry blushed. "No, you look like a girl."

"Thank you. I'll take that as a compliment."

That comment totally baffled Barry. He stood silently for a moment, then went back to his table to retrieve his hat. He dropped money on the table, then walked out of the door.

"Once again you've baffled a man using your feminine wiles."

Scoffing, Jill asked, "What other men have I baffled with my feminine wiles?"

"Me."

Jill stopped with her coffee cup halfway to her mouth. "How have I baffled you with my feminine wiles?"

"Somehow, you went from boss to friend, to lover, to wife. I've never been sure how that progression occurred."

"Are you unhappy about it?"

"That's the best part. I'm not."

"Don't overthink it. You did the same thing to me."

"I couldn't believe it was happening. I asked if you wanted to watch a movie and snuggle. You opted for a shower and the bed. I was too astounded to resist."

Debbie came out of the kitchen with our breakfasts. She set the bowls and plates out, then paused. "Conversations rarely stop that quickly when I arrive unless the people are talking about me."

Jill blushed.

I replied, "We were just reliving our first date."

Debbie picked up the tray. "It must've been a doozy because Jill is as red as Santa's suit. Were you messing around on the kitchen table or something?"

"Quiet little South Dakota ranch girls don't do things like that," I replied.

Debbie snorted. "Are you saying South Dakota girls are more refined than Wyoming girls like me?" She walked away, laughing.

Jill spread the raisins on her oatmeal and started eating without saying anything.

"Did I embarrass you?"

Jill leaned forward. "You left her thinking we got busy on the kitchen table!"

"I didn't say that!"

"You didn't correct her."

I took a bite of bacon. "Neither did you, dear."

Debbie was back a minute later with coffee refills. Instead of retreating to the kitchen, she sat down at the table. "I'm sorry if I embarrassed you, Jill."

Jill waved off her apology. "We got married later in life and Doug's jaded past sometimes embarrasses me."

"You've both lived through divorces?"

Jill shook her head. "Doug's been divorced. This is my first marriage."

Debbie took a coffee mug from a neighboring table and poured a cup for herself. "Lucky you. Not making the stupid young girl mistake of marrying the first guy who kissed you."

"Is that what you did?" I asked.

"Yup. Grade school sweethearts who married between junior and senior year in high school."

"You didn't wait until after graduation?" Jill asked.

"Shotgun wedding. I was pregnant." Debbie chuckled to herself. "I actually thought we were in love. As it turns out, getting pregnant, married, then dropping out of school aren't the best life choices."

"I came close to that scenario," Jill said. "Then I decided getting beaten up every time he got mad or drunk wasn't the life I wanted. Luckily, we parted ways before the pregnancy or marriage."

"What's your deal, Doug?"

"I was a stupid rookie cop who married a hippie. She thought she could reform me. I paid for her college education through a Ph.D., then she ran off with another hippy. I crawled into a booze bottle for a while. I moved to Arizona, got my shit together and met Jill. Now, here we are."

"I've never met cops who were both married. At least not to each other. How does that work?"

Jill pushed her oatmeal bowl aside and wiped her mouth. "He's a cynical bad cop. I'm a diplomatic good cop."

"Yin and Yang," Debbie said, nodding. "Doug, why are you dressed like a cowboy today? Have you gone to the dark side?"

Jill poured coffee for all three of us, then weighed her words. "We can't share information about a police case."

"Why does a police case involve you two? You're like Park Service cops, right?"

I pushed my plate to the side and leaned on the table. "I can only say that Jill and I are going to spend a lot of time here, drinking coffee and looking like bored locals."

"That's why you're wearing scuffed boots and a sweaty hat?"

I nodded. "It'll be best if we didn't look like cops. That way we can keep whatever happens from getting out of hand."

"You're scaring me." Debbie looked at the door like she expected someone to walk in. "I think we should just lock up until tomorrow. What do you say?"

Jill put on her best reassuring smile. "You'll be safer here than in your living room. Okay?"

The bell over the door jingled and Debbie jumped up, ready to run. Randy Pannell walked in. "Geez, Debbie. I'm a little scary, but you and I have known each other for a long time."

Randy took a clean mug from another table and joined us. Pouring himself a cup of coffee, he sat down. "Take it easy. There will be so many cops in Aladdin within the next couple of hours, it'll look like a convention."

"Is this the thing you can't talk about?" Debbie asked. She paused, then looked concerned. "Coffee refills are free, and cops aren't known as big tippers."

I slid my coffee cup over for a refill. "You have a new policy as of today. Cops pay for refills and there's a twenty-percent tip automatically added to every bill."

Debbie looked at Randy. "Really?"

He laughed. "If Doug says that's the way it's going to be, that's how we'll do it."

Jill pulled a charge card out of her back pocket. "Start a tab for us. Put every cop's cup of coffee, doughnut, and cinnamon roll on this charge card. We'll settle up before we leave."

Randy's eyes lit up. "I'll take a cinnamon roll."

Debbie fingered the charge card, drew a breath and straightened up. "Do you want me to warm that roll up for you?"

"Please."

Debbie nodded and went to the glass counter where an assortment of sweets were displayed. Randy smiled and nodded, then glanced at Jill. "Debbie's going to be a problem."

Jill smiled and nodded, then said through her teeth. "Yup. She told us she pees her pants when she's afraid."

"What's she going to do when the shooting starts?"

I leaned close. "No shooting."

"You can say that, but we both know that if Tanya's husband pulls a gun, we're not going to rely on Jill's diplomacy to defuse the situation."

Debbie set down Randy's roll and took the coffee carafe behind the counter for a refill.

Jill watched her leave, then said, "Tanya's real name is Sarah Streed. Her husband is Patrick Streed. He owns a gun range, and by all accounts, he's a good shot."

"Well shit, that's probably why Hank sent the two bulletproof vests in my trunk."

Jill looked at me. "How can we look like two locals drinking coffee if we are wearing vests stenciled *Deputy Sheriff*?"

"We can't."

Jill closed her eyes. "I'm glad that's settled. What's your plan for putting them on before the shooting starts?"

"We'll improvise."

Jill's eyes popped open wide. "What? I want a plan with no improvisation involved."

"Fine. We'll let Randy and the FBI do all the shooting while we hide in the back room, putting on Randy's vests."

"Now you're being a smartass. You can't run for the back room if another cop is being shot at. Your sense of duty doesn't allow you to run if a cop is under fire."

"Probably not, but you can."

Randy snorted. "Have you two ever considered doing a comedy act?"

Jill was about to give Randy a piece of her mind when the door jingled, and Jess Pond walked in looking like he'd just climbed off a horse. He stood next to the door, smiling. "What's a cowboy got to do to get a cup of coffee in this place?" Joining us at the table, he smiled. "Deputy Pannell, I heard the Cheyenne DCI office is unhappy with you."

Randy grimaced but didn't reply.

"What happened, Randy?" Jill asked.

"You know how they were going to get a forensic team to go through Foster's house, garage, and office?"

"Yes," I replied.

"The search didn't go as planned," Randy replied. "The animal we heard scurrying around in the garage *was* a skunk. One of their agents got sprayed. I got a nasty call asking why I hadn't warned them there was a skunk. They didn't believe me when I told them we never actually *saw* a skunk."

Jess grinned. "I bet that's not the end of the story."

Randy shook his head. "Foster's office was a mess. I got a call telling me the office had been ransacked. I guess they rethought that and decided that Foster's filing system was throwing paper in piles on the floor. There were notes scribbled on scraps of paper and paper napkins."

Jill frowned. "Did he transcribe his notes onto his computer?"

"Foster had an Apple desktop computer the DCI guy called antique. After trial and error, they found a spreadsheet showing his time, expenses, and billings, but there wasn't any investigative information on it." Randy paused. "The DCI guy said if we ever sent him to a shithole like that again without checking it first, he'd deliver all the paper to the sheriff's office and let us sort through it ourselves."

Sheriff Hank Stoddard walked in looking like Marshal Dillon, fresh off the set of *Gunsmoke*. Wearing worn jeans, a denim shirt, and wearing his gold badge pinned to a leather vest, he walked to our table and pulled up a chair. With all of us staring, he frowned and asked, "What?"

Jess smiled. "Did you tie your horse to the hitchin' rail, sheriff?"

Stoddard's eyes sparkled. "As a matter of fact, my Bronco is parked in front of the bar, where every good cowpoke ties his ride." He picked up an empty mug from a nearby table and raised it, signaling Debbie for coffee.

Arriving with a carafe in hand, Debbie filled his mug. "Howdy, Sheriff. Are you having a cinnamon roll?"

Stoddard smiled. "I bet they're fresh out of the oven."

Debbie glanced at the remnants of rolls sitting in front of the rest of us and smiled. "I'll warm it in the microwave, and we'll pretend it just came out of the oven."

"That works for me!" With Debbie gone, the sheriff leaned close. "I assume Randy filled you in on the searches at Foster's places."

"Yeah," I replied. "It sounds like his office was as messy as his trailer."

"The DCI folks are reading through his notes, but his filing system left some room for improvement. What kind of private investigator keeps notes on bar napkins and deposit slips?"

We were chuckling when Debbie arrived with the sheriff's cinnamon roll. The frosting had melted and was running onto the plate. "Oven fresh," she said, setting the roll in front of the sheriff.

Stoddard peeled a piece off the roll and dipped it in the hot frosting. We watched silently. "What?" he asked.

"We're just watching your look of appreciation," Jill replied.

"Why aren't you all down in the bar, drinking rot gut whiskey like the gunslingers do while waiting for the bad guys to ride into town?" the sheriff asked as he broke off another piece of the cinnamon roll.

Jess sighed. "Hank, you've watched too many old westerns. No smart cowboy went into a gunfight with alcohol slowing his reflexes."

"I suppose it depends on his point of view. Alcohol also dulls the pain of being shot."

I gestured toward the cops sitting around the table. "I think our plan is to not get shot, so numbing the pain isn't an issue." I paused, then added, "Those old westerns were pure fiction."

Hank smirked. "Like the shootout at the OK Corral?"

"Okay, I'll give you that one. But the rest are pure Hollywood. Butch Cassidy and the Sundance Kid never jumped off of a cliff."

"No, but they did ride to Bolivia to escape the US warrants for their arrest."

Jill looked annoyed. "Is there a point to this discussion?"

Dipping the last of his roll in the puddle of frosting, Stoddard nodded. "We're killing time. There's no point in staring at each other for hours while waiting for something that might happen."

"This is part of law enforcement boredom," I replied. "Cops tell stories as a way to get to know each other."

"Ah," Jill said. "This is male bonding."

"This is cop bonding," Stoddard replied. "If we were male bonding, there'd be profanity and dirty jokes."

"Like the cowboys in the ranch bunkhouse," Jill replied. "I used to listen to them while sitting on the back step."

"I bet you learned a lot about the world," Stoddard replied, wiping his fingers on a paper napkin.

"Mostly I learned that cowboys are foul-mouthed misogynists."

Debbie returned with the coffee carafe in time to hear the end of Jill's remarks. She topped off our coffee and said, "It's not just cowboys who are like that. My experience is that most men fall into that category." She looked at all of us, waiting for an argument. When it didn't come, she added, "until they prove otherwise. I think this group might be an exception to that rule."

Jess Pond shook his head. "Can I get a cinnamon roll while we try to convince you that we're not jerks?"

Debbie's mouth curled into a hint of a smile. "A nice tip would go a long way toward improving my view of you."

Jill raised her finger to interject a thought. "I've already given Debbie my charge card. The coffee and rolls are on me." She looked at Debbie and added, "And there will be a generous tip included."

"I already knew Jill was okay. The jury is still out on the rest of you."

Hank reached for his wallet, pulled out $20, and threw it on the table while Debbie watched. "I've got the tip. I have to live here after the rest of you go home."

Snatching the money from the table, Debbie put it into her apron. "The problem with Hank is, I never know if he's a genuinely nice guy, or if he's trying to get re-elected."

We laughed as Debbie walked away and Hank searched for a response.

Chapter 17

Jess Pond's cell phone buzzed. He stood and wiped the cinnamon from his fingers as he walked out of the door. He was back two minutes later with an update.

"The Assistant US Attorney has been interviewing Sarah Streed all morning. They've agreed to an immunity deal. It's early in the process, but Sarah's already given them enough to arrest Patrick Streed and two of his co-conspirators on a variety of charges, including racketeering."

Jill smiled. "Has someone in your Portland office arrested Sarah's husband?"

Jess shook his head. "The FBI Portland field office sent two special agents to the gun range. They were told 'the boss took off a couple of hours ago.' They went to his house, but there's no one home."

"Have you issued a national BOLO to have him stopped by any agency that sees his car?" I asked.

"He's not in his own car. All his vehicles are either at the gun range or parked at his house. We don't know if he's borrowed a car, rented a car, is riding with someone else, or if he decided to cash in his chips and took an Uber to the airport to catch a flight to Havana."

Sheriff Stoddard stared at the ceiling. "He's in the wind."

"It seems so," Jess replied. "We're checking the car rental companies, airline passenger manifests, and have provided the TSA with his passport picture for facial recognition in case he's using a false identity. It's possible that he's in a borrowed vehicle driving in this direction or is driving south to Mexico or north to Canada. There's no reason to believe he knows anything more than Sarah is somewhere in this region, so if he's smart, he's going somewhere his money is stashed or where the US doesn't have an extradition treaty."

"If he's not smart enough to run away, it'll take him days to check out every motel in northeast Wyoming and southwest South Dakota," the sheriff opined. "If he starts with the bigger motel chains in the bigger cities, it'll take him weeks to work his way down to Aladdin."

"She's not registered at the motel," I said. "He'll never locate her that way."

We sat brainstorming and throwing out possible scenarios until the sheriff's cell phone rang. Still sitting at the table, he took the call. Leaning back, he looked surprised. "The farrier?" he asked.

Jill looked uneasy. "Streed's looking for Sarah's horse as a way of locating his wife.

He knows she wouldn't go anywhere without Bill."

Stoddard disconnected the call. "The dispatcher had a call from Kris Roberts, the Hulett farrier. She had a call last night from a man who told her his ex-wife had stolen his horse. The caller described Sarah Streed's horse, said he's called Bill, and asked if an unfamiliar woman had brought a horse fitting that description into the area. Kris told him she'd replaced a shoe on a Sorrel overo named Bill, for a woman who recently moved to Aladdin."

"Aw shit," Jess said. "Why would she give a stranger that information?"

"Apparently, the caller sounded quite distressed and described Sarah's horse perfectly. Kris thought about the call overnight and was suspicious enough to call the dispatcher this morning to tell her that someone should check out a possible stolen horse in Aladdin."

"Is Pat Streed vindictive enough to chase down his wife rather than taking off to save his own skin?" I asked.

"Do we think he knows Sarah is baring her soul to the Assistant US Attorney?" Randy asked.

"What would make him think that she'd turn over the information she knows now, when she's been gone for months?" Jill replied. "He believes Sarah's so intimidated by his threats that she won't talk to any cops."

Stoddard stared at Jess Pond. "Do you think he's on his way here?"

Jess looked disgusted. He pushed the remainder of his cinnamon roll to the center of the table. "I don't think he's vindictive. I think he sees Sarah as a loose end that has to be tied up before he runs. How long does it take to drive from Portland to Aladdin?"

Jill picked up her cell phone from the table and punched in information. "Google says it's 1,200 miles. That's eighteen hours of driving."

"That's without gas, meal, or bathroom stops," Randy added.

Jess looked at the sheriff. "What time did the farrier get the call?"

"The farrier got the call yesterday, just after lunch."

We all glanced at the clock near the door. Jill did the math the quickest. "That was nineteen or twenty hours ago."

"Shit," Jess said as he stood and walked away from the table. He was punching a phone number into his phone as he walked out of the café's door.

Stoddard picked up his phone and dialed dispatch. "Monique, start calling everyone who's not on duty. Have them drive their personal vehicles to Aladdin as quickly as they can."

Jess walked back inside shaking his head. "I've got a couple of partial tactical teams packing up their vehicles in Rapid City. They're waiting for four people who are driving in from home. I told them to send whoever was ready to move immediately. Two agents will be here within two hours. The rest will be an hour or two behind them."

Debbie arrived with the coffee carafe and started pouring refills. "Does anyone want another cinnamon roll or doughnut?" Seeing the looks on everyone's faces, she froze. "Someone's coming for Tanya, aren't they?"

"We're not sure," I said, trying to sound sincere.

"Bullshit. You're all worried and something bad is about to happen. It's written all over your faces." She left without waiting for our doughnut order.

Stoddard wrapped his hands around his coffee cup. "We need a plan."

I drew a breath. "We need two plans. What are we going to do until the deputies and FBI agents arrive, and how will we deploy everyone when they get here?"

Jill looked at Randy. "Have you got a spare handheld radio?"

"I've got one in the car. What are you thinking?"

"I'll take a radio, saddle up Bill, and ride toward the interstate. If I see any suspicious out-of-state vehicles approaching, I'll relay that to Randy and the sheriff."

"Wear a vest," I said.

"I'll be on a horse. Without a vest, I'll look like any other cowgirl out for a ride."

"Don't be stubborn. Wear a vest."

That comment brought a round of chuckles. Jill glared at me but acquiesced. "I'll see if Randy's spare vest fits under my jacket."

Randy stood and nodded to Jill. "I've got an extra-large *Hulett Red Devils* hoodie you can wear over the vest.

The sheriff called out to Randy. "Call your buddy, the outfitter."

Stopping at the door, Randy asked, "Do you mean, Zane, the guy we used for tracking?"

"Yeah, him. Call him and ask him to bring over a string of horses in case something goes *western*. I'd like to be prepared in case Streed figures out some way to come in from behind the store. We can put a couple of deputies with Zane on horseback."

Jill stood and kissed my cheek.

"What's that for?" I asked.

"In case things go western," she replied. Nodding to Randy, she walked out of the door he held open for her.

The sheriff stared at me, then at Jess. "You didn't put out a BOLO, right?"

"I couldn't. We don't know what he's driving," Jess replied.

Stoddard called dispatch again. "Monique, I need you to do two things. Put out a BOLO for an eastbound car or SUV with Oregon plates on I-90. It'll have at least one male occupant. Approach with caution, the driver is armed and dangerous. Next, call

243

the Wyoming Highway Patrol. I want their nearest trooper at the I-90 welcome stop on Highway 111 for backup. Tell them we will be attempting to arrest an armed criminal near Aladdin."

Jess was also on his phone. "How far away is my tactical team?" He waited, then responded, "They're only in Sturgis? Tell them lights and sirens. Our operation may be going down in the next hour or maybe less. Call the South Dakota State Patrol. Tell them we may need them for backup in northeastern Wyoming."

Randy walked in carrying a bulletproof vest and an AR-15 rifle. He leaned the rifle against a chair at the next table and handed the vest to me.

"Is Jill wearing a vest?" I asked.

"Yes, she put it on under my sweatshirt."

I glanced at the rifle. "I take it we're not trying to make a discreet arrest anymore."

Randy wobbled his head. "You know how it is with guns. You don't need one often, but when you do need it, you need it alongside you, not in the trunk of your car parked outside."

"And the discreet part?" I asked.

Randy looked down at his uniform. "I'll take the rifle and walk into the kitchen if an unfamiliar car pulls up outside."

I nodded and looked at Stoddard. "We're still trying to do this without any shots being fired, right?"

"We're going with that plan until a gun clears leather."

"Until I gun clears leather? Are we in an episode of *Gunsmoke*?"

"Let's hope not."

Debbie returned with the coffee carafe. She was pouring Jess' coffee when she noticed Randy's rifle leaning against the chair. Her hand began to shake, and she spilled coffee on the table. I snatched the carafe out of her hand and poured coffee for the rest of us while she wiped up the spilled coffee with a rag. Handing her the nearly empty carafe, I asked, "Are you okay?"

"I'm not sure. Are we still pretending nothing is going on?"

"That's the plan."

She nodded toward the rifle. "A few people carry pistols, but I've never had anyone bring an assault rifle into the café before."

Stoddard smiled at her. "Pretend it's a long-barreled pistol."

Debbie's look was memorable. "Sure." She took a step away and looked back at us. "John's shotgun is loaded with slugs. He keeps it next to the back door for shooting bears."

Jess looked at me. "I hope he doesn't hit us with any friendly fire. A shotgun slug leaves a large ugly scar."

Randy finished a sip of coffee and said, "I've shot a few bears and injured elk with a slug. None of them lived to develop a scar."

I leaned forward. "No shooting will be required."

Through the front café windows, I saw Jill ride through a gate in the fence on the other side of the road, then she turned Bill south. "There goes our lookout."

Stoddard got up and stretched. "I'm getting too old to sit around drinking this much coffee. I'm going to empty my bladder so I'm ready for action."

Randy smiled at me. "Doug, you must have a gallon-sized bladder. You drink coffee all day and I've never seen you go to the bathroom."

"I spent a lot of time on stakeouts while I was with the St. Paul Police Department. I learned how to hold my coffee."

Jess stood. "I've never mastered that skill. It must be something only local cops can do." He left for the restroom.

Randy leaned close to me. "Is your heart pounding?"

"I'll save the adrenaline for later."

"This is exciting. I spend most shifts driving around without a single call. On a busy night, the only calls I usually get are cars hitting deer and drunks running into guard rails after the bars close."

"That's police work, Randy. Hours of boredom and moments of terror."

"Only moments of terror?"

"Most cops never fire their weapons anywhere except on the range. The ones who do find themselves in a shooting situation are in a confrontation with someone who's less than ten yards away, and the incident is over in less than three minutes."

Randy whistled. "Our response times average thirty minutes, more if we're at the far edges of the county. My backup would arrive in time to deal with the cleanup."

"That's how it often happens, even in the big city."

The sheriff returned to the table just as Jill's voice came over the radio. "A red Jeep Wrangler is driving toward you."

"That's probably Wayne Olson. He's the off-duty deputy who lives closest to Sundance." Randy was ready to respond when another male voice came over the radio. Indeed, the Jeep was driven by a deputy responding to the sheriff's call for backup.

Five minutes later, I saw the jeep approaching when Jill's voice came over the radio again. "A boxy gray SUV is approaching on Highway 111. It might be a Mercedes."

Randy keyed the mic on his radio. "How far are you from Aladdin?"

"I can't see the rest area yet, so I'm probably halfway to the interstate."

Randy reached for the rifle. "Nobody around here owns a Mercedes. If it's not made in America, local folks won't buy it."

The sheriff chuckled. "If your rig isn't made in America, you can't find anyone to fix it without driving to Rapid City."

Jill came over the radio again as the red Jeep parked in front of the café. "The gray Mercedes is pulling over."

Randy turned his head toward the shoulder-mounted mic. "How far are you from the road? Can you see his license plates? Are they from Oregon?"

"I'm too far away to see plates. Wait, two men are getting out of the Mercedes."

"Getting out of the vehicle alongside the road?" I asked, rhetorically.

"Maybe they have to pee," Jess said as he returned to the table.

"Shots fired!" Jill's voice was panicked and jerky like she was riding a galloping horse.

Randy was out of his chair first, grabbing the rifle and running toward the door. I was right behind him, and literally bumped into him when he stopped abruptly. "What the hell, Randy?"

"They're beyond the ranch and hills." He hesitated, then added. "Wait, here they come. They're turning the corner toward us."

"Get Jill on the radio," I ordered.

Randy keyed his mic, "Jill, are you there?"

There was a long pause before she answered, "Yeah. I'm riding in a swale toward you. I can see the roof of the Mercedes once in a while. They're turning at the 'T' where the highway ends."

Randy rushed to his car, but instead of jumping into it, he returned with binoculars.

"What the hell is going on? Why would a random vehicle shoot at a woman riding out on the prairie?"

"Jill's riding Sarah's horse," I replied. "They probably think they're shooting at Sarah."

"What? Jill doesn't look anything like Sarah," Randy replied as he scanned the prairie behind the nearest ranch house for Jill.

"She's wearing your red sweatshirt over a vest. She must look like any other woman from a couple hundred yards away."

Riding out of the swale at a full gallop, Jill raced across the pasture, spurring Bill on.

"What the hell are you doing?" I asked rhetorically.

Randy turned toward me. "What?"

"I was talking to Jill."

The gray Mercedes braked hard and stopped near the only driveway between the highway and the store. Two men jumped out, pulled their pistols, and started firing wildly at Jill who was still over 100 yards away from them.

I drew my pistol and fired toward the Mercedes, knowing my chance of hitting them was close to zero, but that the shots would distract them from Jill. Jess Pond ran toward his pickup, and the sheriff radioed a broadcast that shots were fired. Randy raised his rifle, clicked the safety off, and leaned against the café to steady his aim.

Although my pistol fire hadn't hit them, the gunfire got the attention of the men in the Mercedes. They ducked behind it and were ready to fire at us when Randy fired off a methodical pop, pop, pop, pop of shots from the assault rifle. I replaced my empty magazine, preparing to start firing from my exposed position on the sidewalk in front of the café when Randy emptied his rifle.

Between Randy's shots, I could hear his bullets impacting the Mercedes. The windshield shattered and the front tire slowly went flat. The men stayed hidden during Randy's methodical firing.

A cloud of dust behind the shooters distracted me for a moment. "Sheriff, do you have someone coming in on an ATV?" I asked as I took aim at the Mercedes.

"All of my people are coming in trucks or Jeeps. They live too far away to drive here on an ATV."

A second rifle started firing at the Mercedes. I looked over and saw Wayne Olson firing over the hood of his Jeep with a lever-action deer rifle. The sheriff shoved me behind Chet's pickup. "You crazy bastard, where's the vest Randy brought you?" he muttered as he drew his pistol. "They're a long way off, but one of them might make a lucky shot and hit you."

Randy's magazine ran out and he took two quick steps across the sidewalk and jumped alongside the sheriff and me.

Kneeling while leaning his back against the pickup, he inserted a full magazine.

"What the hell is that guy doing on the ATV?" the sheriff asked.

"I don't have a clue," I replied as the gunfire from the Mercedes resumed and one of the café's front windows shattered. I heard a bullet impact Chet's truck, but the steel stopped the bullet from reaching us.

Randy scampered to the pickup's rear bumper and was about to start firing again, then he pulled back. "I can't shoot. That damn ATV rider is right in my line of fire."

I peeked over the hood of the pickup as the ATV raced toward the gray Mercedes. It disappeared from my sight seconds before I heard the thud of an impact, followed by a single gunshot. I watched, waiting to see what was going on. With the gunfire from the gray Mercedes stopped, I risked standing upright to see what happened.

The ATV came into view as it slowly rolled into the road from behind the Mercedes. I recognized Barry, struggling to stay upright on the ATV's seat. He twisted to get something out of the basket tied behind him. A moment later, I heard three more shots as I watched his body jerk from the bullets' impacts.

Enraged, I put my gun in the holster and pulled Chet's keys out of my pocket. "Randy, get in the pickup bed!"

Cranking the engine, I was surprised when the passenger door opened, and Hank Stoddard climbed in. "Go!" he yelled.

"I'm in," Randy yelled from behind me as I shifted into reverse and quickly backed onto the highway.

The sheriff pointed ahead of us. "Someone's taking the ATV!"

A man dressed in blue jeans and a tan shirt limped from behind the gray Mercedes. He shoved Barry's body aside, struggled onto the ATV's seat, then studied the apparently unfamiliar controls until the ATV lurched ahead, almost throwing him off.

"He's riding into the timber, not after Jill."

I accelerated as fast as Chet's old pickup would go. With the engine screaming, I shifted gears and raced toward the Mercedes as the ATV sped across a small strip of prairie before disappearing into the timber. "He's injured and switched from fight to flight mode."

"Forget the ATV," Stoddard ordered as the ATV disappeared into the trees. "This old rig isn't going to be able to climb through the timber after him."

I braked to a stop near Barry's inert body lying in the road. Jumping out, I saw blood soaking his camouflage jacket and puddling on the ground. His unseeing eyes stared at the cloudless sky. Hearing a noise to my left, I drew my pistol and leaned on the gray

Mercedes' hood. "Put your hands where I can see them!"

The response to my order was a groan. Randy moved behind me, aiming his rifle at the male body near the Mercedes' back door. The man's legs were twisted in unnatural directions and blood oozed from a gash on his head. A black pistol lay in the dirt a few inches from his hand.

Putting his hand on Randy's shoulder, the sheriff said, "He's no longer a threat." He paused, then said, "Doug, kick that pistol out of his reach, then check him for other weapons."

The man on the ground groaned again, each motion seeming to cause him pain. Through clenched teeth, he said, "Jesus, call an ambulance."

Jess Pond's pickup braked to a stop alongside us as I searched the man's pockets. "Give that man first aid. I want him alive and handcuffed to a hospital bed."

I pulled a wallet from the man's back pocket and flipped it open. "Meet Lawrence Mettler, from Portland, Oregon."

My announcement was met with another groan. "Where's Pat? Tell him to call an ambulance."

Randy, who'd seen his share of roadkill animals, rested his rifle over his shoulder. "Sorry, Larry. Your buddy, Pat, took off with the ATV and left you here. Tough luck for you. The only people here to save your sorry ass are cops."

Jess was becoming annoyed. "Hank, call your dispatcher and have her send an ambulance."

The sheriff put his pistol in the holster. "The quickest way to get him to the hospital is in the bed of a pickup. It'll take an ambulance half an hour to get here."

Jess clenched his eyes shut as if he was counting to ten. "Fine. Put him in the back seat of my pickup. I don't want someone taking an unnecessary detour on the way to Sundance." Looking at Randy he added, "Radio the Sundance hospital. Have someone waiting for me at the ER entrance with a gurney."

Reluctantly, Randy keyed his mic and relayed the request that the hospital be notified.

Chapter 18

With significant effort, the four of us got the injured man into the second-row seat of Jess Pond's crew cab pickup. His legs were shattered, and every motion caused him to scream out in agony. With squealing tires, Jess took off toward Sundance as Randy radioed dispatch to tell the hospital to look for a blue pickup and to arrange for helicopter transport to the higher-level trauma facility in the Rapid City hospital.

The sheriff knelt next to Barry's lifeless body and sighed. He looked at Randy and said, "Have the dispatcher send the coroner."

With the adrenaline fading from my system, I looked around for Jill and the horse. "Where's Jill?"

Randy spoke into his radio mic, "Jill Fletcher, can you read me?"

"Yeah," Jill replied, sounding off.

"What's your location?"

"Bill and I are walking to Aladdin."

I unclipped the mic from Randy's shoulder. "Why aren't you riding?"

"We're going to need a vet to look at a bullet wound."

"Bill was hit by the gunfire?"

"His crest was grazed, through his mane."

"Are you okay? Did you get thrown when he got hit?"

There was a long pause. "We owe the sheriff a vest."

"You were hit?" I asked, too emphatically.

"I've got mighty sore ribs, but beyond that, I'm fine."

I scanned the horizon and spotted Jill and the horse crossing the highway, walking toward the Aladdin store. "Stay where you are."

"No. I'm putting Bill in the shed until the vet gets here."

"Wait. You were crosswise to the gunfire when you were riding toward Aladdin. There's no Kevlar on the sides of a vest. It's all in the front and back."

"I'm fine. Meet me at the horse shed."

I was about to climb into Chet's pickup when the sheriff pointed down the highway to our west. "I think that's Zane with his horses. I hope he's ready to lead a posse into the timber."

Randy was leaning over Barry's body, in a prayer-like pose. He looked up. "I think we should let that city-slicker ride that ATV so deep into the wilderness that he'll never be seen again."

I looked toward the timber. "That's right. There's nothing there except trees most of the way to Montana. He could be lost for days."

Randy nodded. "It'd save everyone a lot of bother and taxpayer money if he's never found."

The sheriff shook his head. "With my luck, he'll accidentally circle around and end up right back here. We've got to look for him."

I drove back to the store and met Jill at the shed. She was on her phone, apparently speaking to someone doing triage at a Sundance veterinary clinic. "The bullet went all the way through his crest. The bleeding has stopped." She listened while looking at me. "He's inside now. I'll clean and sterilize it. No, I don't know if he's had his tetanus shot. Is there a way someone can see him before morning?"

"Tomorrow?" I asked.

She nodded as she ended the call. "They're busy. It's calving season. The vet is going to a nearby ranch in the morning. He'll stop then."

"Can I leave you here with Bill?"

Jill froze. "Why? There was a lot of shooting. What happened? Are you okay? Is Randy okay?"

"All the cops are fine." I drew a breath, steeling myself for the delivery of the bad news.

Jill sensed what was coming. "What's the 'but?'"

"Barry raced in on his ATV and ran down the guys who were shooting from the Mercedes."

"Was he hurt in the collision?"

I shook my head. "He was shot and killed by Patrick Streed."

"Barry is dead?"

"Streed jumped on Barry's ATV and rode into the national forest. Zane is here and we're going to track him down on horseback."

Jill gently patted Bill's shoulder. "Let someone else do this, Doug."

"I need to see it through to the end. You know that."

Jill grabbed my arm. "There are deputies who are horse people. Let them take over."

"Only Wayne has shown up so far. I'm sure Zane saddled up Rascal for me."

Jill pulled aside Chet's coat. "Where's your vest?"

"Things got crazy. It's probably still in the café."

"Put it on."

"Yeah, that's probably a good idea." I hugged Jill and kissed the top of her head. "Don't worry."

"Try to return unscathed this time. Adding another scar wouldn't be a good idea."

I kissed her and squeezed her hand for a second. "Rascal is probably waiting."

Randy was holding Rascal's reins when I walked to the front of the general store. "Where's Zane?" I asked.

"He and Wayne took off a couple of minutes ago. We'll be able to catch up."

Using the boardwalk, I climbed into the saddle without embarrassing myself. Rascal was following Randy and Hercules before I got my right toe in the stirrup. I leaned forward and patted Rascal's neck. "We're buddies now. You don't need to cut under any low-hanging branches or rub against any trees, okay?"

I took his lack of response as assent and followed Randy as Hercules started up the hill behind the general store.

Zane's tracking skills weren't required to follow the ATV trail through the crushed pine needles and broken branches under the pines. The horses walked while Randy and I scanned ahead and to the sides, not that I expected the ATV to sneak past us. Randy slowed as we rode into a canyon. Pointing ahead, he showed me where Zane and Wayne were riding up a steep ridge across from us. "I'm surprised that ATV went up that slope without flipping over backwards."

Rocking with Rascal's steps, I nodded. "Too bad it didn't roll. Our search would be over."

It took us half an hour to reach the top of the ridge where we'd seen Zane. Randy reined in Hercules and waited for me to catch up. "There's something strange," he said, nodding toward two sets of ATV tracks. "Zane went right, so we'd better follow him."

"I wonder how Zane chose this set of tracks over the ones going straight?"

Randy snorted. "I'll bet our city slicker from Portland is lost. He probably circled back over his own trail."

"Either that or he hit a dead end."

Randy gave me the same look I sometimes got from Jill when I said something stupid. "We call that a box canyon out here."

The timber opened to an area of rocky prairie, and we got a glimpse of Zane and Wayne only a hundred yards ahead. Much to my disappointment, Randy spurred Hercules to a trot so we could catch up. Rascal needed no encouragement. Apparently feeling peer pressure, he trotted along behind Hercules.

Zane and Wayne were barely back into timber when we caught up with them. Zane reined his horse and waited for us to ride alongside them. "Can you smell him?"

Thinking Zane must have a nose like a bloodhound, I sniffed the air. To my surprise, I smelled ATV exhaust. "Yes! Let's go!"

Zane put up his hand to stop me. "But I can't hear him."

I shook my head, not understanding what he was trying to communicate.

"He's stopped, and not very far ahead of us," Zane added.

"Ah, and you don't think we should ride straight ahead in case he's set up an ambush."

"If you want to walk straight ahead, I'll let you. But I won't let you ride Rascal into a situation where he might get shot."

"Believe me, I don't want either of us to get shot."

Randy nodded. "Especially since you left that nice bulletproof vest hanging on your chair in the café."

I patted my chest reflexively.

Zane shook his head. "So, are you bulletproof under that coat?"

"I don't want to find out."

"I was being facetious," he replied, spurring Puma ahead.

Randy was next to me as we followed them. He frowned and asked, "Why does Zane use those damn long words I don't understand?"

"I think he's trying to get some use out of the vocabulary he learned in college."

"Maybe so, but it doesn't mean anything if I can't understand what he's telling me."

Zane put up his hand to stop us, then swung down from his saddle. After putting a finger to his lips, he made a hand gesture for Randy to look over the ridge ahead of us. I held Hercules' reins as Randy walked, duck walked, and then crawled to the top of the ridge. Edging ahead on knees and elbows, he slid ahead until he appeared to have a view of whatever was ahead of us, over the ridge.

Hercules snorted and Zane grimaced before reaching out and putting his hand on the horse's neck. "Easy," he whispered.

Randy shifted his position and pulled a pair of binoculars out from under his coat. We all waited expectantly for some sign from him. Right up until the gunshot rang out.

Randy flopped over, making me think he'd been hit. After a half roll, he pushed himself up on one elbow and said, "I think he knows we're behind him." He slid partway down the hill, then stood up and walked to us. "The ATV is just sitting there like it ran out of gas or died. Streed is behind a tree just past the ATV. It appears he dragged himself to the tree, so I think he's crippled up."

I looked at Zane. "What do you suggest?"

"Well, if that asshole was a wounded game animal, I'd suggest we leave him where he is overnight. He'll stiffen up in the overnight cold and might bleed out entirely. Either way, he'd be easier to deal with in the morning."

I hung my head. "As appealing as that sounds, we have an obligation to provide first aid to an injured suspect. What do you think, Randy?"

"There's nobody out here to second guess what we do. I vote for letting him stiffen up."

"The problem will come when we're asked to testify under oath. I'm afraid I'd have to tell the truth. We need to make every reasonable effort to capture him and render first aid."

Zane shook his head. "There's always one of those moralistic religious types in every group. Why don't you go up there and try to reason with him, Doug?"

"I'm not wearing a vest."

Randy raised one eyebrow. "Let me give you a piece of advice. Don't go showing him any part of you that would normally be covered by a vest. Hell, I'd argue against sticking the top of your hat above the ridgeline."

"How far away is he?" I asked.

"I'd estimate about one hundred and fifty yards."

"That's a tough shot with a pistol," I replied.

Randy didn't appreciate my answer. "Doug, you're talking about a guy who owns a gun range. He probably practices one-hundred-yard shots regularly. Do you?"

"No. I assume any of my encounters will be at seven yards or less."

Zane nodded toward his horse. "I've got a rifle you can borrow."

"I'm trying to find a way to bring him back to face a jury," I replied.

Closing his eyes and looking disappointed, Zane said, "I won't disabuse you of your noble intentions, but I'm not convinced your suspect has the same plan."

Wayne frowned. "What in hell is that supposed to mean?"

"Zane doesn't think that Streed wants to surrender," I replied.

"Why in hell don't you just say shit in English, Zane?" Randy asked.

Zane smiled. "Because I know it irritates you and Wayne."

I hiked up the hill, then squatted down short of the ridge line with my back against a tree. "Streed, this is Doug Fletcher. I'm an investigator with the US Park Service. I'd like to talk about your situation."

A shot rang out, the bullet zipping through pine boughs a foot or more over my head.

"I can sit here until you run out of ammo."

"Good luck with that, Fletcher. I own a gun range. I've got plenty of ammo."

"I saw you jump on that ATV. Your hands were empty."

Another shot rang out, this one kicking up dirt on the ridge line. "That's true, but how many magazines were on my belt?"

"Our guide has suggested leaving you here overnight to stiffen up. He thinks you'll be more amenable to discussing your return in the morning."

"Do whatever you've got to do, Fletcher. It makes no difference to me. But I suggest you find the stupidest flunky in this backwater police department to be the first one to peek over the ridge in the morning because he's going to die."

"Let's reason this through."

Another shot zipped over my head. "What's to reason through? You watched me shoot the ATV's owner. Unless I'm mistaken, Wyoming has a death penalty for murder."

I looked down the hill at Randy and Wayne, who nodded their agreement. I flopped onto my back and stared at the sky as I yelled, "Streed, how do you see this ending?"

"With me, and two or three of you, being packed out in body bags. I'm going to die here. How many of you are willing to join me?"

Zane waved to beckon me back down the hill. Upon my arrival at the horses, he offered me a drink from a canteen. "I've got an offer you might not like."

"I'm generally open to suggestions," I replied.

"If you guys keep him focused on this ridge, I'll slip around into that little ravine to our left. I can take him out from there."

"Take him out as in, *kill him*?"

Zane frowned. "I'm not going to run through a hundred yards of open forest, then tackle that sonofabitch." He waited a moment, and when I didn't respond, he said, "That man's no better than a rabid skunk. The best thing you can do is kill him before someone else gets hurt or killed."

Randy looked at me. "It's turkey season, so it's not just us up here. Some unsuspecting turkey hunter could walk over the hill and get shot."

Wayne and Zane nodded their agreement.

I closed my eyes and thought for a moment.

"Doug?" Randy asked.

"Can't you come up with a better plan?" I asked.

Randy looked me in the eye. "You've always said that you're here to support us. Right? We are in charge of the investigations and your role is assisting us."

"Right," I replied.

"Has that changed?"

"No."

Randy pointed at Zane. "As the senior deputy on scene, I deputize you to take lethal action to neutralize the threat to these officers and any civilians who may be in the area." He turned to me and asked, "Are you going to argue that decision, Doug?"

I looked at the pine needle bed on the timber floor while wrestling with my answer. "No, Deputy Pannell. It's your murder, and you're in charge. I'll support whatever decision you make."

Zane walked to Puma and pulled a rifle from a leather scabbard. He looked at Randy. "Create a diversion."

Randy reached out his hand. "Give me your coat, Doug."

I shrugged Chet's coat off my shoulders and handed it to him. "Why do you want my coat?"

Randy tugged at the zipper on his uniform jacket. "Do you have any idea how much these jackets cost?"

Before I could protest, Randy handed me the horses' reins. He and Wayne scampered up the hillside, stopping just short of the ridge line. "Streed!"

"That doesn't sound like Fletcher."

"This is Deputy Pannell, of the Crook County Sheriff's Department. I'm here to bring you in."

Streed laughed. "Are you the dumbest sonofabitch who's going to be the first one shot?"

"That's not my plan. But one way or another, you're coming back with us to Aladdin."

A shot rang out and a twig fell off a tree somewhere over Randy's head. "Pannell, did you see that twig break off?"

"What of it?"

"That was the twig I was aiming at. I'm thinking any part of you coming over that ridge is going to be bigger than that twig."

"Well, I'm not coming alone. You're going to have to shoot a bunch of us."

Streed laughed. "So far, I've heard you, Fletcher, and a couple horses. That makes four bullets. Come on over."

Randy gestured for Wayne to move to his right, then they low crawled up to near the top of the ridge. Randy looked toward the ravine where Zane disappeared, then drew his pistol from its holster. Popping his hand over the ridge, he fired half a dozen shots in the direction of Streed's voice. His shots were met with a return volley of fire that tore up clumps of pine needles, rocks, and twigs around Randy's spot on the ridge.

"You better try aiming better next time, Pannell. I think you might've killed a red squirrel."

Randy nodded to Wayne and together they reached over the top of the ridge, firing a few rounds, then pulling back. More return volleys came, kicking up dirt near each of them.

"That was fun," Streed yelled. "Like a shooting gallery at the fair. You know, I always won the biggest stuffed bear for my girlfriend."

Randy nodded to Wayne, and they fired a few more shots, then Randy waved my jacket, which garnered a couple more shots. Randy held it toward me, showing me two bullet holes.

"I'm getting bored of this game, Pannell. Are you guys going to get serious, or do I need to come over there and give you..."

A single rifle shot rang out and Streed never finished his taunt.

* * *

Zane sent Randy, Wayne, and me back to Aladdin while he tied Streed's body to Puma's saddle. We were met at the general store by the sheriff, Jess Pond, and two FBI agents in black garb whom I assumed were part of Jess' tactical team. Hank Stoddard walked over to meet us, looking concerned. "Randy, where's Zane?"

"He's tying Streed to his saddle. I have to bring Rascal back so he can ride out."

The sheriff looked among us. "We heard a lot of gunfire. You're all unhurt?"

Randy chuckled as Jill trotted out from behind the general store. "Well, we took one casualty. Doug, show them your coat."

I got down from Rascal, then took off my coat, holding it up so everyone could see the bullet holes. The sight of the holes brought Jill running. "Where were you hit? Did the vest stop the bullets?"

I handed Rascal's reins to Wayne and spread my arms wide. "No visible injuries. Randy waved my coat as a diversion to draw Streed's fire."

Jill looked at my chest, then put her hands on her hips. "Where is the vest Randy gave you?"

"The posses' departure was rushed."

I walked to Jill who was simmering. Opening my arms, I hugged her. "Ow. Ow. Ow."

Releasing my hug, I asked, "What's wrong?"

Reaching across her chest with her right hand, she held her left side. "I have bruised ribs."

I held her left hand. "Sorry."

"Aside from not remembering to wear a vest, what made you decide not to be the hero today?"

I looked at Hank Stoddard. "Randy convinced me this was his department's operation. My job was advising them."

The tiniest smile curled Jill's lips. "And you listened to him?"

"How's Bill the horse?"

"I can tell he's hurting, but he'll be okay unless he gets an infection."

Jess motioned for his team to get out of their tactical gear and stow their weapons. Steering Jill and me toward the café, he asked, "Your advice was for them to ventilate your coat?"

"There was a discussion about the cost of a deputy's uniform jacket compared to the value of this moth-eaten coat I borrowed from Jill's uncle."

The sheriff peeled me away from Jess and Jill, taking me a couple of steps away from the café entrance. "What in hell happened up there?"

"I tried to reason with Streed. When he refused to surrender, Randy took over. I can't really tell you what happened from there."

The sheriff studied my face, then said, "Bullshit."

"They left me holding the horses while they brought the operation to a conclusion."

The sheriff and I watched as the two carpenters we'd seen the first morning covered the café's broken windows with plywood. "But Streed is definitely dead?" Stoddard asked.

"Definitely. I'm one hundred percent positive he'll be coming back across the saddle, not sitting on it."

Stoddard studied my eyes for a moment, trying to determine if I was lying. "Good," he said, steering me into the café. "Can I buy you a cup of coffee, or would you prefer to walk down to the saloon where we can have something stronger?"

I nodded to Jill, who pulled out a chair next to her. "Coffee would be great. Thanks."

Debbie brought coffee as soon as we sat. Nodding toward the vest hanging on an empty chair she said, "Glad to see you're in one piece, Doug. Why didn't you take that bulletproof vest along when you went chasing the bad guys?"

I smiled and changed the topic. "You found carpenters to cover your window quickly."

Debbie looked toward the front of the café where the second piece of plywood was being screwed into place. "They heard our window was broken, so they showed up with plywood sheets."

"They showed up without you calling them?"

Debbie cocked her head, apparently surprised at the question. "Friends do things like that for their friends."

Jill reached out and squeezed my hand. "It's a small-town thing."

Chapter 19

Waking to a nightmare about Randy and Wayne being shot by Streed, I sat up. Jill was still asleep in the fold-out bed, where she'd slept alone so I wouldn't bump into her injured ribs. She'd reluctantly let me see the bruise when she changed into her flannel nightgown. Although the borrowed bulletproof vest had saved her life, the bullet had still done damage, leaving her with a painful black bruise that would eventually fade to purple and blue over time.

Not wanting to disturb her sleep, I put on my clothes from the previous day and slipped out of the door, closing it as silently as I could. Aladdin was quiet as the morning twilight lit the sky east of the motel. There were already three pickups parked in front of the café. I looked to the right and saw the gray Mercedes, now wrapped with yellow CRIME SCENE tape, still parked on the shoulder of the road. Aside from the Mercedes' flat tires, the damage caused by hundreds of bullets wasn't visible in the dim morning light, nor were the hundreds of bullet casings the Wyoming DCI had collected, bagged, and tagged the previous night.

Walking down the sidewalk, I stopped next to Chet's pickup to remove a piece of yellow crime scene tape peeking out from the tailgate remaining after the rest had been removed when the DCI had finished taking pictures and collecting the spent bullet casings shot by Randy, the sheriff, and me. During the excitement of the shootout and our return, I hadn't noticed the three bullet holes in the driver's side of the pickup. One bullet hit high on the fender enclosing the pickup bed, probably a shot aimed at Randy or the sheriff. The other two were lower, in the driver's door and in the front fender. Like the shots that had broken the café's front window, they'd been poorly aimed, intended primarily to keep our heads down. I raised the pickup's hood to make sure none of the hoses had been hit. The only engine damage was a dented valve cover, leaving the truck serviceable. After closing the hood, I walked to the café.

The two carpenters who'd installed plywood over the broken window were eating rancher's breakfasts. Instead of staring at me, wondering who the stranger was as they had our first day in Aladdin, they smiled and nodded at me. I nodded back and found my usual table near the back corner. I glanced at Barry's empty table and felt a pang of guilt. *There's nothing you could've done to change the outcome of Barry's confrontation with the Oregon killers,* I said to myself as Debbie walked over with coffee.

"Jill's not up yet?"

"I let her sleep in."

"Do you want to order now, or wait until she gets up?"

"Bring me the usual," I said, testing Debbie's memory.

"Two eggs, sunny side up. Bacon and whole wheat toast with jelly."

"That sounds good. Thanks."

Debbie paused. "Do you want me to put this on the tab Jill opened yesterday?"

"Sure. And I'll pay for the carpenters' breakfasts too."

A sly smile crept across Debbie's face. "If you're trying to make friends, a free breakfast will take you a long way."

I nodded to Barry's table. "It's sad to see the empty corner table."

Debbie turned and looked at the corner. "Yeah, Barry provided a dependable portion of our morning sales. I'll miss him in many ways."

When Debbie left, I punched the sheriff's department non-emergency number into my phone. The dispatcher answered on the first ring. "Is Sheriff Stoddard in?"

"He sure is. As a matter of fact, he was asking if we'd seen any of the Park Service people yet."

"Tell him only one of us is up, then ask if he's got a second to talk."

The instrumental version of a Barry Manilow tune played while the dispatcher searched for the sheriff. "Hey, Doug. How are you feeling this morning?"

"Aside from some saddle sores and a blister from wearing borrowed boots, I feel fine. How are your people?"

"About that. You and Jill need to come into the courthouse to make formal statements about yesterday's events. There are a lot of cartridge cases on the ground that need to be accounted for."

"I only took a few of those shots. I think your people are responsible for ninety percent of the good guys' shots."

"Just the same, your statement will go a long way with explaining that we were acting in self-defense and protecting innocent civilians."

"There's a veterinarian coming sometime this morning to look at Sarah Streed's horse. We'll drive into Sundance after he's checked out the animal."

There was a pause in the conversation while I heard footsteps and the closing of a door. "Doug, I'm not going to belabor the point, but your assistance was above and beyond what I expected of you and Jill. You both stood up right beside my guys when we needed you, and you didn't ask anything of us that you weren't willing to do yourself. Hell, according to Randy, he made you stand down when they created a diversion for Zane. He also pointed out that you did all that while not wearing the bulletproof vest he brought for you.”

“Yeah, well, things got a little crazy and I never found the time to put on that vest.” I paused. “I suppose the Park Service owes you for the cost of the vest Jill was wearing. They’re not reusable once they’ve stopped a bullet.”

“All things considered; the cost of a vest will be lost in all the paperwork that we’ll have to fill out for the DCI investigation.”

“So, you’re waiting for the DCI to complete their investigation. Is that why the Oregon Mercedes is still parked here?”

“The DCI shooting investigation team is driving in from Cheyenne this morning to interview Zane, me, and my deputies. They’ll tow the Mercedes to their lab so they can count the bullet holes and process the interior for fingerprints and such.”

“I suppose they’ll want to interview Jill and me.”

“Jill never fired her weapon, and your shots didn’t hit anyone. We can take your statements and add them to the file. As you’ve pointed out, your role was advisory, so the DCI will focus on my department’s actions.”

“I appreciate that. Tell them there are three holes in our borrowed pickup. The one you, Randy, and I were using for cover.”

“They took photos of your borrowed pickup last night. You don’t need to hang around waiting for them to process it.”

Debbie arrived with my breakfast. "My breakfast arrived so I'm going to disconnect and eat while it's still hot."

"There's one other thing before you go. We searched the ATV last night. One of the shots hit the ATV's gas tank, so Streed ran out of fuel, which is why he stopped where he made his last stand."

"That's convenient. I wonder how far into the national forest he would've driven if he'd had a full tank of gas?"

"We'll never know what he had in mind." The sheriff paused, then added, "We found a blood-stained lariat, camouflage cap, and a pistol in a box mounted in the ATV. Unless I miss my guess, the blood on the lariat belongs to the PI. I expect the gun and the shells in the magazine will have the PI's fingerprints on them, and the cap will have his DNA."

"That'll wrap up the PI's murder case, but we still don't know how he got to Aladdin."

The sheriff sighed. "The ATV Barry was riding is registered to Jacob Foster, the PI. I've got a search warrant for Barry's family ranch. I expect Foster's pickup and his trailer will be found in one of the ranch's outbuildings or somewhere on a remote part of their ranch."

Debbie was standing next to the table, waiting for something. I asked the sheriff to hold on, then put my hand over the phone. "Do you need something from me?"

"No, I just wanted to remind you that I still have Jill's charge card."

"Thanks. She'll pick it up after she pays for our breakfasts." With Debbie out of earshot, I returned to the sheriff. "You're 100% certain that Barry killed Jake Foster?"

"Make that 99% sure. According to Debbie, Barry had a crush on Tanya. I think he caught the PI spying on her and took action to protect her. The PI's gun and cap were prizes he kept from the encounter."

I spread jelly on my toast. "Barry was certainly fearless, and possibly protective of his friends. He rammed the two guys who were shooting at the café without any regard for his own safety."

"We'll never know Barry's motives. I'm turning my conclusions over to the district attorney and closing the Foster murder case."

I ended the call, then mulled over the sheriff's comments as I ate. My thoughts were interrupted when the two carpenters walked over, both young and slender with worn, but clean jeans and shirts. The first guy took off his hat and held out his hand. "Thank you kindly for buying our breakfast."

I stood and shook his hand. "Thanks for coming to Debbie's aid after the shootout."

The second carpenter took off his hat, too, exposing the white bald head hidden under the Stetson that contrasted with the tan of his unprotected forehead. "Yeah, thanks. That was just being neighborly. If you ever need a shed built or a barn repaired, we'd be happy to do it for you."

"I'll keep you in mind," I replied. Returning to my breakfast, I was warmed by their thanks. I felt accepted. It was a feeling I generally felt only when around our friends, Matt and Mandy. I flashed to Jill's comments about retiring in the Black Hills and felt less negative about the prospect than before.

Debbie topped off my coffee and cleared my plate.

"Has Barry always driven around in an ATV?"

"He has for the last few months. He used to ride his horse over before that."

"Do you remember exactly when he started riding the ATV?"

"He rode it all winter. He said riding the ATV was easier than saddling the horse every day."

As Debbie walked away, my mind swirled with all the new information about Barry, the ATV, and Foster's murder. *Could it be that simple? Barry's crush on Tanya precipitated Foster's murder and all that followed. No, it was my call to the Portland police sergeant that led to Streed's appearance in Aladdin. Streed would've eventually put the pieces together, but I may have been the catalyst that moved his discovery ahead. Without Streed's arrival, would Foster's murder have been solved?*

I debated about continuing to drink coffee against waking Jill to tell her the news about the evidence found in the ATV's box linking Barry to Foster's murder. The coffee won out. I was leaning back, taking in the comfortable feel of the café when my phone rang. I answered without looking at the caller ID, assuming it was either Jill looking for me or the sheriff with more questions. I was surprised to hear Jess Pond's voice.

"Did I wake you?" he asked.

"Oh, hell no. I'm in the Aladdin café drinking coffee. I suppose you want me to drive to Rapid City to make a statement about yesterday's gunfight?"

"That's a Crook County crime. It's not an FBI case."

"Two guys driving from Oregon to Wyoming and shooting up a town isn't an interstate FBI case?"

"Nope. I've got bigger fish to fry."

"Ah, Sarah Streed's inside information about money laundering and human trafficking."

"Sarah is smarter than she lets on."

I chuckled. "She explained how she'd used a dumb blonde act while her husband and his cronies talked business."

"Oh, she's way smarter than that."

"I don't understand."

Jess paused, apparently closing his office door. "We've been played."

"By Sarah?"

"Yes, by Sarah. She appears to have been the brains behind the money laundering scheme."

"You've arrested her?"

"I can't. She negotiated an immunity agreement with the Assistant US Attorney. She immediately started outlining the human trafficking, illegal gun sales, and how the money was laundered."

"What makes you think she was a major player?"

"Two things. We spoke with Patrick Streed's buddy, who is recovering from two shattered legs in the Rapid City Hospital. He told us that he and Patrick were dispatched by the people running the human trafficking to 'deal with' Sarah and recover their money before she spoke with the cops."

"What's the other thing?" I asked.

"The money is gone."

"We knew she'd cleaned out her joint accounts with Patrick."

"That's peanuts. She cleared out the money that was being laundered. It's gone. She stashed it somewhere offshore, and our forensic accountants haven't found it."

"Are we talking millions?"

"We're talking ten or a hundred times that! And we're certain she knows where it is."

"If she's got millions stashed, why was she living in an RV in Aladdin, Wyoming?"

"Because the people she burned want all their money back, and they've got people scouring every outpost of the planet trying to find her. She claims that anywhere in the world where people can hide money is under surveillance. She couldn't go to Switzerland, the Caribbean, Hong Kong, Singapore, or anywhere she might've made untraceable deposits. As crazy as it sounds, Aladdin, Wyoming is possibly one of the most remote places on earth when you're hiding big sums of cash."

"I'm having a hard time believing that someone who has millions and millions of dollars would *choose* to live in Aladdin."

"She wasn't planning to stay there forever. Her internet search history shows that she was looking at remote places to live all over the world, from Lapland to southern Argentina."

"She fed us a sad story about not being willing to leave Bill, her horse behind."

"That horse was the sticking point in all her plans. She couldn't figure out how to get the damned horse to one of these places without setting off bells and whistles with the people searching for her. When you've got enough money, getting a fake passport and travel visas for yourself is relatively easy. It's damned hard to sneak a horse around. You have to charter a big plane and every country requires veterinary certificates. A lot of countries require you to put the horse in government quarantine for weeks or months when it arrives in the new country. Bill the horse is her Achilles heel!"

"With her immunity deal, is there any way to charge her?"

"I've got FBI forensic accountants going over the gun range's books. The Alcohol, Tobacco and Firearms people are looking at the range's gun inventory and sales. The Internal Revenue Service is combing her tax returns. The Security Exchange Commission is looking for her investments. The Treasury Department is looking at overseas money transfers and wire fraud. It appears she invested millions in some cryptocurrency, and everyone is trying to figure out how to track that. If all those smart folks can't find something to charge her with, we've got the State Department talking to the Philippine ambassador about kidnapping charges in their country. Someone will figure out how to put her behind bars, probably on state charges rather than federal."

"Will she be safe in prison?"

"I don't think US women's prisons are as predatory as men's prisons. On the other hand, she's not going to be taking cooking classes from Martha Stewart. If The Philippine's government charges her with kidnapping and trafficking, her incarceration will probably be very unpleasant."

"I suppose she can afford the best attorneys that money can buy."

Jess chuckled. "She's just about tapped out the money from her personal accounts. To get at her stolen money, she'd have to tip her hand about the accounts we can't find. I think she'll be stuck with a public defender, at least for now."

The bell over the café door tinkled and a man walked in. The new patron spoke with Debbie, who pointed at me. "I've got to run. I think Bill's veterinarian just arrived."

Jess laughed. "You'd better take good care of Bill. He's worth millions, at least to Sarah."

"About Bill, do you have a place to keep him while you investigate Sarah?"

Jess snorted. "The FBI doesn't have a barn."

After ending my call, I guided the veterinarian outside the café. He looked like any other working man except for his truck which was covered with compartments. Behind the truck was a trailer that looked like it was meant to restrain an unruly bull. "I'm Doug Fletcher," I said, shaking his hand.

"Doc Perkins." His handshake was firm and his hands calloused. "I spoke with Jill Fletcher last night. Is she your daughter?"

I laughed and gestured toward the parking lot between the café and the general store. "Jill's my wife. She was riding Bill when he was shot."

To my surprise, Jill was waiting for us near the shed housing Bill. "Doctor Perkins? Bill is in here."

The vet walked up to Bill's stall and put out his hand. "I hear that you're hurting."

Bill nuzzled the vet's hand as if he recognized him. Gently running his hand along Bill's neck, the vet whispered softly to the horse until they obviously trusted each other. Unlatching the stall, the vet walked in and closed the gate while Jill leaned on the top rail.

"What do you think, Doc?" she asked as the vet gently lifted Bill's mane to inspect the wound.

"It's hardly more than a nick. It appears you cleaned it up nicely last night. The bleeding has stopped and there isn't any sign of infection. I think a tetanus shot and antibiotics will suffice for now. Beyond that, keep the wound clean and let me know if Bill seems distressed or if there's any discharge from the injury."

Jill held the gate for the vet, then closed the stall.

We watched the vet walk to his truck and open a side compartment. "I talked to Jess just before the vet arrived. Sarah won't be released soon."

Frowning, Jill said, "She has an immunity agreement with the US Attorney."

"It appears that Sarah was more than an innocent witness to the crimes going on at the gun range. She was apparently the brains behind the money laundering until she decided to stash all the money offshore and run."

The vet returned with two huge syringes. Letting himself into the stall, he talked to the horse in a reassuring voice. Bill never reacted to the injections.

Jill let the vet out of the stall. "What do we owe you?"

"I've treated Bill before. I'll leave Tanya the bill."

I followed the vet to his truck. "Tanya won't be back for a while, if ever."

The vet seemed unsurprised by the news, continuing to pack up his gear. "What are you two to Tanya?"

I opened my coat, exposing my badge. "We're here investigating a crime. Tanya asked Jill to look after Bill when she left."

"Seems kind of cruel to stick you two with a vet bill for being Good Samaritans."

I removed my wallet and pulled out a federal credit card. "Can you take a credit card that charges the government? I'll submit your receipt with my expense voucher."

A hint of a smile appeared on the vet's face. "I'd be delighted to bill the government for my services."

Jill appeared at my side. "What's going on?"

"The government is paying the vet's bill."

Jill grimaced. "That's not going to fly. Think about the problems we had paying for hay in Arizona."

"Jack signed the voucher and the auditors whined but left us alone."

The vet returned with the receipt and my card. "It's a pleasure to charge Uncle Sam for my services."

I nodded toward the café as the vet drove away. "Breakfast is being served, and Debbie wants to return your charge card."

Jill sighed. "Great. That'll be two expense vouchers that'll bring auditor scrutiny."

I updated Jill as we walked to the café, "The sheriff called. All the evidence points to Barry being Jake Foster's killer."

Jill froze. "Why would Barry kill Jake Foster?"

Gesturing toward the café, we walked on. "Barry had a crush on Tanya. The sheriff thinks Barry caught Jake Foster spying on Tanya, so he took action to protect her. It was Foster's ATV that Barry's been riding around all winter. They also found incriminating evidence in the ATV."

Debbie met us at the table with an empty cup and more coffee. "How are you today, Jill?"

Stunned by the revelations about Barry, it took Jill a moment to respond, "Bruised and sore."

"I imagine it takes a while to recover from being shot." Debbie's comment turned the heads at a nearby table filled with turkey hunters. The waitress turned to the six men and placed her hands on her hips. "Yes, this woman was shot yesterday yet here she is, sitting up and taking nourishment. She's one tough mama. Don't mess with her."

Jill chuckled, then grabbed her ribs. "Stop. It hurts when I laugh."

"What would you like? I can have John whip up a bowl of oatmeal, or we have the usual specials."

"How are they specials when it's the same menu everyday?" I asked.

"Listen Mr. Smarty Pants. If you want to climb on a chair to erase that board and write in new specials every day, you go right ahead. As long as I'm in charge of it, the specials aren't changing."

Jill wrapped her arms around herself and put her head down. "Stop it. You're killing me." She drew a shaky breath. "How about a couple of scrambled eggs and whole wheat toast."

One of the turkey hunters stood and excused himself as Debbie took Jill's order to the kitchen. Instead of walking to the restroom, he came to our table. "Do you guys own the pickup with the bullet holes that's parked outside?"

Jill looked at me with panic in her eyes. "I didn't notice. Are there bullet holes in Uncle Chet's pickup?"

I put my hand on Jill's arm and looked up at the hunter. "As you've probably surmised, yes, the pickup is ours."

"What the hell happened? We drove past the Mercedes that looked like Swiss cheese when we arrived this morning. Then, we overheard the waitress say this lady had been shot. The front windows are boarded up. There are bullet holes in the siding. It looks like a war zone.”

“There was a little disagreement that got out of hand.”

“Out of hand seems like a major understatement.”

Jill nodded. “It’s an ongoing investigation. We’re not allowed to comment.”

“You’re cops?”

“Park Service investigators,” I explained.

“Looking at all the bullet holes, you’re lucky someone wasn’t killed.”

I nodded, not wanting to tell him about Barry, Streed, and the gunfight in the timber. “Yeah, lucky.”

The hunter walked to the restroom.

“What’s our plan for the day?” Jill asked.

“The sheriff called. He wants our statements.”

“That won’t take long. Anything else?”

I raised my eyebrows. “We should stop at Vore Buffalo Jump to let them know that the murder has been solved. After that, I’ve got no plans.”

“Let’s drive up through the Bear Lodge Pass and visit Devils Tower. We can tell Nikki Beardsly the Buffalo Jump body has been identified.”

“We could do that.”

Debbie delivered Jill’s breakfast and set the charge card on the table.

Jill unfolded a paper napkin and set it on her lap. "I'll need a receipt for my expense voucher."

"There aren't any charges. The sheriff left a hundred-dollar-bill on the counter and told me he was paying for all the coffee and rolls."

Jill slid the card back to Debbie. "That's not enough. Put the rest of it on my card."

Debbie shook her head. "Your money's no good here. You put yourself on the line for us. The least we can do is give away some coffee."

Jill pushed the card closer to Debbie. "Look closely. It's a government charge card. The Park Service is paying the bill. All I need is a receipt for my travel voucher."

"Oh, that's a horse of a different color," Debbie said, picking up the card. "I'm sure I can whip up an itemized bill for coffee, rolls, and doughnuts."

"Thank you," Jill replied.

"It's amazing how willing people are to take our cards when they find out the federal government is paying the bill."

Jill took a bite of her eggs and said, "I don't think Jack will sign a bill for entertaining a bunch of cops."

"The worst he can do is say no, then make us pay out of pocket. We can afford it."

"Speaking of affording things, who is paying for Bill's board while Sarah is in custody?"

"I don't know. We'll have to ask Jess or the sheriff."

Jill spread jelly on a slice of toast. "I don't think either of those agencies has a horse boarding budget."

"Probably not."

Jill's eyes twinkled and she smiled, showing her dimples.

Suspecting where Jill's thoughts were going, I said, "We're not in charge of Bill."

"I promised Sarah I'd look after him."

"You promised to watch him for a few days, not the rest of his life."

"My promise didn't have an end date. We can bring him back to Spearfish and he can hang around the ranch with the rest of Dad's horses. Besides, Sarah will have to forfeit all her assets. Bill and her RV are the only items of value she has."

"No."

Jill reached out and squeezed my hand. "It's no big deal. One more horse on the ranch is no extra work. We'll have to pay Dad for a few extra bales of hay."

"No."

"It was my promise to Sarah. I intend to keep it."

Taking out my phone, I said, "Let me call your dad. I'm sure he'll refuse."

Jill stopped me. "Let me call Dad. He won't say no to me."

I put my phone away. "Have you always been so sly and devious?"

Jill's dimpled smile was her reply.

I shook my head. "Let's have lunch in Hulett on our way to Devils Tower."

Jill gestured toward her plate. "Doug, I haven't even finished breakfast, and you're already talking about lunch. Your life revolves around food."

"It's one of the staples of life. Food, sleep, and…"

Jill looked at me. "And…"

"With your sore ribs, we'll be skipping the third item for a while."

"I appreciate your consideration. Besides, I think we'll be spending the next few nights with my parents."

"I think you crying out in pain might put a damper on our love life."

"How sweet of you to give up sex because it might cause me pain."

I rolled my eyes. "I am housebroken."

Jill wiped her mouth, "I'd say partially housebroken." She set the napkin on her plate, stood, then looked panicked.

"What?"

"You owe Dad and Chet bottles of good bourbon."

"I never played cribbage. I don't owe them anything."

Jill gestured toward the door. "Maybe not, but they will be disappointed if you don't show up with some good whiskey for them."

I held the door for Jill and asked, "Do you think Sundance has a liquor store?"

"I'm sure they do. I expect they sell more beer and Christian Brothers Brandy than expensive bourbon."

I nodded. "And Hulett will be the same."

"Don't make me laugh. It hurts."

"I see a stop in a downtown Spearfish liquor store in my future."

Chapter 20

After packing our bags, I paid our motel bill while Jill checked on Bill. We took Highway 24 west. The drive through the Bear Lodge Pass was pretty, and driving through the sleepy town of Alva reminded me of how close to poverty many Black Hills residents live. We reached Hulett well before noon and Jill looked at me when I slowed near the restaurant.

"It's too early for lunch and too late for another cup of coffee. Let's drive to Devils Tower and eat lunch in Sundance."

I sighed in mock disappointment, continuing through town without stopping. Within minutes, Devils Tower was visible ahead of us. It seemed huge, even in the distance, but became more impressive the closer we got.

"Those boulders at the bottom looked like rocks a few miles ago," I commented as we drove.

"As I recall, a lot of them are the size of boxcars," Jill replied.

Turning into the park entrance road, we passed a restaurant and a rustic store. A mule deer doe with her spotted fawn grazed, uninterested in us, as we approached the visitor check-in kiosk. Stopping at the window, I showed my badge to the young man collecting entrance fees.

"Is your passenger a Park Service employee, too?"

Jill held up her badge and asked, "Is Nikki Beardsly working today?"

"She should be at the information desk in the visitor center. Just follow the road. You can't miss it."

Jill looked over her shoulder as we pulled away from the kiosk. "Really? I'm sure we won't miss it. As I recall, the road ends at the visitor center."

"I think there's a paved walking trail that could be confused with a driveway."

The entrance road wound through an area of timber, providing glimpses of the huge stone tower. A sign announced that we were a half mile from the stoplight.

"What the hell?" I asked. "They have a stoplight inside a national monument?"

"I'm more intrigued with the announcement that we're half a mile from the stoplight." A moment later we passed another sign announcing our location as a quarter mile from the stoplight. "I suppose that means the traffic gets backed up this far during the peak tourist season."

We passed the stoplight, which wasn't operating in early April, and passed an empty gravel parking area before arriving at the one-way loop that passed the rangers' quarters and the visitor center.

The ranger from the kiosk must've notified the visitors center that we had asked about Nikki, because she met us at the door. "Welcome to Devils Tower National Monument."

"We were here a couple of years ago," Jill said as we walked through the door Nikki held open for us. "We investigated the fall of a climber."

"We have a couple of falls a year. None have been fatal recently." Nikki followed me in, and we stopped in front of the main desk. "Would you like a tour while you're here?"

"Would you join us on a walk around the tower loop?" I asked.

"Sure, if I can find someone to watch the desk while I'm gone." A minute later, Nikki reappeared, wearing a Park Service green coat and Smokey Bear ranger's hat. "Aggie is watching the desk. Let's go!"

Nikki led us across the parking lot to the paved trail and explained that the tower was the core of an ancient volcano. "What you see was left after all the material around it eroded away. This was a riverbed for a rushing river as the glaciers melted following the last ice age."

Jill walked alongside Nikki and I stayed a step behind. "We identified the man whose body was found behind the Buffalo Jump Museum. He was a private investigator from Moorcroft."

Nikki stopped. "You were able to identify him? I mean, he was a mess."

"The coroner used dental records."

"How did he get from Moorcroft to the Buffalo Jump?"

Jill paused to frame her response. "He was involved in an investigation that went awry. I can't expand on the circumstances other than to say it's tied to yesterday's police action in Aladdin."

"Someone said there'd been an Old West shootout by the Aladdin store. I thought they were kidding, or that someone was filming a movie there."

"The investigator's murderer and one other person were killed. I'm sure the sheriff will have a press conference and the information will be available online later today."

"Wow. I suppose you guys were bummed that you missed the excitement."

Jill glanced at me and made a discreet head shake. "I think we're more relieved than disappointed. It's never pleasant when there are shootings and people are injured and killed."

"Are you going to stop at the Buffalo Jump to tell Peggy and Charlie?"

"Do you think they'd be there?"

"I think they have a school group touring there today. I'm sure Peggy will be there to make sure everything runs smoothly." Nikki smiled. "I'll call Peggy's cell phone to let her know that you're stopping by."

"We need to talk to the sheriff in Sundance first, but we'll plan to stop at the museum on our way back to South Dakota."

"And we have a horse to pick up in Aladdin," Jill added.

"Thanks for stopping here to let me know. All of the board members have been chatting about the dead guy. It's probably the most exciting thing that's happened since the surveyors found the buffalo bones."

Nikki pointed out climbers going up the narrow *chimney* where the visitor had fallen to his death prior to our earlier investigation. Other climbers were taking easier approaches on the opposite side of the tower.

We shook hands in the parking lot and Nikki hesitated. "I heard Jill used to be an interpretive ranger, then a park superintendent. I suppose being an investigator is more challenging."

Jill smiled. "Being an investigator has its moments."

"Did you move around a lot before becoming a superintendent?"

"I was at a different park every few years. It was fun seeing new areas and experiencing the different cultures of each property."

"I graduated from SDSM&T in Rapid City. I'm not sure I'm interested in moving around the country."

"There are people who spend their entire careers in the same park. They stay where they're happy. On the other hand, you could move from here to Jewel Cave, Wind Cave,

The Badlands, or even the Minuteman Missile site and still be in the Black Hills."

"Thanks for pointing that out," Nikki said as we stopped next to Chet's pickup. She froze when she saw the bullet hole in the door, then noticed the other holes in the fenders. "Were you guys driving this during the gunfight?"

"Those are old holes from hunting season," I lied.

Nikki put her finger on the hole in the door. "It's not rusty. That's brand new."

"Huh," I said. "I wonder how that happened."

Nikki grinned. "You are such a bad liar."

* * *

South of Devils Tower, we turned left onto Highway 14 traveling south into Sundance. Jill took out her phone and punched in a number. "Who are you calling?"

"I thought we could buy Randy and Hank lunch if they're close to town."

The dispatcher answered and transferred the call to the sheriff. "Are you two coming in to make your statements?" he asked.

"We thought we'd buy you and Randy lunch if you're available."

"I'm pretty much always available for someone who is buying lunch. I'll have to see if Randy's around. He's on paid leave until the shooting investigation is complete." We agreed to meet at the steakhouse, like everything else in Sundance, it was located a few blocks from the complex housing the Crook County Courthouse, jail, and sheriff's office.

Jill ended the call and put her phone away. "I don't have much to say about yesterday's events."

I frowned and glared at her. "I think you need to document your spotting of the gray Mercedes, being shot, and your non-life-threatening injury."

"Oh, that." Jill thought for a moment, then turned to me. "What are you going to say about the events in the national forest?"

"The truth usually works well."

"I like to believe everything is black and white. You've taught me there are shades of gray."

"I'll be committing the sin of omission. I won't lie, but there are details that don't need to come from me."

"Okay, what might you omit?"

I thought for a moment. "My ears were ringing from all the gunshots, and I was ordered to stand down with the horses. I couldn't see what happened from my vantage point."

"Zane fired the kill shot."

I looked at Jill. "I couldn't see Zane from where I was standing. I saw Randy and Wayne take a lot of shots toward the fugitive. I can honestly say I don't know who fired that fatal shot. I never saw Zane fire a weapon."

"But you assume..."

"All I can testify to is what I saw. I never saw Zane shoot."

"The DCI will determine that the suspect was killed by a rifle shot. Randy and Wayne were carrying pistols."

"The last thing I saw when I mounted Rascal was Randy carrying Zane's rifle."

"Zane handed it to him."

I nodded. "I'm sure Zane did hand that rifle to Randy. I saw Zane take it out of a case on his saddle. I don't know if he handed Randy the gun before or after the shot, and that's God's honest truth. It's up to Randy, Wayne, and Zane to say exactly what happened."

Unhappy with my answer, Jill looked out the side window at the passing terrain. "You don't want to contradict something Randy said."

"I can't, because I didn't see what happened. If I have to testify in court, that's what I'll say."

"Will Zane get in trouble if Randy says it was him who fired the shot that killed Pat Streed?"

"I'm not up on Wyoming law, but in most states, a Good Samaritan who acts to protect the life of a law enforcement officer is shielded from prosecution. Besides, I think Randy deputized him before everything went south."

"In South Dakota, they'd probably pin a medal on him. No Wyoming prosecutor would take that case to trial. I think Zane's safe."

We beat the sheriff to the steakhouse and found a parking spot around the corner from the restaurant before walking to the entrance. We sat at a table near the kitchen, leaving the chair facing the door for the sheriff. Randy and Hank Stoddard walked in together. Seeing us wave, they joined us. In a fatherly gesture, the sheriff squeezed my shoulder as he walked past. He bent down and whispered something to Jill.

"Thanks. I'm bruised, but okay," she responded.

The waitress brought us menus and took our beverage orders before we could talk. When she retreated, the sheriff leaned over the table and whispered, "Yesterday was a nightmare. It's going to take the DCI days just to fingerprint all the spent brass in the Aladdin parking lot, around the gray Mercedes, and in the forest. We're damn fortunate that Jill was the only lawman hit by gunfire, and that her injuries are only bruises."

Jill sighed. "Barry died."

Frowning, the sheriff said, "Don't shed many tears for Barry. He killed the PI."

"He thought he was protecting Tanya," Jill replied.

"He could have chased him off or called us in. Barry didn't need to kill that man. That crime is on him and no one else."

Our beverages arrived, ending the conversation. We placed our orders and waited until the waitress left before speaking.

"Is Zane in trouble?" Jill asked.

Stoddard shook his head. "Zane is a member of the sheriff's posse and Randy deputized him."

Jill said, "I thought he was just Randy's friend?"

"We've used him for searches a few times. He has a badge and everything."

"Good," Jill replied, ending that conversation.

Stoddard looked at me. "You fired your weapon, so I need to take your statement about the shootings in Aladdin. You also negotiated with Streed. I need a statement about that unsuccessful negotiation."

"Randy put me in charge of the horses, so I didn't see any of the final shootout."

Stoddard looked at Randy, who nodded. "Doug was out of it."

A hint of a smile curled Stoddard's mouth. "So, you don't have anything that will contradict what Zane, Randy, and Wayne have said?"

"I was holding the horses. There was a whole bunch of shooting and hollering, then it stopped." I paused, then pointed to my coat. "Someone waved my jacket around and the assailant put two bullet holes in it. I don't suppose I'll get reimbursed for the cost."

Stoddard leaned back. "You have an expense account. Let the government reimburse you for that ratty sheepskin."

Jill looked at me. "There's also the issue of the bullet holes in Chet's truck."

"That's not going to be a problem," I replied. "Chet wouldn't let me fix them if I offered to. Can you imagine the number of stories he's going to tell the old farts in Spearfish? By the time that story dies, I'm sure it will be Chet standing behind the pickup shooting the bad guys while the cops cowered behind cover."

Jill turned to the sheriff. "Doug's right. Can you say something about my Uncle Chet not being in Aladdin when you hold your press conference?"

The sheriff laughed. "I hadn't planned to cover who wasn't in Aladdin. I will mention the assistance and support of our two Park Service liaisons. I sent an email of thanks to your boss this morning."

"Thank you," I replied. "You're not going to make us stand behind you at the press conference, right? My uniform got wrinkled in the suitcase."

Stoddard shook his head. "You two do whatever you think is right. You're welcome to join me at this afternoon's press conference, or you can disappear into the sunset. It's your call."

I looked at Jill. "In our case, we're going to disappear east, into the sunrise."

* * *

A school bus was parked in the Vore Buffalo Jump parking lot, along with a car and three pickups. After parking Chet's pickup in the back of the lot, we walked across the parking lot to the teepee that served as the entrance. Jill looked around before we walked in. "It's quiet. Where are the kids?"

"I suppose they're in the museum, down below."

"Groups of schoolchildren are never quiet."

I opened the door, and we were met with three smiling faces. Peggy Landin gestured for us to enter. "Nikki called a couple of hours ago to tell us you had news about our mystery man. She wasn't sure when you'd arrive."

Wayne Smith nodded. "We've been here on pins and needles waiting for you."

"She didn't give you the news?" Jill asked.

All three of the board members shook their heads. Wayne spoke up, "Is this related to all the shooting up north yesterday?"

I leaned on the counter. "We identified your John Doe as a Moorcroft private investigator. I can't get into any detail other than to say that both he and his murderer have been identified.”

“What was his name?”

“I think the sheriff will be releasing that information after the next of kin are notified.”

“And you’ve already arrested his killer?” Peggy asked.

Jill gave me a look, encouraging me to expand. “The murderer is deceased.”

Wayne nodded. “That was all the gunfire up in Aladdin?”

“I’m sorry, but I can’t comment until the sheriff releases that information.”

Peggy gave me a conspirator’s grin. “Why was the victim left here?”

“The answer to that question died with the murderer.”

Wayne shook his head. “Well, hell, you’re not giving us any gossip at all.”

Jill smiled and said, “You know everything we’re authorized to say. I suspect there will be a news conference this afternoon. The sheriff will release what details he can.”

Peggy reached out and put her hand on mine. “This has been the most exciting thing to happen at this site in about two hundred years. Thanks for your part in solving the mystery.”

“Two hundred years?” I asked.

“That’s roughly when the last herd of buffalo were driven over the rim. Once the native tribes got rifles, they didn’t need to chase the herds over the cliff. They could shoot them one at a time from a distance."

A memory popped into my mind. "They called the 1873 Winchester the gun that won the West."

Politely nodding, Jackie replied, "The Winchester '73 was the first reliable repeating rifle. There were rifled muzzle-loaders before that and single-shot rifles capable of taking down a buffalo became widely available shortly after the Civil War."

Jill looked at her watch as if we had a pressing engagement. "We need to be in Spearfish shortly. Thanks for your hospitality."

Peggy smiled. "Thanks for injecting excitement into our ancient history."

After leaving the Buffalo Jump, we drove to Aladdin and parked behind the store. I hooked Tanya's horse trailer to Chet's pickup while Jill retrieved Bill from his stall in the shed. Showing no apparent trauma from his bullet wound, Bill followed Jill to the horse trailer and climbed in without hesitation.

"You did call your father and tell him we're bringing a horse, right?"

Jill smiled. "He'll be okay with this."

"My mother would've had a fit it I'd shown up with a dog or cat."

"You're not daddy's little girl. We get away with a lot more than sons do."

Chapter 21

Al Rickowski met us on the back step as we walked to the house. "Why are you hauling a horse trailer?"

Jill put her hand on her father's arm. "I have a four-legged friend who needs to be put into a stall. I'll unload him and be in after a bit."

"Why are you standing out here in the cold?" I asked as we watched Jill unload Bill from the horse trailer.

"Your mother is on the warpath."

"Why?"

Al looked amused as Jill led Bill to the barn. "She's unhappy about what happened in Aladdin. She assumes you two were in the middle of it."

"I have no control over what the bad guys decide to do," I replied.

"That's not how your mother sees it." Al paused as Jill disappeared into the barn. "Where did you find the horse?"

"Bill's an orphan."

Al smiled. "Jill has always been a magnet for stray and orphaned animals."

"Why are you smiling at me? I'm neither a stray nor an orphan."

"Are you sure about that?" Al asked as Jill walked out of the barn.

We walked in and Jill was swarmed by our mothers. She fought off their attempts to hug her, explaining that her ribs had been bruised during a 'horse-riding incident.'

My mother pulled me aside and stood nose-to-nose with me. "We watched the news conference. The sheriff said you and Jill assisted with the investigation and arrests. You were in the middle of all that *commotion* in Aladdin, weren't you?"

I pulled Mom into a hug and squeezed her. "I'm fine. Thanks for asking."

Mom pushed me back and relaxed slightly. "I worry about you two."

"I know you do. But we have jobs to do, and they're occasionally dangerous. We try to minimize the risks, but sometimes there are events out of our control."

Al set out lowball glasses and Chet pulled a bottle out of one of the bags I'd delivered, and he read the label. "This isn't bourbon! What's Pendleton's?"

Putting my arm over Mom's shoulder, I walked to the table. "The selection in Sundance was limited. The guy behind the counter said this was the finest sipping whiskey he had."

Chet held up the bottle for Al to see. "I suppose if it's got a bucking bronco on the label, it's probably okay."

Al took the bottle, uncorked it, and poured two glasses half full. He held up his glass to us. "Let's face it, any free whiskey from my son-in-law will taste good."

Molly walked over and slid her shoulders under my other arm and slipped her arm behind my back as the men sipped the whiskey and smiled. "You made Al and Chet mighty proud."

"I did?"

"We watched the Crook County Sheriff's Department news conference on television. He called you and Jill out by name as key people in solving the murder and bringing in a bunch of bad people."

"That was kind of him."

Jill stood alongside the table and watched the whiskey sampling.

"Honey," I said, "were you going to talk to Chet about the damage to his truck?"

Jill shook her head. "I don't deal with mechanical things." She gestured toward the door.

Jill walked to the door, held it open, and ignored the questions. "Dad, let's look at the barn situation."

I sat next to Chet. "I assume the sheriff mentioned the gunfire in Aladdin during his news conference, right?"

"It sounds like it was a mess. Were you and Jill involved in that?"

"Your truck was parked in front of the café where some of the shots were fired. It has a couple of bullet holes."

Chet waited for me to indicate I was joking. When he realized I was serious, a smile spread across his face. "Hot damn! Now I'll have a story for the guys at coffee!"

My mom rolled her eyes and crossed her arms, obviously less excited about telling stories to the guys at coffee.

Molly looked at the door with concern. "What's going on with Jill and the horse?"

"The horse Jill borrowed in Aladdin is an orphan after yesterday. She offered to take care of him."

Chet laughed. "That's just like Jill. She was a sucker for lost puppies, farm kittens, and strays." Chet walked to the door. "Come on, show me the bullet holes in my truck."

"Um, Chet, before we rush out, we need to talk about your coat, too."

Chet got up and walked over to the hats and coats hung near the door. Reaching for his sheepskin, he asked, "What about my coat?"

"It suffered some damage, too."

Hefting the sheepskin coat, he spread it for everyone to see, then he whistled. "Damn. You weren't wearing it when this happened, were you?"

"No. I'm fine."

Chet poked his finger through one of the holes. "Wow! This may make a better story than the pickup."

Mom came over and hugged me before I walked outside. "Between the booze and bullet holes, I think you've made the day for a couple of old coots. Thanks."

"You're not going to yell at me?"

"I've given up. You and Jill do what you're going to do. There's nothing I can say to change you, is there?"

"It's taken a long time for you to get to this point."

Mom drew a breath. "I can't say I'm happy about your career, but you seem to be. And so does Jill. I suppose that's what is important."

Al, Chet, and Jill were standing in the driveway having a discussion when I walked out. Jill walked over to me and took my hand, leading me toward the barn. Inside the barn, she led me to a stall filled with mechanical stuff, saddles, and tack.

She pulled me close and leaned her head against my shoulder. "Quit acting like you're angry. You'll be happy to have something to keep you busy while Dad, Chet, and I are familiarizing Bill with his new pasture."

"I'll walk along."

Jill squeezed me. "Give me some alone time with Dad and Chet. Chet also wants to talk to me about his ranch."

I chuckled. "Their little girl has grown into quite a woman."

"Let's say they're finally getting there."
Jill let go of me, smiled, and gave my
shoulder a nudge. "Besides...you don't like
horses."

The End

Other Dean Hovey mysteries from BWL Publishing Inc.

Whistling Pines cozies
Whistling up a Ghost
Whistling Pirates
Whistling Bake Off
Whistling Artist
Whistling Fireman
Whistling Wedding (coming in 2024)

Doug Fletcher mysteries
Stolen Past
Washed Away
Dead in the Water
Death in Shifting Sands
Devils Fall
Prairie Menace
Down River
Burnt Evidence
Gator Bait
Grave Survey
Dead End Trail
The Last Rodeo
Peril in Paradise

Pine County Mysteries
Killer Secrets
Deadly Mixture
Fatal Business
Taxed to Death
Conflict of Interest (coming in 2024)

Dean Hovey is the award-winning and best-selling author of three mystery series. He uses his scientific background, travel, extensive research, and consultants to add reality and depth to his stories. One reader said his characters are like people he'd like to invite over for a beer and discussion.

Hovey's Doug Fletcher mysteries follow U.S. National Park Service investigators Doug and Jill Fletcher as their investigations take them to national parks from coast to coast. The Whistling Pines mysteries are humorous cozies set in a northern Minnesota senior residence, following Peter Rogers, the Whistling Pines recreation director, as he stumbles through the investigation of murders in his small town. The Pine County mystery series follows sheriff's deputies Pam Ryan, Floyd Swenson, and CJ Jensen as they investigate murders in rural Minnesota.

Dean and his wife split their year between northern Minnesota and Arizona.